18/12

Hi Nicole,

I read this book in German and really liked it — I hope you do too!

John Airlie.

With compliments

Starkmann Library Services Limited
6 Broadley Street
London NW8 8AE
Telephone 01-724 5335
Telefax 01-724 9863
Telex 94013987 SLSL G

Jakob the Liar

Jurek Becker

JAKOB THE LIAR

*translated from the German
by Leila Vennewitz*

PICADOR

published by Pan Books

First published under the title *Jakob der Lügner* in 1969
by Aufbau-Verlag, Berlin and Weimar
This Picador edition first published in 1990
by Pan Books Ltd, Cavaye Place, London SW10 9PG

9 8 7 6 5 4 3 2 1

© Aufbau-Verlag 1969

Translation © Jurek Becker and Leila Vennewitz 1990

ISBN 0 330 30447 X

Phototypeset by Input Typesetting Ltd, London
Printed and bound in Great Britain by
Billing & Sons Ltd, Worcester

Translator's acknowledgement

*My husband William has contributed
his knowledge and patience unstintingly
to the work of this translation,
and for this I warmly thank him.*

I can already hear everyone saying, A tree? So what's a tree – a trunk, leaves, roots, some beetles in the bark and a shapely crown at best, so? I can hear them saying, Don't you have anything better to think about to give you that rapturous look like a hungry goat being shown a nice juicy bunch of grass? Or maybe you mean one tree in particular, a special one that for all I know gave its name to a battle, the Battle of the Black Pine, say, do you mean one like that? Or was someone special hanged from it? No, not even that? Oh all right, it seems pretty inane, but if you get such a kick out of it we can go on playing this silly game for a bit, it's up to you. Maybe you mean that soft sound people call rustling, when the wind has found your tree and improvises a tune on it? Or do you mean the number of board feet your tree yields? Or the well-known shade it casts? It's a funny thing, but at the very mention of shade everyone thinks of trees, although buildings or blast furnaces cast much more shade. Do you mean the shade?

No, all wrong, I say then, you can stop guessing, you'll never get it. I don't mean any of that, although its heating potential is not to be sneezed at. Quite simply, I mean a tree. I have my reasons. First of all, trees have played a certain role in my life, a role I may be overestimating, but that's how it appears to me. When I was nine I fell out of a tree, an apple tree incidentally, and broke my left hand. It healed up fairly well, though there are a few intricate movements I can no longer perform with my left hand. I mention this merely because it had always been taken for granted that I would one day be a violinist, but that's really not important. First my mother had the idea, then my father wanted it too, and finally all three of us wanted it. So: not a violinist.

A few years later, I must have been about seventeen, I lay for the first time in my life with a girl, under a tree. This time it was a beech tree, a good fifteen metres tall; the girl's name was Esther – no, Moira, I think, at any rate it was a beech tree, and a wild boar disturbed us. Could have been more than one, we didn't have time to look back. Then a few years later my wife Chana was executed under a tree. I can't say what kind of a tree that one was, I wasn't there, I was just told about it, and I forgot to ask about the tree.

And now the second reason why I get that rapturous look when I think about that tree, probably or even certainly the more important reason of the two. It so happens that trees are not allowed in this ghetto (Ordinance No. 31: 'It is strictly prohibited to maintain any kind of ornamental or edible plants within the confines of the ghetto. The same applies to *trees*. Should any wild plants have been overlooked during the establishment of the ghetto, these are to be removed immediately. Offenders will be. . . .').

Hardtloff dreamed this up, God knows why, perhaps because of the birds. Countless other things are prohibited too, of course – rings and other valuable objects, keeping pets, being out in the street after eight at night – there's no sense in listing them all. I try to picture what would happen to a person who, wearing a ring, is found with a dog on the street after eight p.m. Actually no, I don't try to picture that at all, I don't even think about rings or dogs or the time of day. I think only of this tree, and my eyes get that rapturous look. I can see their point of view; I mean, theoretically I can understand it: You are Jews, you are less than dirt, why do you need rings, why do you have to hang about in the street after eight p.m.? We have such-and-such plans for you and intend to carry them out in such-and-such a way. I can see their point of view. I weep over it, I would kill them all if I could, I would wring Hardtloff's neck with this left hand of mine whose fingers can no longer perform intricate movements; still, I can see the logic of it. But why do they forbid us to have trees?

I've tried hundreds of times to unload this blasted story, without success. Either I tried it with the wrong people, or I made some mistake or other. I mixed up a lot of things, I got names wrong or, as I said, they were the wrong people. Every time I have a few drinks, it comes up again, I can't help myself. I mustn't drink so much, every time I think these must be the right people, and I think I've got it all nicely together, nothing can go wrong when I tell it.

Yet Jakob, to look at him, isn't the least bit like a tree. There are men, after all, of whom one might say, 'sturdy as an oak', tall, strong, a bit awe-inspiring, men one would like to lean against every day for a few minutes. Jakob is much shorter, he'd hardly reach the shoulder of any sturdy oak of a fellow. He is scared like all the rest of us, he is really no different from Kirschbaum or Frankfurter or me or Kowalski. The only thing that distinguishes him from the rest of us

8

is that without him this whole damn story could never have happened. But even there one can be of two minds.

So it is evening. Don't ask about the exact time, only the Germans know that, we have no clocks or watches. It's been dark for some time now, a few windows show light: that's all I can tell you. Jakob is hurrying, there's not much time left, it's been dark for quite a while. Then suddenly there's no time at all, not even half a second, for there he is, bathed in light. This happens right in the middle of the street, the Kurländischer Damm, close to the ghetto boundary, where most of the dressmakers used to be located. There stands the sentry, fifteen feet above Jakob, on a wooden tower behind the barbed wire stretched clear across the street. At first the sentry says nothing, just holds Jakob in the beam of his searchlight, right there in the middle of the street, waiting. To the left, on the corner, is what used to be the store belonging to Mariutan, an immigrant Romanian who has meanwhile had to go back to Romania to safeguard the interests of his country at the front. And on the right is the business that used to belong to Tintenfass, a local Jew now living in Brooklyn, New York, and continuing to make high-class ladies' dresses. And between them, standing on the cobblestones and alone with his fear, is Jakob Heym, really too old for such a test of nerves. He snatches off his cap, can't make out a thing in the light; all he knows is that somewhere in this dazzle there are two soldier's eyes that have found him. Jakob mentally runs through all the obvious transgressions and can't think of any he has committed. He has his identity card on him, he hasn't been absent from work, the yellow star on his chest is on exactly the prescribed spot – he glances down at it again – and he sewed on the one for his back only two days ago. If the man doesn't shoot right away, Jakob can answer all his questions satisfactorily: just let him ask.

'Am I mistaken, or is it forbidden to be on the street after eight o'clock?' the soldier says at last. One of the easy-going kind, the voice doesn't even sound angry, quite mild in fact; one might feel like having a chat, a touch of humour might not be out of place.

'It is forbidden,' says Jakob.

'And what time is it now?'

'I don't know.'

'But you ought to know,' the soldier says.

Jacob might now say, That's true, or he could ask, How could I? or What time is it, then? Or he could say nothing and wait, which is what he does, as that seems the most advisable course.

'Do you at least know what that building is over there?' asks the soldier, having realized, no doubt, that this partner is not the kind of person to keep a conversation going. Jakob knows. He hasn't seen in which direction the soldier has nodded or pointed; he sees only the blinding searchlight, and beyond it are quite a few buildings, but, the way things are at the moment, only one can be meant.

'The military office,' Jakob says.

'What you do now is go in there and report to the duty officer. You tell him that you were out in the street after eight o'clock and you ask him for a well-deserved punishment.'

The military office. Jakob doesn't know much about this building; he knows that it houses some sort of German administration – at least that's what people are saying. As to what is being administered there, nobody knows. He knows that the tax department used to be there; he knows there are two exits, one to the front and one leading out of the ghetto. But above all he knows that the chances of a Jew leaving this building alive are very poor. To this day, no such case has ever been heard of.

'Anything the matter?' asks the soldier.

'No.'

Jakob turns and walks away. The searchlight follows him, draws his attention to uneven spots in the paving, makes his shadow grow longer and longer, makes his shadow climb up the heavy steel door with its round peep-hole when Jakob still has many steps to go.

'And what do you ask for?' says the soldier.

Jakob stops, turns round patiently, and replies: 'For a well-deserved punishment.'

He does not shout; only people lacking in self-control or respect shout, but neither does he say it too softly, so as to be sure the man in the light can hear him clearly across the distance. He takes pains to find exactly the right tone; it should indicate that he knows what he is to ask for, all he needs is the question.

Jakob opens the door, quickly shuts it again between himself and the searchlight, and looks down the long empty corridor. He has been here often; there used to be a small table just inside the entrance on the left, with a minor official seated behind it. As long as Jakob can remember, it was always Mr Kominek, who used to ask each visitor: 'What can we do for you?' 'I've come to pay my semi-annual taxes, Mr Kominek,' Jakob would reply. But Kominek would behave as if he had never seen Jakob before, although from October to the end of April he had been in Jakob's little shop almost every week and eaten potato pancakes there. 'Occupation?' Kominek would ask.

'Tradesman,' Jakob would answer. He never showed his annoyance, not even a trace; Kominek invariably managed four pancakes, and sometimes he would bring his wife along too. 'Name?' Kominek would ask next. 'Heym, Jakob Heym.' 'Letters F to K, Room 16.' Yet whenever Kominek came to his shop he had never bothered to order pancakes, he would simply say: 'The usual.' For he was a regular.

Where the table once stood there is now no longer a table, but the places where its legs used to be still show the four marks on the floor, whereas the chair has left no trace, probably because it never stood as consistently on the self-same spot as the table had. Jakob leans against the door to catch his breath. The last few minutes have not been easy, but what does that matter now? The smell in this building has changed, somehow for the better. The acrid odour of ammonia that at one time pervaded the corridor has gone; instead there is, inexplicably, a more civilian smell. There is a hint of leather in the air, female sweat, coffee, and a trace of perfume. At the far end of the corridor, a door opens, a woman in a green dress comes out, walks a few steps; she has nice straight legs, she goes into another room, two doors are left open, he hears her laugh, she comes out of the room again, walks back, the doors are closed again, the corridor is empty once more. Jakob is still leaning against the steel door. He wants to go outside again, maybe the searchlight is no longer waiting for him, maybe it has sought out something new, but maybe it is still waiting, it seems rather unlikely that it is not waiting, the soldier's last question had sounded so final.

Jakob walks along the corridor. There is nothing on the doors to indicate who is behind them, only numbers. Perhaps the duty officer has the room formerly occupied by the bureau chief, but one can't be sure and it is not advisable to knock at the wrong door. What do you want, some information? Did you hear that? He wants information! We have such-and-such plans for him, and he comes wandering in here and wants information!

Behind Number 15, formerly 'Tradesmen A-E', Jakob can hear sounds. He puts his ear to the door, tries to listen, can't understand anything, only single words that make no sense; but even if the wood were thinner it wouldn't help much, for no one is likely to address another person as 'Duty Officer'. Suddenly the door opens – what else but Number 15! – but fortunately the doors here open outwards so that the person coming out doesn't see Jakob, who is hidden by the door. Fortunately, too, the person leaves the door open, he'll be back in a moment; when people think there's no one else around they leave doors open, and Jakob is concealed. Inside the room a radio is turned on; it crackles a bit, one of their 'people's radios' no doubt, but there is no music. Since being in the ghetto Jakob has never heard any music, none of us have, except when someone happened to be singing. An announcer is reporting trivialities from some headquarters, someone has been posthumously promoted to lieutenant-colonel, next comes a bit about assured supplies for the population, and then the announcer reads out a bulletin that has just come in: 'In a fierce defensive battle our heroically fighting troops succeeded in halting the Bolshevist attack twenty kilometres from Bezanika. In the course of the action our side. . . .'

Then the fellow is back in his room; he closes the door, and the wood is too thick. Jakob doesn't move, he has heard a great deal, Bezanika is not that far away, more than a stone's throw but certainly not an enormous distance. He has never been there, but he has heard of Bezanika, a very small town; if you travel south-east by train via Mieloworno and the district town of Pry, where his maternal grandfather once had a chemist's shop, and you then change trains for Kostawka, you eventually arrive in Bezanika. It may be all of four hundred kilometres, maybe even five hundred, not more, he hopes, and that's where they are now. A dead man has heard some good news and he is happy, he would like to go on being happy, but in his situation – the duty officer is waiting for him and Jakob must move on.

The next step is the hardest; Jakob tries to take it but is stymied. His sleeve is caught in the door, the fellow who came back to the room has pinned him there without the slightest malice aforethought: he simply closed the door behind him, and Jakob was caught. He gives a cautious tug, the door is well made, it fits perfectly, no superfluous gaps; you couldn't slip a sheet of paper through. Jakob would like to cut off that piece of sleeve, but his knife is at home, and using his teeth, of which half are missing, would be a waste of time.

It occurs to him to take off his jacket, simply take it off and leave it stuck in the door – what does he need a jacket for now anyway? He has already slipped out of one sleeve when he remembers that he does still need the jacket. Not for the approaching winter – when you're in the ghetto the oncoming cold doesn't scare you. The jacket is needed for the duty officer, if he ever finds him, the duty officer, who doubtless can stand the sight of a Jew without a jacket – Jakob's shirt is clean and only slightly mended – but hardly the sight of a Jew without a yellow star on his chest and back (Ordinance No. 1). Last summer the stars were on the shirt, you can still see the stitch marks, but not any more, the stars are now on the jacket. So he puts it on again, sticks with his stars, tugs more firmly, gains a few millimetres, but not enough. The situation is, one might say, desperate; he tugs with all his might, something rips, making a sound, and the door opens. Jakob falls into the corridor, a man stands over him, in civilian clothes and very surprised; the man laughs, then turns serious again. What does Jakob think he is doing here? Jakob gets up and chooses his words very carefully. Not that he's been out in the street after eight, no, the sentry who stopped him had told him it was eight o'clock and he was to report here to the duty officer.

'And then you stopped to listen at this door?'

'I wasn't listening. I've never been here before and didn't know what room to go to. So I was just about to knock here.'

The man asks no more questions and nods his head towards the end of the corridor. Jakob walks ahead of him until the man says 'Here': it is not the bureau chief's room. Jakob looks at the man, then knocks. The man walks away, but there is no answer from inside.

'Go in,' the man tells him and disappears behind his own door after Jakob has pressed down the latch.

Jakob in the duty officer's room: he stays by the door, he hasn't put his cap back on since he got caught in the searchlight. The duty officer is quite a young man, thirty at most. His hair is dark brown, almost black, slightly wavy. His rank is not apparent as he is in shirtsleeves; his jacket is hanging from a hook on the wall in such a way that the shoulder-boards cannot be seen. Hanging over the jacket is his leather belt with his revolver. Somehow this seems illogical, it should really be hanging under the jacket; surely a man first takes off his belt and then the jacket, but the belt is hanging over the jacket.

The duty officer is lying on a black leather sofa, asleep. Jakob believes he is fast asleep; Jakob has heard many people sleeping, he has an ear for it. He isn't snoring, but he is breathing deeply and regularly; somehow Jakob must make his presence known. Normally one would clear one's throat, but that won't do here, that's something one does when visiting good friends. Although actually, when visiting a very good friend one doesn't clear one's throat; one says: 'Wake up, Salomon, I'm here,' or simply taps him on the shoulder. But, even so, throat-clearing won't do, that's somewhere between here and Salomon. Jakob is about to knock on the inside of the door, but drops his hand when he sees a clock on the desk, its back to him. He has to know what time it is; there is nothing he has to know more urgently right now than this. The clock says seven thirty-six. Jakob walks softly back to the door. They've been having you on, or not *they*, just that one fellow behind the searchlight, he's been having you on, and you fell for it.

Jakob still has twenty-four minutes left; if they are fair, actually twenty-four minutes plus the time his stay here has already cost him. He still doesn't knock. He recognizes the black leather sofa the duty officer is lying on; he has sat on it himself, it used to belong to Rettig, Rettig the broker, one of the richest men in the town. In the fall of 1935 Jakob borrowed some money from him, at twenty per cent interest. The whole summer had been so cool that he could hardly sell any ice-cream at all. His takings had never been so low, not even his famous raspberry ice-cream had sold well. Jakob had had to start selling potato pancakes as early as August but hadn't yet made enough money for the potatoes, so he had to borrow. And he had sat on the sofa in February 1936 when he returned the money to Rettig. It had stood in the outer office; Jakob had sat on it for an hour, waiting for Rettig. He remembered how surprised he'd been at the extravagance, there was easily enough leather for two overcoats or three jackets – and in the outer office!

The duty officer turns on his side, sighs, smacks his lips a few times; a cigarette lighter slips out of his trouser pocket and drops on to the floor. Jakob simply must wake him up now; it would be a bad thing for him to wake up without Jakob rousing him. He knocks on the inside of the door, the duty officer says 'Yes?', moves, goes on sleeping. Jakob knocks again, how can anyone be that fast asleep, he knocks louder, the duty officer sits up before being properly awake, rubs his eyes and asks: 'What time is it?'

'A few minutes after half past seven,' says Jakob.

The duty officer has stopped rubbing his eyes, sees Jakob, rubs his eyes again, doesn't know whether to be angry or to laugh: it's quite incredible, no one's going to believe him. He stands up, takes his belt from the hook, then the jacket, puts it on, buckles on his belt. He sits down behind the desk, leans back, stretches both arms wide apart.

'To what do I owe this honour?'

Jakob tries to answer, but he can't, his mouth is too dry: so that's what the duty officer looks like.

'No false modesty, now,' says the duty officer. 'Out with it! What's the problem?'

A bit of saliva has collected in his mouth, this seems to be a friendly fellow, maybe he's new here, maybe he isn't even aware of this

14

building's terrible reputation. For a moment it occurs to Jakob that possibly he miscalculated the distance, maybe Bezanika isn't that far, maybe barely three hundred kilometres, or even a good deal less; maybe the man facing him is scared. The smart thing is to be prepared, there must be a natural explanation for everything. But then he remembers that the report has only just reached the announcer, the duty officer has been asleep and can't have heard it yet. On the other hand it might be just as well if he hasn't heard it; the report mentioned that the Russians had been halted, the Germans have succeeded in stopping the advance, you lot have had a success, maybe this fellow thinks that the Russians are still advancing. Jakob has been speculating too long, the duty officer is getting impatient, that's not smart, the man is beginning to frown.

'Don't you speak to Germans?'

Of course Jakob speaks to Germans, why wouldn't he speak to Germans, that's the last impression he wants to give for God's sake, we're all sensible people after all, of course we can speak to each other.

'The sentry on the tower on the Kurländischer Damm told me to report to you. He said I was out in the street after eight o'clock.'

The duty officer looks at the clock in front of him on the desk, then pushes back his sleeve and looks at his watch.

'And that's all he said?'

'He also told me I was to ask for a well-deserved punishment.'

That answer can't do any harm, Jakob thinks, it sounds obedient, disarmingly honest. Someone who carries his frankness to such an extreme might be entitled to fair treatment, especially when the offence of which he is accused was never committed: any clock can bear witness to that.

'What's your name?'

'Heym, Jakob Heym.'

The duty officer takes paper and pencil, writes down something, not only the name, goes on writing; he looks at the clock again, it's getting later and later, he goes on writing, almost half a page, then puts the paper aside. He opens a little box, takes out a cigarette, and gropes in his trouser pocket. Jakob walks to the black leather sofa, bends down, picks up the lighter from the floor, and puts it on the table in front of the duty officer.

'Thanks.'

Jakob goes and stands by the door again; a glance at the clock on the desk has shown him that it's already past seven forty-five. The duty officer lights his cigarette, takes a puff, his fingers fiddle with the lighter. He flicks it on a few times, then snaps it shut again, the flame is already quite small.

'Do you live far from here?' he asks.

'Less than ten minutes.'

'Go on home.'

Should he believe it? How many people had the duty officer said that to without their ever getting out of here? What will he do with his revolver when Jakob turns his back? What's out there in the corridor? How will the sentry react when he sees that Jakob has eluded his well-deserved punishment? Why should Jakob Heym of all people, that insignificant, trembling little Jakob Heym with the tears in his eyes, be the first Jew able to describe what the inside of the military office looks like? Six new days of the Creation would be needed, as the saying goes; the confusion has grown even worse than it was at that time.

'Come on now, beat it!' says the duty officer.

The corridor is empty again: one can almost rely on that since it is one of the minor sources of danger. But then the door to the outside: had it made any noise before when he opened it, did it open without a sound, or did it squeak or creak or grate? Go ahead, take in every detail, quite impossible if only one knew in advance that the result would really matter! Matter? In practical terms it makes absolutely no difference whether it can be moved quietly or not. If it doesn't squeak, Jakob will open it; and if it does squeak, is Jakob supposed to stay where he is? At ten minutes to eight?

Gently he presses down the latch. Too bad there's no other word for gently – maybe very gently or infinitely gently, all equally far from what is meant. One might say, Open the door quietly; if he hears you it could cost you your life, the life that has suddenly acquired meaning. So he opens the door. And then Jakob is standing outside: how cold it has suddenly become, the wide square lies before you, a joy to step on to it. The searchlight has become tired of waiting, it's having fun somewhere else, is at a standstill, perhaps resting up for new adventures. Mind you keep close to the wall, Jakob, that's it; once you've reached the corner of the building you must grit your teeth for the twenty metres across the square. If he does notice anything he'll first have to swing the beam around and search, but here's the corner already, only a measly twenty metres to go.

It is almost exactly twenty metres, I've measured the distance: to be precise, nineteen metres and sixty-seven centimetres. I've been there, the building is still standing, completely undamaged, only the watchtower is gone. But I had someone show me the exact spot, right in the middle of the Kurländischer Damm, and then I paced off the distance – I have a pretty good feeling for a metre. But it wasn't accurate enough for me so I bought a tape measure, then went back and measured it again. The children looked on and took me for an important person, and the grown-ups watched in amazement and took me for a madman. Even a policeman turned up, asked me for my identity card, and wanted to know what I was measuring here. In any case it's exactly nineteen metres and sixty-seven centimetres, no doubt about that.

The building has come to an end, Jakob gets ready to take off: almost twenty metres have to be covered a few minutes before eight, it's a safe bet, and yet. A mouse is what one ought to be. A mouse is so insignificant, so small and quiet. And you? Officially you are a louse, a bedbug, we are all bedbugs, by a whim of our Creator absurdly overgrown bedbugs, and when was the last time a bedbug wanted to trade places with a mouse? Jakob decides not to run, he'd rather creep, it's easier to control the sounds that way. If the searchlight starts moving he can still speed up. Half-way across he hears the sentry's voice – don't panic, it's not directed at him, the sentry says 'Yessir!' Again he says 'Yessir', and again: there's only one explanation, he's on the phone. Maybe it's a call from another sentry who is also bored. But he wouldn't keep saying 'Yessir' to him, of course he wouldn't. So it's the sentry's superior giving him some sort of orders? Actually quite irrelevant, but, assuming the best, it's the duty officer on the line. What the hell are you thinking of – have you gone crazy, giving poor innocent Jews a scare like that? ('Yessir'.) Couldn't you see the man was half out of his mind – his legs were trembling with fear! Don't ever let me catch you at it again, is that clear? ('Yessir'.) At the fourth Yessir, Jakob has reached the opposite corner; let the fellow go on talking till he's blue in the face. Then, in less than ten minutes, Jakob is home.

J akob shares a room with Josef Piwowa and Nathan Rosenblatt. They met for the first time here, in this room. None of them likes the others much; cramped quarters and hunger make for discord, but in all fairness it must be said that even the very first meeting was quite stiff.

Rosenblatt died well over a year before Jakob's safe return. He had eaten a cat that was careless enough to ignore the warning notices along the barbed wire, and one day there it lay in the yard, dead of starvation. Rosenblatt was the first to find it and, as I was saying, he ate it, and that's what he died of. Piwowa has only been dead for three months. His passing was accompanied by certain mysterious circumstances; all that is known is that he was shot to death by a guard in the shoe factory where he worked. He became insolent, uttered words that even in normal times are better left unspoken to a guard, and, predictably, the enraged man shot him. One theory is based on the fact that Piwowa could never control his temper: he had always been subject to sudden rages and was bound to come to such an end. Others, however, maintained that a violent temper and emotions were no explanation here; they said it was a case of a perfectly ordinary though very skilfully provoked suicide. One way or the other, Piwowa has been dead for three months, Rosenblatt for well over a year. His bed went up the chimney last winter, while Piwowa's bed, chopped into neat lengths, is still in Jakob's cellar waiting for the cold times ahead. So far no replacements for his room-mates have appeared: supplies have been used up, damned or blessed be all cats and guards – in any case they hadn't liked each other. At least Rosenblatt is silent when he is at home, sitting with closed eyes on his bed and praying; he is the last to go to bed and the first to get up because his debates with God consume all his time. Even after his death he didn't give up this habit, but at least he is silent, sitting silently with closed eyes and only an occasional furtive glance.

Piwowa is quarrelsome. The last to be billeted, he behaves as if he were the first. Changes everything round, has to sleep with his feet towards the window, our bread rations have to be hidden from him. To be frank: Piwowa used to work in the woods, as a poacher. His father before him had been a poacher, but he himself was an even better one; he has no children.

So Jakob comes home. The day has been a great strain: many things experienced, endured, suffered, heard, with much trembling. Rejoice, brothers, go wild with joy, the Russians are twenty kilometres from Bezanika, if that means anything to you! Open your eyes, Nathan Rosenblatt, stop quarrelling, Piwowa, the Russians are on their way, don't you understand? Twenty kilometres from Bezanika! But Rosenblatt goes on praying, Piwowa goes on lying with his feet towards the window; let them lie there and quarrel and pray and be dead, Jakob is home, and the Russians had better hurry.

★

We're going to have a little chat now.

We're going to have a little chat, as befits any self-respecting story. Grant me my little pleasure, without a little chat everything is so sad and gloomy. Just a few words about doubtful memories, a few words about the carefree life; we're going to whip up a cake with modest ingredients, eat only a mouthful of it and push the plate to one side before we've lost our appetite for anything else.

I am alive, there can be no doubt about that. I am alive, and no one can force me to have a drink and remember trees and remember Jakob and everything to do with his story. On the contrary, I am offered some nice things, I am told to enjoy myself for a few days: we only live once, my friend. Wherever I look, diversion: new cheerful worries interspersed with a little unhappiness, women, that's not over yet, reforested woods, well-tended graves that at the least excuse receive such quantities of fresh flowers as to look almost overdone. I don't want to be demanding. Piwowa, whom I never saw, was demanding: supplies of game and bread had to be protected from him, but I am not Piwowa.

Chana, my quarrelsome wife, once told me: 'You're wrong' – that's how she began almost everything she said to me – 'a person is only undemanding when he is content with what he's entitled to. Not with less.'

Seen like that, I must be very content. Sometimes I even feel privileged, people are kind, obliging, make every effort to look patient. I can't complain.

Sometimes I say, 'That was the whole story, thank you for listening, you don't have to prove anything to me.'

'That's not my intention. But you must realize that I was twenty-nine—'

'You don't have to prove a thing to me!' I say again.

'I know. But when the war was over I was just—'

'Kiss my arse,' I say as I get up and leave. After five steps I could kick myself for being so rude, so needlessly insulting, and it hadn't meant a thing to him. But I don't turn round, I walk on. I pay the waiter and, as I go out, look back over my shoulder towards the table and see him sitting there with a baffled expression, what's got into me, and I shut the door behind me and refuse to explain.

Or I'm lying in bed with Elvira. To make this clear: I am forty-six, born 1926. I am lying in bed with Elvira; we work in a factory, she has the whitest skin I have ever seen. I imagine we'll get married one day.

We are still panting, we have never mentioned it, then suddenly she asks me: 'Tell me, is it true that you. . . .'

God knows who told her. I can hear the pity in her voice and go crazy. I go into the bathroom, sit down in the tub, and start singing, to stop myself from doing what I know I will regret after five steps. When I come back after half an hour she asks me in surprise what suddenly came over me, and I say 'Nothing' and give her a kiss, turn out the light and try to fall asleep.

The whole town lies in a green belt, the surroundings are incomparable, the parks well cared for, every tree invites my memories, and I make ample use of this. But when it looks into my eyes, that tree, to see whether they have that rapturous look I have to disappoint it, for it's not the right tree.

Jakob tells Mischa.

He hadn't come to the freight yard with the intention of telling anyone, but neither had he planned not to tell anyone. He came to the station with no intentions at all. He knew he would find it hard to keep the news to himself, almost impossible: after all, it was the best possible news, and good news is there to be passed on. On the other hand we know how it is: the informant is held responsible for all the consequences, in time the news becomes a promise, you can't prevent it. At the other end of the town they'll be saying that the first Russians have already been sighted, three young ones and another who looked like a Tartar; the old women will swear to it and so will anxious fathers. Someone will say he heard it from so-and-so, and that person heard it from so-and-so, and someone down the line knows that it came from Jakob. From Jakob Heym? Inquiries will be made about him, everything connected with this most vital of all questions must be most carefully investigated; an honourable, reliable fellow, seems respectable enough, is said to have once owned a modest restaurant somewhere. Rejoicing seems to be in order.

Then days will pass, weeks if God finds it necessary – three hundred kilometres or five hundred are a fair bit of country – and the looks Jakob encounters will no longer be quite as friendly, not quite. On the other side of the street there will be whisperings, the old women will commit the sin of wishing him ill; the ice-cream he has sold will gradually turn out to have been the worst in the whole town, even his famous raspberry ice-cream, and his potato pancakes never quite kosher: that can happen.

Jakob is lugging crates with Mischa to a freight car.

Or let's look at another possibility. Heym says he has heard that the Russians are advancing, are already four hundred kilometres from the town. So where does he claim to have heard that? That's the point: at the military office. At the military office?! A look of horror may follow, answered by a slow nod, a nod that confirms the suspicion. Who would ever have believed that of him, Heym of all people, never! But that's how wrong one can be about a person. And the ghetto will have acquired one more suspected informer.

Well, anyway, Jakob didn't come to the freight yard with any firm intentions. It would be wonderful if they already knew about it without him, if they had met him with the news: that would be ideal. He would have rejoiced with them, wouldn't have let on that there were three people already in the know: Rosenblatt, himself and Piwowa. He would have kept his mouth shut and, at the most, asked after a few hours who had brought the news. But as soon as Jakob arrived at the freight yard he realized that they didn't know yet; their backs were enough to tell him. The lucky break hadn't happened, indeed it would have been crazy to count on it; two lucky breaks in such a short time can only happen to Rockefeller on a Sunday.

They haul the crates to a freight car. As a carrying-mate Jakob is not particularly sought after; no one is eager to have him. Making pancakes is hardly conducive to producing giants, and the crates are heavy. The station is full of such people no one is eager to have; giants are scarce. Everyone is eager to have the giants, but the giants don't negotiate, preferring to haul together. Don't give me that stuff about camaraderie and all that rubbish; anyone who talks like that has no idea of what goes on here, not the slightest. Personally I am not one of the giants; I've cursed and hated them like the plague when I've had to haul with another fellow like myself. But if I had been one of them I would have behaved exactly the same, exactly the same and not one bit differently.

Jakob and Mischa are hauling a crate to the freight car.

Mischa is a tall fellow of twenty-five, with light-blue eyes, a great rarity among us. At one time he did some boxing at the Hakoah, but only three fights, two of which he lost, and once his opponent was disqualified for hitting below the belt. He was a middleweight, or rather, more of a light heavyweight, really, but his trainer advised him to lose those few pounds in training, there being too much competition in the light-heavyweight class. Mischa took his advice, but it didn't help much; he didn't do all that well even as a middleweight, as was proved by his three fights. He was already toying with the idea of eating himself into a heavyweight; maybe he would have done better in that class. At about eighty-five kilos the ghetto interfered with his plans, and ever since then his weight has gradually been going down. Even so, he is still in pretty good shape; he really deserves a better partner than Jakob. Many people believe that one day his good nature will cost him his head, but no one tells him that; maybe some day that person will suffer a similar fate.

'Stop gawking and look where you're going, or we'll both trip and fall,' says Jakob. He is furious because the crate is so heavy, in spite of Mischa, and what annoys him most is the knowledge that Mischa will be the first person he tells; the trouble is, he doesn't know how to begin.

They heave the crates onto the edge of the freight car. Mischa's mind really isn't on his work; they go back to the pile to pick up another crate. Jakob tries to follow Mischa's gaze, the fellow is driving him crazy the way he keeps looking sideways. The station looks the same as always.

'That freight car over there,' said Mischa.

'Which one?'

'On the next-to-last track. The one without a roof.' Mischa is whispering, although the nearest sentry is at least twenty metres away and not even looking in their direction.

'What about it?' asks Jakob.

'There are potatoes in that car.'

Jakob grumbles all through the next haul. So there are potatoes in it, what's so special about that, potatoes are only interesting when you have some, when you can cook them or eat them raw or make pancakes out of them, but not when they're lying around in some freight car or other at a station like this one; potatoes in that freight car over there are the most boring thing in the world. Even if they were pickled herrings there or roast goose or millions of pots of *Cholent* . . . Jakob goes on and on, trying to get Mischa's mind off the subject and draw him into conversation.

Only Mischa isn't listening; the sentries' relief will soon show up, something they always turn into a little ceremony, standing at attention and reporting and shouldering arms, and that is the only moment at which to try. Jakob's objections aren't to be taken seriously, Mischa says, of course there's a risk – all right, even a great risk, so what? Nobody's saying the potatoes are as good as eaten, every opportunity is a risk, must one explain that to a businessman? If there were no risk there would be no opportunity either. Then it would be a sure thing, and sure things are rare in life; risk and the chance of success are two sides of the same coin.

Jakob knows that time is running out; Mischa is in a state in which no normal conversation is possible with him. And then he sees the relief column marching up: now he has to tell him.

'Do you know where Bezanika is?'

'Just a moment,' says Mischa tensely.

'Do you know where Bezanika is, I said.'

'No,' says Mischa, his eyes following the column as it covers the last few metres.

'Bezanika is about four hundred kilometres from here. . . .'

'Oh yes.'

'The Russians are within twenty kilometres of Bezanika!'

Mischa manages to tear his gaze for a moment from the marching soldiers; his unusual eyes smile at Jakob; actually this is very nice of Heym, and he says: 'That's nice of you, Jakob.'

Jakob almost has a fit. Here you overcome all your scruples, ignore all the rules of caution and all your misgivings, for which there are reasons enough, you carefully choose a blue-eyed young idiot to confide in, and what does that snot-nose do? He doesn't believe you! And you can't simply walk away, you can't leave him standing there in his stupidity, tell him to go to hell and simply walk away. You have to stay with him, save up your rage for some later occasion, and you can't even relish the vision of such an occasion. You have to beg for his indulgence as if your own life depended on it, you have to prove your credibility although you shouldn't need to, he's the one who needs to. And you have to do all that terribly fast, before the sentries face each other, slap their rifles onto their shoulders, and exchange the information that there is nothing special to report.

'Aren't you glad?' asks Jakob.

Mischa smiles at him kindly. 'That's fine,' he says in a voice that, while sounding a little sad, is also intended to convey a certain appreciation of Jakob's touching efforts. And then he has something more important to watch again. The column is approaching, it has already passed the little red brick building used by the railwaymen and the sentries.

Mischa is trembling with excitement, and Jakob tries to get his words out faster than the soldiers can approach. He tells his story in a shortened version – why hadn't he started it earlier? He tells about the man with the searchlight, about the corridor in the military office, about the door that opened outwards and hid him. About the report he heard coming from the room, word for word as he has been repeating it to himself a thousand times during the night, nothing added and nothing withheld. He omits his brief imprisonment in the door jamb, keeps to essentials, nothing either about the man who took him to the duty officer, a minor figure in the story; only about the duty officer himself, who must have been human and hence a weak link in the otherwise logical chain of evidence. He had looked at the clock like a human being and then, like a human being, told Jakob to go home.

And then to his horror Jakob sees that there is no stopping Mischa now, the only way is through certainty, and already the soldiers are facing each other. The enemy must be caught off guard, when his attention is at a low point. Mischa is crouching, ready to leap, certainty and the Russians are far away, the only thing left for Jakob to do is grab Mischa and hold on to his leg. They both fall to the ground, and Jakob sees the hatred in Mischa's eyes: he has ruined his chance, at least he is trying to. Mischa wrenches himself free, nothing can stop him now, and he thrusts Jakob away.

'I have a radio!' says Jakob.

It's not the sentries who have fired. So far, busy with their change-over ritual, they haven't seen a thing – Jakob has fired, a bullet straight to the heart. A lucky shot from the hip without taking proper aim, yet it found its mark. Mischa sits there motionless: the Russians are four hundred kilometres from here, near some place called Bezanika, and Jakob has a radio. They sit on the ground staring at each other: there never was any freight car with potatoes, no one has ever waited for the sentries to be relieved, quite suddenly tomorrow is another day. Although it is still true, of course, that opportunity and risk are two sides of the same coin, one would have to be crazy to overlook the fact that there must be some sort of healthy relationship between the two.

They go on sitting there for a bit, Mischa with a blissful smile in his eyes, the result of Jakob's handiwork. Jakob gets up, they can't sit there indefinitely; he is angrier than ever. He has been forced to launch irresponsible claims, and it's that ignorant idiot there who has forced him, just because he didn't believe him, because he suddenly had a craving for potatoes. He'll tell him the truth all right, not this minute but some time today, no matter whether that freight car is still there tomorrow or not. Within an hour in fact, an hour at most, maybe even sooner, he'll tell him the truth: let the fellow enjoy a few more carefree minutes – not that he's deserved them. Soon he won't be able to live without that happiness, then Jakob will tell him the truth, and then he will have to believe what went on at the military office; after all, that doesn't change anything about the Russians, he'll have to believe it.

'Pull yourself together and get up. And above all, keep your trap shut. You know what that means, a radio in the ghetto. Not a soul must find out about it.'

Mischa couldn't care less what that means, a radio in the ghetto. Even if a thousand regulations were to prohibit it on pain of death, let them – does that matter now, when suddenly tomorrow is another day?

'Oh, Jakob. . . .'

The corporal in command of the sentry detail sees a lanky fellow sitting on the ground, just sitting there, hasn't even collapsed, propping himself on his hands and staring up into the sky. The corporal straightens his tunic and comes striding towards them, little fellow that he is.

'Watch out!' Jakob cries, nodding towards the danger approaching in all its dignity.

Mischa regains his senses, comes down to earth, gets up, knows what is about to happen, but can't keep the look of pleasure off his face. He busies himself with the crates, is about to tip one on its side, when the corporal hits him from the side. Mischa turns towards him, the corporal is a head shorter than he and has trouble reaching up to hit Mischa in the face. It almost verges on the comical, not suitable for a German newsreel, more like a scene from an old slapstick silent movie when Charlie the little policeman tries to arrest the giant with the bushy eyebrows, and, try as he will, the big fellow doesn't even notice him. We all know that Mischa could lift him off the ground and tear him to pieces. If he wanted to. The corporal hits him a few more times – by now his hands must be hurting – then shouts something or other that nobody's interested in and only lays off when a thin trickle of blood runs out of the corner of Mischa's mouth. Then he straightens his tunic again and belatedly notices that in the excitement his cap has fallen off; he picks it up, puts it on, goes back to his men, and marches away with the off-duty sentry detail behind him.

Mischa wipes the blood from his mouth with his sleeve, winks at Jakob, and reaches for a crate.

'All right, let's get on with it,' he says.

They lift up the crate, and, as they carry it, Jakob's anger flares up again, almost tearing his teeth apart. He's not superstitious and there's

no such thing as a higher power, but in some inexplicable way –
perhaps only because it verged on the comical – he feels that Mischa
deserved the beating.

'Oh, Jakob. . . .'

We know what will happen. We have some modest experience in the
course events are apt to take; we have some imagination so we know
what will happen. Mischa won't be able to keep his mouth shut. Never
mind that he has been forbidden to talk: it won't be spite that will
make him break his silence or not even try to remain silent; it won't
be some malevolent desire to get Jakob into trouble – it will be joy, pure
and simple. Stop taking your own lives, you'll soon be needing them
again! Stop living without hope, our days of misery are numbered!
Make an effort to survive, you've had plenty of practice in that, you're
familiar with all the thousands of tricks one can use to cheat death –
after all, you've managed so far. Just survive the last four hundred
kilometres, then survival will be over, then life will begin.

Those are the reasons why Mischa won't be able to keep his mouth
shut. He'll be asked for his source, he will reveal it, what's wrong
with that? Soon even the children in the ghetto will know the big
secret, in the strictest confidence of course; they will hear about it
when their parents in their joy forget to whisper. People will come to
Jakob, to Heym the possessor of a radio, and want to hear the latest
news; they will come with eyes such as Jakob has never seen before.
And what on earth is he going to tell them?

Half a day has passed, the big crates have been stowed away in the
freight cars, now it's time for the smaller ones, the kind that one man
can carry alone, and Jakob has lost sight of Mischa – well, not literally
lost sight of him, they see each other every few minutes but always a
few metres apart, in passing, with their backs under a load or while
on their way to another crate. The opportunity for a word of
explanation hasn't come yet; one can't simply take him aside and say,
This is how things really are. Whenever they see each other, Mischa
winks at him or smiles or makes a face or waves at him surreptitiously,
whether carrying a crate or not, it hardly makes any difference to him;
each time some confidential gesture, we both know what it's all about.
Once Jakob forgets himself and winks back, but he recovers himself
immediately – that would be going too far, that would block the way
to the opportunity. But he can't help himself; each time they pass

his anger subsides. After all, the fellow has a right to be happy: why shouldn't he be happy after all that has happened?

The day is bright blue, as if specially chosen for the joyous occasion. The sentry by the wooden shed is sitting on a few bricks, having taken off his rifle and placed it beside him; he is leaning his head against the wall with his eyes shut, basking in the sun. He is smiling, one could almost feel sorry for him.

As Jakob walks past he gets a good look at him; walking quite slowly he studies that face with its closed eyes. He takes note of the smile, the prominent Adam's apple, the wide gold signet ring on the sentry's little finger. Jakob walks on and discovers, so he has told me, that he has changed. From one day to the next his senses are suddenly far more alert; he is beginning to observe. The apathetic despair has not survived the excitement of the previous night, nothing is left of that numbness. Now it is as if one must remember everything exactly as it was so as to be able to tell about it afterwards. Afterwards.

Jakob invents an innocent little game. On his way to the freight car or on his way back to the crates he always passes very close to the drowsing sentry. So close that he almost walks over his outstretched legs, each time depriving him for a brief moment of the sun. The sentry, of course, doesn't notice, doesn't even open his eyes although he is not asleep; he moves his head once slightly, or twitches his mouth – in annoyance, it seems to Jakob – or does nothing at all. But each time Jakob passes him he loses a moment of sunshine. Jakob carries on his little game until he has to turn to another pile of crates. The sentry is no longer in Jakob's path; he would have to make a detour, and for that the joke is too slight and the risk too great. Jakob sees with satisfaction that a few little clouds are carrying on his prank. Then it is noon.

A man in railway uniform emerges from the red brick building, the same man ever since we've been working here. He has a stiff leg that makes a noise with every step like a pebble falling into water, obviously a wooden leg. We call him the Whistle, not at all disparagingly for we know nothing about his human or professional qualities. The only thing we have against him is that he happens to be a German which, strictly speaking, of course, should not be reason enough for a low opinion, but that's how unfair one's plight can make one. As soon as he emerges from the building he pulls from his breast pocket a whistle fastened with a black cord to his buttonhole and proceeds to blow it at a remarkable volume, a signal that it is now noon. This is the only sound we have ever heard from him, apart from the pit-pat of his wooden leg. That's why we call him the Whistle. For all we know he may be mute.

We form a line, very disciplined and with no jostling. That's how they've taught us, under the threat of no food. It must look as if at the moment we had absolutely no appetite: What, food again? A fellow hardly has a chance to settle into the job before he is interrupted yet again by another of these many meals. So we form a line, without haste; you look round and make sure you're all standing in an imaginary straight line. With outstretched arm you check the distance to the man in front of you, then correct it by a few centimetres to create the impression that you are among well-mannered people here. The spoon is taken out of the trouser pocket and held in the left hand against the left trouser seam. Then the handcart appears round the corner of the shed, with the tin bowls piled beside the two steaming green cauldrons. The cart stops at the head of the greedy queue. The first man steps forward, opens the cauldron (invariably burning his fingers as he does so), and begins doling out the contents. The Whistle stands to one side, mute and staring fixedly, to see that everything is done fairly.

On this bright blue day I do the doling. I know nothing, I'm always the last to find out, the sun gets on my nerves, I'm furious. I'm annoyed at the extra work, my burned fingers are hurting, I'm the last to get my food. I slap the ladleful of soup into their bowls, the men move off, I discover nothing unusual in their faces, in none of them, but then I'm not paying attention. I don't even see who I happen to be giving soup to, I just look down at the bowls.

Jakob has drawn his ration, as they put it; he is looking for Mischa, who was far ahead of him in the line. Noon would be such a good opportunity for a private word with him, a little correction that does nothing to alter the actual facts. Mischa is nowhere to be seen; it is a large area, and the men have spread out with their bowls. The break is too short for a long search. Jakob sits down on a crate and swallows his hot soup. He's only human, his thoughts roam far away from the bowl, what's going to happen and how long will it take, and then what. The sun is shining on him, and no one is casting a shadow. Then Kowalski arrives.

Kowalski arrives.

'Is there a spot of room for me here too?' asks Kowalski.

He sits down beside Jakob and begins to spoon up his soup. Kowalski is marvellous. He thinks he is a real fox of a fellow who knows all the ins and outs, yet his expression can conceal nothing; it tells all. You only have to be slightly acquainted with him to know what he's going to say before he has even opened his mouth. His words are always merely the confirmation of long-held assumptions, if you're only slightly acquainted with him. At the freight yard everyone is slightly acquainted with Kowalski, and Jakob has known him since they were at school together. Here, in these grim times, they have rather lost sight of each other, which is easy enough to explain. Neither of them is a giant; a crate doesn't get any lighter when the one at the other end is an old friend, so it's simply due to circumstances. And otherwise there is virtually no opportunity. Two people get thrown together, or they don't. They hardly ever did, and now here comes Kowalski with his bowl, saying, 'Is there a spot of room for me here too?', and sits down beside Jakob and starts to eat.

Kowalski had been Jakob's most frequent customer. Not his best, his most frequent. Every day, just before seven, the shop bell would tinkle and, sure enough, there was Kowalski. He would sit down in his usual place and eat potato pancakes until the sight made you dizzy. Never less than four or five, usually followed by a little glass from under the counter, since Jakob didn't have a licence for schnapps. Most shopkeepers would have been ecstatic over such a customer, but not Jakob, for Kowalski never paid, not a penny, not once. Being schoolmates wasn't the reason for Jakob's generosity, what kind of a reason would that be, and generosity simply didn't enter into it. In a stupid moment one tipsy evening they had made a bargain. Kowalski's barber shop was only a few doors away; they met almost every day anyway, and the bargain had seemed advantageous to both of them. You don't pay at my place, and I don't pay at yours. Later they both regretted it, but a bargain is a bargain, and one man alone can't ruin another man. They both tried.

At first, potato pancakes were Kowalski's favourite dish, a fact that probably accounted in part for his suggestion, but that soon changed. After a while he grew sick and tired of them, and the only reason he went on eating four at a time was that, out of habit, Jakob set them down in front of him without a word. Much more important to him by this time was the little drink that followed.

Jakob, on the other hand, suffered at first from the inescapable fact that, although one can eat potato pancakes every day, one can't have one's hair cut every day. After much thought the idea of getting a shave occurred to him. He even sacrificed his sparse little beard, although he felt bad about that. His best times were the summers; fortunately Kowalski's stomach could not tolerate ice-cream, and for a while Jakob was the only beneficiary of their bargain. However, as time passed his ambition subsided; other worries were really more important, he let his beard grow again, and the whole thing quietly petered out except for an occasional flare-up.

But that's old history. Kowalski is sitting beside him, spooning up his soup – how much longer in silence? – a single suppressed question imprinted in red spots on his gaunt cheeks. Jakob stares into his empty bowl, thinking. Perhaps it's only a coincidence, funny coincidences do happen. How are you? would sound idiotic, he thinks. He carefully licks his spoon clean and puts it in his pocket; there's no reason to get up yet, they still have a few minutes left on their break. The last men in the line are just getting their soup. Putting his bowl aside he props himself on his hands, leans back and closes his eyes, his head tilted back: to be a sentry for a few moments and enjoy the sun.

Kowalski stops eating; through his closed eyes Jakob can hear that his bowl is not yet empty: he hasn't scraped the bottom yet. So Jakob can hear that Kowalski is looking at him; it can't go on much longer, he just has to find the right beginning.

'Any news?' Kowalski asks casually.

When Jakob looks at him he starts eating again, the suppressed thoughts still on his cheeks but his innocent eyes fixed on the soup. He says it as if you had just entered his barber shop, sat down on the only chair facing the only mirror, while he shakes the black hairs of the previous customer from the cape and ties it round you – as always, much too tight. 'Any news?' Mundek's son has won his first court case, it looks as if he's going to do well, but that's no longer news, Hübscher had already been talking about it the day before. But what you don't know yet: Kwart's wife has left him, no one knows where she's gone, but then no normal person can get along with Kwart. It sounds so familiar that Jakob feels tempted to say: 'Not as short in the back as last time, please.' 'Well?' Kowalski asks, his eyes threatening to drown in the soup.

'What do you mean, news?' says Jakob. 'Why ask *me*?'

Kowalski raises his face towards Jakob, that fox's face that is like an open book. He turns it towards Jakob with an expression of mild reproach, of some understanding of Jakob's caution, and the implication that in this particular case caution might well be considered misplaced.

'Jakob! . . . Aren't we old friends?'

'What's that got to do with it?' says Jakob. He's not sure whether his attempt to play dumb is convincing; after all, Kowalski has known him a long time. And he can imagine that basically it doesn't much matter whether he's convincing or not: if Kowalski knows something, no acting talent in the world will help him. If Kowalski knows something, he won't let go; he can hound you almost to death.

Moving a little closer, Kowalski lets his spoon float in the soup and grabs Jakob's arm with his free hand to prevent him getting away.

'All right then, let's speak plainly. . . .' Lowering his voice to the level at which secrets are discussed, he whispers: 'Is it true about the Russians?'

Jakob is shocked at the tone. Not at the whispering: people whisper on all sorts of occasions, that doesn't frighten him. He is shocked at the seriousness; he can see that it's not going to be a picnic, nothing to be taken lightly; he is shocked at the quaver in Kowalski's voice. It holds an expectation that will not tolerate ridicule; certainty is demanded here, a man is asking – a man who wants only this one question answered, there's no escape, just this one question, nothing else, for all time. And yet Jakob makes one last, vain attempt.

'About what Russians?'

'About what Russians! Must you insult me like that, Jakob? Have I ever done you any harm? Remember, Jakob, remember who's sitting beside you! The whole world knows he has a radio, and to me, his only, his best friend, he refuses to tell anything!'

'The whole world knows?'

Kowalski backs down. 'Not exactly the whole world, but one or two people do know about it. Has someone told me, or do I have second sight?'

In Jakob's head, one annoyance displaces the other. Kowalski is upstaged by Mischa: that blabbermouth is going to land him in an impossible situation. Suddenly it is no longer necessary to take Mischa aside for a correction – totally superfluous. The fire can no longer be contained – who knows how many others would now have to be taken aside! And even if he were to try his best with every single one of them, try with the patience of an angel to explain to each individual the crazy route by which the glorious news has fluttered into the ghetto, into their very ears: what else could they do but not believe him? With all due respect and much sympathy for his situation? Or does anyone seriously believe that Kowalski could afford to be fobbed off with a story so manifestly full of holes?

'Well?'

'It's true about the Russians,' says Jakob. 'And now stop bothering me.'

'Are they twenty kilometres from Bezanika?'

Jakob rolls up his eyes and says: 'Yes!'

He gets to his feet: that's how they sour one's joy, yet Kowalski is as entitled to it as all the rest of them. He would give anything for Kowalski to have been spotted by the sentry on the Kurländischer Damm, Kowalski or anyone else. What on earth made him go there? All good citizens are in bed, but at that dark hour he has to roam the streets because the walls of his room are closing in on him, because once again Piwowa and Rosenblatt have become unbearable, because a stroll after work seems to bring a strange, faint whiff of normal times. A stroll in a town one knows, has known since they used to sit you up in your pram with a pillow at your back. The buildings tell you about almost forgotten trifles: over there you once fell down and sprained your left ankle, at this corner you finally told Gideon the truth to his face, in that building there was once a fire in the middle of winter. A longed-for whiff of normal times, that's what he had promised himself: he hadn't been able to enjoy it for long, and now this.

'Will you at least keep it to yourself?'

'You know me!' answers Kowalski. He wants to be left in peace, for the time being. The break is short, and he has enough just coping with his own emotions and with what is suddenly looming ahead of him.

Jakob picks up his bowl from the ground and walks away. He carries Kowalski's expression with him, the face tilted to one side, no war far and wide, the eyes fixed on a distant point that no one else can see. He hears Kowalski's lips whispering rapturously: 'The Russians. . . .' Then Jakob reaches the handcart: he adds his bowl to the others and glances back again at Kowalski, who is now fishing his spoon out of his soup. The whistle shrills, even Kowalski hears it, and a little tower of bowls is quickly erected. To Jakob it seems that all the men are looking at him strangely, differently from the day before, somehow with the secret in their eyes. Maybe it's an illusion, in fact it must be: they can't possibly all know about it already, but there may well be one or two who do.

I would like, while it's still not too late, to say a few words about how I came by my knowledge, before any suspicions arise. My principal informant is Jakob; most of what I have heard from him will turn up in this story somewhere, I can vouch for that. But I say 'most', not all, I say it deliberately, and in this case the reason is not my poor memory. After all, *I* am telling the story, not Jakob: Jakob is dead, and besides, I'm not telling his story but a story.

He told me, but I am talking to you. That's a big difference, because I was there. He tried to explain how one thing followed another and that he couldn't have acted any differently, but I want you to know that he was a hero. Not three sentences would pass his lips without his mentioning his fear, but I want you to know about his courage. About those trees, for example, about those non-existent trees I'm looking for, that I don't want to think about but have to, and my eyes grow moist when I do: he had no inkling of that, that's simply and solely my concern. I can't quite piece it all together, but there are some things that he knew nothing about, when he might have asked me how I got such ideas in my head, but somehow I feel that it is all part of it. I would like so much to tell him why I feel that, I owe him an explanation, and I think he would say I was right.

Some things I know from Mischa, but then there is a big gap for which there are simply no witnesses. I tell myself that it must have happened more or less in such and such a way, or that it would be best if it had happened in such and such a way, and then I tell it and pretend that's how it was. And that *is* how it was; it's not my fault that the witnesses who could confirm it can no longer be found.

For me, probability is not a determining factor; it is improbable that I of all people should still be alive. Much more important is my feeling that it could or should have happened this way, and that has nothing whatever to do with probability, I can vouch for that too.

I t wasn't at all a bad idea of Mischa's, to speak to Rosa during the ration-card distribution, to pluck up his courage and ask her whether they couldn't walk part of the way home together, and luckily she agreed. At first it was only her face that loosened his tongue – how many girls have been addressed merely because of their bright eyes! – but one thing led to another, and today, about a year later, he loves all of her, just the way she is. The first steps were awkwardly silent; his head felt hollowed out. He received no help at all from her, not even an encouraging glance; she looked straight ahead shyly, apparently waiting for something important to happen. But nothing happened until they reached her front door; her mother was already standing anxiously at the window, wondering what was keeping her only daughter. With lowered eyes Rosa hurriedly said goodbye, but she must have just had time to hear where exactly he would be waiting for her the next day.

At any rate she did show up, which took a load off Mischa's mind. He reached into his pocket and gave her his first gift. It was a little book of poems and songs; by that time he knew them all by heart, and it was the only book he happened to own. Actually he had wanted to present her with an onion, if possible one with a bluish skin; right from the start he was very serious about Rosa, but the idea was too ambitious. In such a short time he was unable to find one, try as he would. At first she was a little coy about accepting the gift at all, the way unsophisticated girls often are, but then of course she did accept the book and tell him how pleased she was. At this point he introduced himself – the day before they had been too excited to get around to that – and now for the first time he heard her name: Rosa Frankfurter.

'Frankfurter?' he asked. 'Are you by any chance related to that famous actor Felix Frankfurter?'

As could later be readily established by means of theatre programmes, this was something of an exaggeration. Frankfurter the actor never got beyond supporting roles. But Mischa, never having seen Frankfurter on stage, had not meant it ironically. He had been to the theatre only once and had merely heard or read about him. And Rosa didn't take it that way either. She blushingly admitted that such was indeed the case, that Frankfurter the actor was her father. They went on to chat a bit about the theatre, about which he knew practically nothing, until he managed gradually with great skill to bring the conversation round to boxing, about which she in turn knew practically nothing. In this way they had a marvellous time together, and that same evening she did not resist Mischa's first kiss on her silky hair.

When Mischa arrives, Felix Frankfurter is sitting at the table playing a game of draughts with his daughter. He is a big man, tall and gaunt; Mischa has described his appearance with much loving care. What was once a massive corpulence has left the old man's skin in folds, which is greatly emphasized by the fact that the clothes he is wearing date from considerably stouter times. Photos prove that some years ago man and skin formed a well-balanced entity: a weighty album that Frankfurter pressed on Mischa during his very first visit, for he

34

couldn't possibly allow the unfavourable impression, of which he was fully aware, to remain. Round his neck a scarf, artistically yet casually arranged with one end in front and one on his back, and in his mouth a pipe, a meerschaum, that has long since forgotten the taste of tobacco.

He is seated at the table with his daughter; the game looks hopeless for Rosa. Mrs Frankfurter is sitting with them, paying no attention to the game; she is altering one of her husband's shirts, making it smaller and perhaps dreaming of some quiet happiness. When Mischa arrives, Rosa has just been grumbling that the game with her father is so boring because he takes such ages contemplating each move, and he has been trying to explain to her that it is better to win one game in two hours than lose five in the same amount of time.

'But why are you taking so long now?' she had asked. 'You're ahead anyway.'

'I'm not ahead "anyway",' he had answered, 'I'm ahead because I give each move so much thought.'

She had made an impatient gesture, any pleasure in the game was now gone. Only obedience keeps her from sweeping the pieces from the board, plus the fact that Mischa hasn't yet arrived, but at that moment there is a knock at the door. She hurries to open it, and Mischa comes in. Greetings are exchanged, Mr Frankfurter offers Mischa a chair, Mischa sits down. Rosa quickly clears away the board and pieces before Mischa can take over her losing game. Many a time he has taken her place, looked for a way out, and in the end had to give up and ask for a return match. Frankfurter would agree, and then they would both sit there lost in thought, and suddenly it was so late that Mischa would have to leave before Rosa could spend any time with him.

'Have you been playing?' asks Mischa. 'So who won today?'

'Who do you think?' says Rosa, making it sound like a reproach. Mr Frankfurter draws on his meerschaum pipe, as content as circumstances permit, and winks at Mischa. 'She plays faster than she thinks. But I'll bet you've noticed that yourself on other occasions, right?'

Mischa disregards the little joke. Today he is not coming empty-handed: he is merely wondering how to convey the news with the greatest possible effect, for there's nothing Frankfurter enjoys more than a story that ends with a punch line. When he talks about the theatre – where, if one is to believe him, the wildest things have happened – every step, every glance, look on stage carries some special implication.

Someone falls down or makes a fool of himself or messes up the performance or doesn't understand why the others are laughing. If that weren't so, Frankfurter probably feels, there would be no point in telling the anecdote in the first place.

'What can one offer a guest these days?' Frankfurter says to his silent wife. And then to Mischa: 'What can one offer a guest apart from one's daughter?'

He smiles, having brought off his little joke, then draws on his pipe again. Anyone can draw on an empty pipe, nothing to it, but not the way Frankfurter does. Included in his performance are the enjoyment, the pleasurable richness of the smoke. Someone not looking too closely might be tempted to wave the smoke away.

There is a thoughtful silence. Any moment now Mr Frankfurter will tell a story, one of his anecdotes at the end of which he puts on such a display of mirth that he slaps his thigh: for instance, about the actor Strelezki, otherwise said to have been a divine Othello, whose false teeth fell out just as he was bending over Desdemona to strangle her. Rosa lays her fingers on Mischa's hands, her mother goes on making the shirt smaller, Frankfurter is rubbing his knees, perhaps he's not in the mood today; and here comes Mischa with such good news, still wondering how best to tell them, as if pondering over a move.

'Have you heard the latest?' Rosa asks him suddenly.

Startled, Mischa looks from one to the other; he gives up his search and is surprised that Mrs Frankfurter doesn't even look up from the shirt. They already know, yet he hasn't noticed till now that they know. He is surprised to find that everything in the room looks just as it did at his last visit. He is amazed at the speed: it was only this morning that he heard it from Jakob, and now it's already here at the Frankfurters, by way of who knows how many intermediaries; but strangest of all is that Rosa should wait till now to bring up the subject. She can't have forgotten it and only just remembered it: impossible. Something's wrong – maybe they have a reason not to believe it.

'You already know?'

'They were talking about it at work today,' says Rosa.

'And you're not glad?'

'Glad?' says Mr Frankfurter. 'We're supposed to be glad? What are we supposed to be glad about, my boy, eh? At one time they could have been glad about it, gathered all the relatives together, got drunk, but today there are a few little things that have changed. In my opinion, it's all a big calamity, my lad, almost a disaster for those people, and you're asking why I'm not glad?'

Mischa instantly realizes that they are talking about something quite different, the only explanation for their mood. Otherwise Frankfurter has taken leave of his senses and doesn't know what he's saying.

'It will be hard to bring up a child,' says Mrs Frankfurter between two stitches.

The first clue, renewed astonishment in Mischa's eyes: they are talking about some child, so news doesn't travel all that quickly. Apparently two crazy people have brought a child into this world, without having heard the news – in normal ghetto times, certainly a subject for discussion. But as of yesterday the times are no longer normal, a different wind is blowing, we can tell you about things that will make you forget child and husband and wife and eating and drinking: as of yesterday, tomorrow will be another day.

Now Rosa is surprised: first she is surprised, then she smiles at Mischa's expression.

'So you really don't know about it yet,' she says. 'But that's what he's like. He can't stand it if other people know more than he does. He's such a know-it-all, while the truth is he doesn't know anything. A child has been born in Witebsker-Strasse. Actually there were twins, but one of them died almost at once. Last night. When all this is over they intend to have the boy registered under the name of Abraham.'

'When all this is over,' says Frankfurter. He lays his pipe on the table, gets up, and starts to pace the room, head bowed, hands behind his back. His disapproving glances are directed at Mischa – surely the boy isn't grinning? They take everything so lightly, including Rosa; perhaps they are too young to grasp it. They speak of the future as if it were a weekend that can't fail to arrive – the whole family goes off to the country with a picnic basket, rain or shine. 'When all this is over the child will have died and the parents will have died. We all will have died, that's when this will be over.'

Frankfurter has finished his pacing and sits down again.

'I think David sounds nicer,' says Mrs Frankfurter gently.

'Dovidl. . . . Do you remember? That's what Annette's son was called. Abraham sounds so terribly old, not at all like a child. Yet it's only for children that names are important. Later, by the time they're grown up, names don't matter so much any more.'

Rosa tends to favour Jan or Roman; she feels it's time to get away from the traditional names. When it's no longer necessary to wear the yellow star, why not choose different names? Frankfurter shakes his head over this women's chatter, and suddenly Mischa wishes he had arrived at this moment instead of earlier – blurting it out the moment he arrived. For it he starts telling them now, they will feel just as he did in his error; Why did he wait till now to tell us? He can't have forgotten it! He's been sitting and sitting while they talk themselves ever deeper into their gloomy mood. Either he doesn't tell them till tomorrow and then pretends that it's the latest news, or he'll have to think up some story to explain why only now and not as soon the door was opened. He decides on today, a little extra punch line for Frankfurter. He gets up, affects reluctance, even he doesn't know whether simulated or real, looks diffidently at Frankfurter, who is already wondering about the lengthy prelude, and formally requests the hand of his daughter.

Rosa discovers something on her fingernail that claims her undivided attention, something so important that her face turns fiery red: they have never discussed it by so much as a syllable, which, of course, is really the way it should be. Mrs Frankfurter bends lower over the shirt, which is nowhere near small enough yet, most of the work being required by the collar because of the great importance of a perfect fit. Mischa relishes his inspiration, successful or otherwise; Frankfurter is taken aback and is about to say something. It is his turn to speak, since a polite question deserves an answer, and, no matter how out of place the question may seem to be at first, Frankfurter will build a bridge to the great news, and this will at the same time explain why only now. That is Mischa's plan, devised in extreme haste and not so bad at that; Felix Frankfurter will build a bridge, it's his turn, they are all waiting for his answer.

So: great astonishment on Frankfurter's part, incredulity in his expression; he has just been drawing on his pipe and has forgotten to puff out the smoke. The father who would give his only daughter to no one but Mischa, loving him as he does like his own son, the man of hard facts who is nobody's fool, is staggered. 'He's gone mad,' he whispers, 'suffering has confused him, it's these cursed times when perfectly normal desires sound monstrous. Why don't *you* say something?'

But Mrs Frankfurter won't say anything. A few tears drop soundlessly onto the shirt; she doesn't know what to say, all important questions having invariably been decided by her husband.

Felix Frankfurter resumes his pacing, inner turmoil, and Mischa looks as hopeful as if the next words could only be: Take her and be happy.

38

'We are in the ghetto, Mischa, don't you know that? We can't do what we want because they do what they want with us. Should I ask you what security you can offer, since she is my only daughter? Should I ask you where you intend to find a place to live? Should I tell you what kind of a dowry Rosa will receive from me? Surely that must interest you? Or should I give you some advice on how to conduct a happy marriage and then go to the rabbi and ask when it would suit him best to perform the *Chassene*? You'd be better off racking your brain for a place to hide when they come for you.'

Mischa remains confidently silent; that still wasn't an answer, after all.

'Just listen to that! His ship has foundered, he's swimming in the middle of the ocean, not a soul in sight to help him. And he's wondering whether he'd rather spend that evening at a concert that evening or at the opera!'

His arms sink to his sides; Frankfurter has said all that was to be said, even throwing in a little allegory at the end. No one need be clearer than that.

But Mischa is not impressed. On the contrary, everything has gone just as he hoped. No help in sight, that's the kind of phrase Mischa has been waiting for – soon you'll all know the real situation. It does make sense to speak of the future, Mischa isn't an idiot after all, of course he knows where we are, of course he knows that one can't get married until – and that's the real issue – until the Russians arrive.

Mischa to me: 'So I simply told them (that was his word: simply) that the Russians were twenty kilometres from Bezanika. You see, it wasn't just a piece of news, now it was also an argument. I had imagined they would be thrilled – you don't hear that kind of news every day. But Rosa didn't throw her arms round my neck, far from it; she looked at her father almost in alarm, and he looked at me. For a long time he didn't say a word, just looked at me, so that I began to get nervous. My first thought was, maybe they need time to grasp it, judging by the way the old man was looking at me, but then I realized it wasn't time they needed but certainty. After all, the same thing had happened to me: I too had thought that Jakob was just trying to divert my attention from the carload of potatoes, and I went on thinking this till he told me the whole truth, how he had found out. News like that without a source simply isn't worth anything, it's no more than a rumour. So I was about to open my mouth and dispel their doubts, but then I decided to wait. Let them ask, I thought: if you have to squeeze something out of another person, you can absorb it better than if he tells it to you on his own and all in one piece. And that's exactly the way it happened.'

So: an endless silence, the needle paused in the middle of a stitch, Rosa's hot breath, Frankfurter's eyes, and Mischa standing there in the spotlight, the audience hanging on his lips.

'Do you know what you're saying?' says Frankfurter. 'That's not something to joke about.'

'You don't need to tell me that,' says Mischa. 'I heard it from Heym.'

'From Jakob Heym?'

'Yes.'

'And he? Where did he hear it?'

Mischa smiles weakly, pretends to be embarrassed, shrugs his shoulders unhappily, which they won't accept. Somewhere there was a promise. That he is not going to keep it is another matter, but the promise was made, and one would like at least to be forced to break it, one would like to have done one's utmost: in my place you wouldn't have acted any differently.

'Where did he hear it?'

'I promised him not to tell anyone,' says Mischa, actually quite prepared to do so, but obviously not prepared enough, at least not obviously enough for Felix Frankfurter. This is not the time to note nuances in a voice; Frankfurter takes two or three quick steps and gives Mischa a slap, a cross between a stage slap and a genuine one, but more likely genuine, for it contains indignation, we're not talking here to pass the time.

Naturally Mischa is a bit shocked, that much force wasn't really necessary, but he can't be offended now – the force, after all, had to assume some form or other. He can't sit down with a stony face, arms crossed on his chest, waiting for an apology: he could wait a long time for that. He can, and he does, remove all doubts: the moment has arrived, his plan has gone up in smoke – no one is going to ask now why he took so long.

'Jakob Heym has a radio.'

Another short silence, a few glances exchanged, the shirt – still too big – floats unnoticed to the floor. It's all right to believe one's own son-in-law. At last Rosa throws her arms round his neck, he's waited long enough for that; over her shoulder he sees her father sitting down exhausted and covering his deeply furrowed face with his hands. There will be no discussion: there is nothing to say. Rosa pulls his ear to her mouth and whispers. He doesn't understand, the old man still has his hands in front of his face, and Mischa looks at her inquiringly.

'Let's go to your place,' Rosa whispers again.

A brilliant idea, she has taken the words out of Mischa's mouth: today one inspiration follows on the heels of another. They tiptoe out of the room with exaggerated care, the door clicks shut, no one hears it. Outside, it is already getting dangerously dark.

Then Frankfurter is alone with his wife, without witnesses. All I know is how it ended, I only know the outcome, nothing in between, but I can only imagine that it was something like this.

His wife finally gets up, at some point. She wipes away her tears, no longer those of the marriage proposal, or she doesn't wipe them away. She goes to her husband, quietly, as if not wanting to disturb him. She stands behind him, puts her hands on his shoulders, brings her face close to his, which is still covered with his hands, and waits. Nothing happens, not even when he lowers his arms. He stares at the opposite wall, and she gives him a little nudge. She is looking for something in his eyes and cannot find it.

'Felix,' she may have said softly after a while. 'Aren't you glad? Bezanika isn't so far away. If they've come that far they'll come as far as here too.'

Or she may have said: 'Just imagine, Felix, if that's true! My head's in a whirl, just imagine that! Not much longer now, and everything will be just the way it used to be. You'll be able to perform again, on a real stage, I'm sure they'll reopen the theatre. I'll be waiting for you beside the notice-board next to the porter's lodge. Just imagine that, Felix!'

He doesn't answer. He gets up from under her hands and goes over to the cupboard. Perhaps he looks like a man who has come to an important decision and doesn't want to waste any time in carrying it out.

Frankfurter opens the cupboard, takes out a cup or a little box, and finds a key in it.

'What are you going to do in the cellar?' she asks.

He weighs the key in his hand, as if there were still something to be considered, possibly the matter of finding the right moment, but the sooner the better. Nothing is the same any more. Perhaps he tells her now what he has in mind, taking her into his confidence while still in the room, but that's unlikely since he has never been in the habit of asking for her opinion. Besides, it makes no difference when he tells her; it won't change anything, the key is already in his pocket. So let us assume that he closes the cupboard without a word, walks to the door, turns round and says only: 'Come.'

They go down into the cellar.

The houses of the poor where formerly one would never have set foot: the wooden stairs are worn, they creak abominably, but he walks close to the wall and on tiptoe. She follows him uneasily, also softly, also on tiptoe – she doesn't know why, just because he's doing it. She has always followed him, without asking; often she has only been able to guess what was to be done, and it wasn't always the right thing.

'Won't you tell me now what we're doing here?'

'Sssh!'

They walk along the narrow cellar passage; here it's all right to put down one's whole foot. The last-but-one cubicle on the right is theirs. Frankfurter turns the key in the padlock and opens the wire door in its iron frame, which is no good as fuel and so is still there. He goes in, she follows hesitantly, he closes the wire door behind her, and there they are.

Felix Frankfurter is a cautious man. He looks for a piece of sacking, or a sack with holes that he can tear, or, if there is no sack, he takes of his jacket and hangs it across the door, just in case. I imagine that for a moment he puts his finger to his lips, closing his eyes and listening, but there is not a sound. Then he goes to work on the little pile filling one corner of the space, a little pile of useless stuff, a small heap of memories.

At the time they received the notice, they spent two days with their heads together considering what they should take along – apart from the prohibited things, of course. The situation was very serious, no doubt about that; they didn't expect it to be a paradise, but nobody had any definite knowledge. Mrs Frankfurter thought in practical terms, too practical for his liking, solely of bed-linen and dishes and things to wear, but he was reluctant to part with many items that she regarded as superfluous. With the drum on which at a highly successful performance he had announced the arrival of the heir to the Spanish throne; or with Rosa's ballet slippers from the time when she was five years old, to this day almost unworn; or with the album of carefully pasted-in reviews in which his name is mentioned and underlined in red. Give me one good reason why I should part with them: life is more than merely eating and sleeping. The problem of transport? In great haste he bought a handcart, at an exorbitant price, for at that time prices for handcarts shot up overnight, and now the little pile fills a corner of their cellar.

He lays aside one item after another, his wife watching him silently, seething with curiosity: What is he looking for? Maybe for a moment he studies the framed photograph of all his fellow actors at the theatre, his portly figure over on the right, between Salzer and Strelezki, who in those days wasn't yet so well known. But that's not what he's looking for; if he did study the picture, he puts it aside again and goes on reducing the pile.

'That Jakob Heym is a fool.'

'Why?'

'Why! Why! He heard some news, marvellous, but that's his affair. Some good news, very good news in fact: then he should just be glad and not drive everyone else crazy with it.'

'I don't understand you Felix,' she says. 'You're not being fair to him. Surely it's a great thing for us to know about it. Everybody should know about it.'

'Women!' Frankfurter says angrily. 'Today you know about it, tomorrow the neighbours know, and the next day the whole ghetto is talking about nothing else!'

She may nod, surprised at his fury, that's how it is: so far no reason at all to reproach Heym in the slightest.

'And all of a sudden the Gestapo knows!' he says. 'They have more ears than you think.'

'Oh, Felix,' she interrupts him, 'do you seriously believe that the Gestapo needs us to find out where the Russians are?'

'Who's talking about that! What I mean is: all of a sudden the Gestapo knows that there's a radio in the ghetto. And what will they do? They'll immediately turn every street upside down, house by house, they won't give till they've found the radio. And where will they find one?'

The pile has been levelled. Frankfurter lifts up a cardboard box, white or brown, in any case a cardboard box containing the reason for a just and valid death sentence. He opens the lid and shows his wife the radio.

She may give a little shriek, she may be horrified, certainly shocked; she stares at the radio and at him and is at a loss.

'You brought our radio along!' she whispers and folds her hands. 'You brought our radio along, they could have shot all of us for that, and I knew nothing about it . . . I knew nothing. . . .'

'Why should you?' he said. 'Why should I have told you? I've trembled enough alone, and you've trembled enough even without a radio. There were days when I forgot it, simply forgot it, sometimes even for weeks at a time. So one happens to have an old radio in the cellar and stops thinking about it. But whenever I did remember I would start trembling, and I've never been reminded of it as I was today. The worst part is that I never listened, not a single time, not even in the early days. Not so that you wouldn't notice – I simply didn't dare. Sometimes I wanted to, my curiosity would almost get the better of me: I'd pick up the key, and you remember how from time to time I'd go down to the cellar. You would ask me what I wanted down there and I told you I wanted to look at photos or read the old reviews again. But that was a lie; I wanted to listen to the radio. I would go down into the cellar, hang something across the door, and didn't dare. I would sit down, look at the photos or read the reviews, just as I'd told you, and I didn't dare. But that's all over now!'

'I had no idea,' she whispers to herself.

'That's all over, once and for all!' he says. 'You were right all the time, it was useless stuff, I don't need it any more. There'll be nothing left, nothing to suggest a radio. Then let them come and search.'

He takes the radio apart, piece by piece, probably the only radio in the hands of any of us; without much fuss he destroys it. The tubes are trodden to dust, an indestructible piece of wire is wound as a harmless cord round a box, the wooden casing is put aside piece by piece and will have to wait a few weeks before being burned. At this time of year any smoking chimney is suspect, but that's no great tragedy: wood is wood, after all.

'Did you also hear that the Russians have almost reached Bezanika?' Mrs Frankfurter asks in a low voice.

He looks at her in astonishment.

'Didn't I tell you I never listened?' may have been his reply.

Mischa enters his room with Rosa, and that is a whole story on its own. If it is a story when somebody must be lied to in order to make her a little bit happy, that's what happened with Rosa; if it is a story when bold ruses must be employed and fear of discovery is present, and there must on no account be any slip-ups, and one's expression must remain solemn and innocent throughout: if all this yields a serviceable story, then Rosa going with Mischa to his room is also a story.

In the middle of the room is a curtain.

Fajngold is the name of the man sleeping in the other bed. Isaak Fajngold is responsible for this elaborate device: he is wiped out with fatigue anyway every night, he's over sixty and his hair is snow white; he really does have other worries, but go ahead and do what you like. At first only the wardrobe had divided the room; to Mischa this seemed enough and to Fajngold more than enough, but for Rosa it hadn't been sufficient. She told Mischa that, even if Fajngold is deaf and dumb, he still isn't blind, and the moon shines so brightly into the room and in any case the wardrobe is too narrow. Mischa cheerfully removed the piece of cloth from the window and fastened it to the ceiling beside the wardrobe. Now the moon could shine in more brightly than ever, but not for Fajngold. The main thing was that Rosa was reassured.

Fajngold is no more deaf and dumb than I or Kowalski or anyone else who knows how to use his ears and tongue, but for Rosa he is as deaf and dumb as a clam. From the first moment Mischa realized fully that Rosa would not set foot near his bed because there was another bed with a strange man in it; the understanding landladies and the discreet little hotels with their hall porters who tactfully look the other way and ask no questions – these can be found only in some other town. He knew that under the circumstances she could only say No, she's not that kind of girl, that's beyond discussion, nor is he that kind of a fellow. But if renunciation is to be the ultimate option, there is still ample time for brooding. No one can fault him for that, and Mischa did plenty of it.

One blessed night he was lying awake in bed thinking of Rosa, with Fajngold about to fall asleep in the other bed, and Mischa began to tell him about Rosa. Who she was, and how she was, and what she looked like, and how much he loved her, and how much she loved him, and Fajngold merely sighed. That's when Mischa confessed his burning desire to have Rosa with him for one night.

'By all means,' Fajngold answered, without going more deeply into the problem. 'I don't mind. And now do let me go to sleep.'

Mischa didn't let him go to sleep. He explained to Fajngold that the point was not whether Fajngold agreed but whether Rosa agreed. Also that he hadn't mentioned him to her, he hardly dared to, and if we can't think of something presumably nothing will come of it.

Fajngold switched on the light and stared at him for a long time.

'You're not serious?' he said in a shocked whisper. 'You can't expect me to hang about in the street until you've finished. Have you forgotten the regulations?'

But Mischa didn't expect that, he'd never thought of such a thing and he hadn't forgotten the regulations either. He was simply looking for a solution, which was nowhere in sight. Fajngold switched off the light and soon fell asleep. It's not we who must come up with something, but Mischa, all by himself.

After an hour or two Mischa woke Fajngold, patiently put up with his abuse, and then told him about his idea. As he has said, Rosa will never spend the night with him if she finds out that there is another man in the room, regardless of whether you're twenty or a hundred. If he doesn't tell her, maybe she will come, then she'll see Fajngold, so she'll leave again and never forgive Mischa. No matter which way you look at it, the only solution is for Fajngold to remain in the room and yet be as good as not there.

'You want me to hide?' was Fajngold's weary response. 'You want me to spend night after night under my bed or in the wardrobe?'

'I'll tell her you're deaf and dumb,' Mischa announced.

Fajngold protested; for days he bitterly resisted the idea, but eventually Mischa managed to convince him of the urgency. At night one can't see much anyway, and if she is also sure that one can't hear anything either, we should be able to manage. So with distinctly mixed feelings Fajngold gave his consent, if it means so much to you, and ever since then for Rosa he has been as deaf and dumb as a clam.

For Mischa, though, there was another worry: from a few hints dropped by Fajngold he became aware that Fajngold had once been listening. True, Rosa hadn't noticed anything and Fajngold had kept his mouth shut, but he must have heard a thing or two not intended for his ears. After all, when two people lie in each other's arms, quite a few words are spoken that are not meant for other ears, and it was very embarrassing for Mischa. Since then he has been studying Fajngold's sleep, often deliberately lying awake to listen to the pitch of his breathing and snoring. No one has ever heard himself sleep; no one can imitate his own sleep. A person can imitate sleeping as such but cannot know anything about his own sleep. And Mischa knows what Fajngold's sleep sounds like: he could swear, he says, that he knows it in every detail. And during the rare nights when Rosa is with him, Mischa always first listens intently as he lies beside her, and only when he is quite sure that Fajngold is asleep behind the screen does he begin

46

to caress her and kiss her, and Rosa forgets her disappointment and stops wondering why he has kept her waiting so long.

On one occasion something terrible happened: while deeply asleep, in the midst of a confused dream, Fajngold suddenly began to speak: clearly audible individual words, ignoring the fact that deaf mutes must be deaf and dumb in their sleep too. This woke Mischa, whose heart almost stopped beating; he looked anxiously at Rosa, who lay asleep in the moonlight and merely turned her head from one side to the other. He couldn't call out: Fajngold, shut up! He could only lie there motionless and hope, and luckily Fajngold stopped his fantasizing before there was a disaster. Dreams last for only a few seconds, people say, and it never happened again.

So much for the mini-comedy: all in all, we see that some bold paths have led Rosa to this room, right beneath these covers, not merely straight down one street, then a turn to the left and a turn to the right. Mischa has found a way, Fajngold has co-operated, Rosa is happy to be here.

She is lying on her back, I know, her hands under her head, tonight as always, even though that's a bit selfish since with a big fellow like Mischa the bed has more than enough to cope with: he has to make do with the edge. There she lies, a faraway look in her eyes; the evening, the most wonderful yet, is over: they have already whispered their sweet nothings into each other's ears. Although Fajngold is deaf and dumb they always whisper; when two people lie as Rosa and Mischa do they would whisper even on a lonely island, if it were absolutely necessary to speak. The night is far advanced; the mute Fajngold has long since been asleep behind the screen of wardrobe and curtain. The hot weather and the news must have worn him out: tonight he was only a brief impediment. After only a few minutes Mischa was satisfied with the sounds coming from the other side and could lavish his entire attention on Rosa.

Rosa gently nudges Mischa, her foot against his foot, persisting until he is sufficiently awake to ask her what's up.

'My parents will be living with us, won't they?' she says.

Her parents. They had never come as far as this room. There had always been only the night when Mischa and Rosa were lying together and making love – that particular night and no other. All the following ones were yet to come, and it would be a waste of time to discuss them. But now her parents are there. Let's look briefly at what may one day happen, let's peek through the hole in the curtain. The parents are there and a premonition of the future; they can't be thrown out, Rosa is adamant.

'They won't be living with us,' says Mischa in the darkness.

'And why not? Do you have something against them?'

Rosa raises her voice – these are not matters that demand to be whispered – raises it so rebelliously, perhaps, that Fajngold might wake up, but of course she never suspects this danger.

'Good heavens, is that so important that you have to wake me up in the middle of the night?'

'Yes,' says Rosa.

All right: he props himself on his elbows. She can pride herself on having finally chased away his sleep; he sighs, as if life wasn't already difficult enough.

'All right: I have nothing against them, nothing whatsoever. I really like them very much indeed, they won't be living with us, and now I want to sleep!'

He heaves himself onto his other side, a minor demonstration in the moonlight: their first tiff. Not yet a real quarrel, merely a foretaste of everyday worries. A few silent minutes pass during which Mischa notices that Fajngold has woken up.

'Mamma could look after the children,' says Rosa.

'Grandmas always spoil children,' says Mischa.

'And I don't know how to cook, either.'

'There are books.'

Now she sighs, let's quarrel later, we'll have all the time in the world. Rosa has to lift her head slightly because he is pushing his reconciling arm under it: now a kiss to make up, then finally back to sleep. But she can't simply close her eyes and run away, what she sees she sees: we've been waiting a long time for this glimpse into the future. When they knock, when they are standing in the doorway, those Russians, good morning, here we are, now we can start, by that time it's too late, we can't wait till then to decide, we must know by then what has to be done first and what next. But Mischa wants to sleep, and Rosa can't: so many things are mixed up, at least some of them should be straightened out. Important matters will somehow take care of themselves, people of consequence who'll take care of those are sure to show up; let's start with our own little affairs, no one's going to look after those for us.

From pondering Rosa progresses to whispering: first of all there would be the house, where one must feel comfortable, but we might also discuss something other than the house, if you can think of

48

anything, anyway let's begin with the house. Not too small, not too big, let's say five rooms, that's not asking too much. Now don't start yelling, that much one can ask for, we've been modest long enough. There'd be one room for you, one for me, and two for my parents. And a children's room, of course, where they can do what they like, stand on their heads or scribble all over the walls. We would sleep in my room, we don't need a special bedroom, that would be giving away space which would be wasted during the day: we have to think in practical terms too. When we have guests we could sit in your room: a sofa in the middle of the room, that's quite modern, a long, low table in front of it and three or four armchairs. Though I don't want too many guests, just so you know right now. Not because of the upheaval, that's no great problem, but I'd rather be alone with you. Maybe when we're a bit older. And no one's going to tell me how my kitchen should be. It has to be tiled, that's always clean and attractive, blue and white is what I'd like best. The Klosenbergs used to have a kitchen like that, just like that, I can't imagine a nicer one. The floor covered with pale grey tiles, on the wall shelves for plates and jugs and ladles, and there must also be a little shelf for all those spices. Nobody knows how many spices there are – saffron, for instance, do you have any idea what saffron is used for? That it makes cakes and noodles yellow?

The rest of it I don't know since just about here my informant Mischa finally fell asleep, in the midst of all the spices. Perhaps Fajngold could have told me more about this particular night, perhaps he lay awake all the way from cellar to attic, but I never asked him.

Then at last it is daytime again, daytime at last. We hurry this way and that in the freight yard with our crates; only a few years earlier it would have been described as cheerful, bustling activity. The sentries behave quite normally, shouting or dozing or shoving as usual; they show no alarm or don't feel it yet. Maybe I am mistaken, but I seem to remember that day very well, although nothing unusual happened, at least not to me. As if it were today, I am standing, so I recall, on a freight car; my job is to take the crates and stack them so that as many as possible will fit into the car. There is another man with me, Herschel Schtamm, and that, come to think of it, *is* something unusual. For Herschel Schtamm has a brother, in fact he has a twin brother, Roman, and the two of them work together and normally are always seen together. But not today; Herschel had a little accident right after starting work. He stumbled while carrying a crate, Roman couldn't hold the crate alone, crate and Herschel crashed to the ground. Herschel had to suffer the usual beating, but that wasn't the worst part: in stumbling he sprained one foot and could hardly walk so he couldn't go on carrying with Roman, which is why he is now standing with me on the freight car.

He is sweating buckets, I have never seen anyone sweat like that, and he won't stop sweating until the Russians have captured this damn ghetto, not a day earlier. For Herschel Schtamm is devout. In his lifetime he was a sexton in a synagogue, we call that a *Shammes*, as devout as the rabbi himself. And then there are the ringlets, the pride of all orthodox Jews: go and ask Herschel whether he is prepared to part with them. Not for all the money in the world, he'll tell you, looking at you as if you were mad, how can you ask such a thing? But the ringlets may only be displayed within one's own four walls, nowhere else. In the street and here at the station one runs into Germans who take a dim view of them: where do we people think we're living for some of us to be running round in a get-up like that? Cases have been known where a grab was made for the nearest pair of scissors, and to the accompaniment of secret prayers and tears of laughter the matter was taken care of on the spot, but there have been worse cases too.

Herschel has taken the only possible way out: he hides his ringlets. He is smuggling them through these times. Summer and winter he wears a hat, presumably one is still allowed to wear a hat: a black fur hat with earflaps that can be fastened under the chin. In the sun the hat is terribly hot, but it was the only one he could get hold of and for his purposes it is eminently suitable. We non-devout ones, even his brother Roman, smiled and made our little jokes only during the first warm week. After that we lost interest: Herschel must know what he's doing.

We hoist a crate onto the very top; he wipes the sweat from his face and asks me, while we are picking up the next one, what I think of that business. I know at once what he is talking about and tell him I'm already wild with joy and can think of nothing else. Everything I once owned will belong to me again, everything except Chana, who was executed. There will be trees again; in my parents' garden I can see myself sitting in the walnut tree, on such slender branches that my mother is almost ready to faint; right there in the tree I stuff myself with walnuts. My fingers turn so brown from the shells that it takes weeks for the stains to disappear, but Herschel doesn't seem that enthusiastic.

Jakob lifts a crate onto the edge of the freight car. Why all the hurry – Jakob strides back to the pile with Mischa at his heels. As of yesterday, Jakob is fortune's darling, one of the elect, everyone is after him, the giants as well as the little fellows; everyone wants to work with him, with the man who has a direct line to God. Mischa was the first in the queue, the first to lend a hand when Jakob's eye fell on a crate, and now he's running after him. The fairest way would be to raffle him off, with so-and-so many blanks and one grand prize; then everyone would have the same chance at the supreme stroke of luck, at what has suddenly become so important: being close to Jakob. Only Jakob looks disgruntled: thanks a lot for that kind of luck, five or ten times today he's already been asked – confidentially and hopefully, even by complete strangers – what the radio has been saying. Five or ten times he hasn't known how to answer, has merely repeated what he said yesterday, Bezanika, or only put his fingers to his lips with a conspiratorial 'Sssh!' or said nothing and walked on in annoyance. And all this annoyance has been foisted on him by that stupid beanpole who is now scurrying after him, all innocence, in unwarranted joyous anticipation. No one could possibly have foreseen that. They are behaving like kids, like people eagerly clustering round a bulletin board. Barring a miracle, it will be at best a few hours before the sentries start noticing. Jakob would have welcomed such a crowd in normal times; his shop was open every day except *shabbes*, all year round, and there was a radio in clear view behind the counter: people could listen to whatever they liked. But there you lot mostly stayed away, each of you had to be treated like a king, otherwise you'd leave and not come back; and now you're treating *me* like a king and won't leave and keep coming back, a fellow needs a bodyguard for protection against you.
   Mischa had no idea what furious thoughts are being ignited so close to him, that it is rage which makes Jakob step out so briskly. They haul a few crates, and Mischa imagines that it will go on like this until noon; he fails to notice the hostile looks directed at him from time to time, more and more often. Until the pot boils over, until Jakob stops in his tracks, in the hope that Mischa will walk on, as far away as

possible. But Mischa stops too, looking puzzled: he really is totally unaware, so he might as well be told.

'Please, Mischa,' Jakob says in an agonized voice, 'there are so many nice fellows here. Do you *have* to haul with me?'

'What's up all of a sudden?'

' "All of a sudden," he says! I can't stand the sight of your face any more!'

'My face?' Mischa smiles stupidly; so far his face hasn't bothered anyone, Jakob least of all. At most there's been the occasional remark about his blue eyes, if people hadn't been able to think of anything better, and now suddenly this little eruption, almost an insult.

'Yes, your face! With that blabbermouth!' Jakob adds, Mischa being so completely in the dark. And now Mischa knows which way the wind is blowing: he is the weak link in the little chain of silence – Jakob is right. Although that's no reason to make such a scene, God knows there have been worse things to endure. Mischa shrugs his shoulders: it just happened, too late to change it now. Without a word, before Jakob can get even more worked up, Mischa walks away, this is none of the sentries' business, later or tomorrow there's sure to be time for a conciliatory word.

So Mischa goes over alone to the crates and quickly finds a new partner; after all, he hasn't been completely downgraded yet. His powerful arms haven't been forgotten, they are still appreciated; if you can't haul with Jakob, at least you can with Mischa. And Jakob also comes alone to the pyramid, doesn't even see who reaches with him for the crate: his eyes are still glued to Mischa, who eventually disappears without turning round, maybe offended, maybe not. But after a few steps Jakob notices that his new partner doesn't hold the crate as firmly as Mischa does, not nearly, and he looks at him and sees that the new man is Kowalski, and he makes a face and knows that he has fallen from the frying pan into the fire: Kowalski won't leave him in peace for long.

Kowalski doesn't say a word, or rather, he is not just silent, he is restraining himself: how long can he keep this up? He hauls and hauls, which is fine with Jakob. But somehow it irritates him, Kowalski being silent; the red spots on his cheeks haven't been caused by the exertion. Three whole crates are moved in silence. If Kowalski thinks he can starve him, he's mistaken: Jakob will never bring up the subject on his own since he has nothing to tell, it's just that it gets on his nerves. We'll outwit you, comes to Jakob's mind, we'll set a trap for you, a harmless conversation could make you forget the question you are holding back for the moment, what should we talk about, the noon whistle will soon blow and then try and find me.

'Do you know of anything to keep from going bald?' Jakob asks.

'What do you mean?'

'Every morning my comb is full of hair. Isn't there something one can do about it?'

'Nothing,' says Kowalski, clearly implying that the subject doesn't interest him.

'Surely there's something? I remember that at your shop you used to treat a customer with some such stuff – I seem to remember it was green?'

'Just a racket,' says Kowalski. 'I treated lots of people with that, but I might just as well have rubbed water into their scalps. Some customers insist on having something rubbed in. And it wasn't green, it was yellow.'

'There's nothing that'll help?'

'You heard me.'

So far so good. They silently keep on hauling. In Jakob the hope is growing that he is mistaken, that Kowalski has no intention of asking him, that he reached for the crate simply because he was the closest, and the red spots might after all be due to exertion or bedbug bites. Why does one often fail to think of the obvious? Unfortunate experiences should not cast doubt on all integrity: Kowalski also has his good sides, as countless memories go to show. After all, they had been almost close friends. Already Jakob looks at the sweating Kowalski more kindly, a secret apology in his glance, secret because, fortunately, the reproaches have also remained secret. Each new crate that is carried wordlessly to the freight car is leading him away from the suspicion that he has apparently been directing at an innocent person.

Then suddenly, just before noon, Kowalski puts his sneaky question. Without preamble and in a humiliatingly innocent voice he says: 'Well?'

That's all, Jakob flinches, we know what is meant. Instantly all his rage returns. Jakob feels deceived, the red spots are the same old ones after all. And Kowalski had not been there by chance, he had been lying in wait for him, working all day towards that infamous 'Well?' Kowalski has not remained silent out of consideration – he doesn't even know what that is; he was silent because he saw Jakob having an argument with Mischa, and he has merely been waiting for a favourable moment, cold and calculating as he is: Jakob was to be lulled into a sense of security.

Jakob flinches; the worst thing in this ghetto is that one can't simply turn one's back and walk away. It isn't advisable to repeat this ploy too often.

'Anything new?' Kowalski asks more pointedly. He is not in the mood for a prolonged exchange of stares. If you don't understand my 'Well?', then so be it.

'No,' says Jakob.

'You're not seriously trying to tell me that in wartime a whole day passes with nothing happening? A whole day and a whole night?'

They lift the crate onto the edge of the freight car and go back to the pile. Jakob takes a deep breath, and Kowalski gives him an encouraging nod; Jakob loses his self-control and raises his voice to an undesirable pitch.

'For God's sake, stop pestering me, can't you? Didn't I tell you yesterday that they're within twenty kilometres of Bezanika? Isn't that enough?'

Of course it is not enough for Kowalski if the Russians are within twenty kilometres of some place called Bezanika and he is here: how could that be enough for him? But he has no time for logical counterblasts, not at the moment. He looks round nervously, Jakob having been less than cautious. In fact a sentry is standing quite close by, they have to walk past him, and he is already looking their way. The uniform doesn't look right on him, he is much too young for it; they have already noticed him several times. He has a loud mouth but so far hasn't done much in the way of beating.

'What have you scumbags got to argue about?' he asks as they are about to pass him. Obviously he hasn't heard any details, only raised voices, which can be quickly explained.

'We're not arguing, sir,' says Kowalski loudly, 'it's just that I'm a bit hard of hearing.'

The sentry looks them up and down and rocks on his toes, then turns round and walks away. Kowalski and Jakob pick up another crate without wasting a word over the incident.

'A whole day has gone by, Jakob. Twenty-four long hours. Surely they must have advanced at least a few measly kilometres!'

'Yes, three kilometres according to the latest reports.'

'And you act as if you don't care? Every metre counts, I tell you, every single metre!'

'So what's three kilometres?' says Jakob.

'I like that! Maybe for you it isn't much, you hear the news every day. But three kilometres is three kilometres!'

The ordeal is over, Kowalski won't bother him again today; he is as mute as Fajngold now that he's found out what he wanted to know.

Jakob admits that it wasn't so bad; actually the words came out quite easily, as he explained to me at length. It was an important moment for him, he told me. The first lie, which may not even have been one, such a little lie, and Kowalski is satisfied. It's worth it: hope must not be allowed to fade away, otherwise they won't survive. He knows for sure that the Russians are advancing, he has heard it with his own ears, and if there is a God in heaven they must also come as far as us, and if there is no God they must also come as far as us, and they must find as many survivors as possible, so it's worth it. And if we should all be dead, it was an attempt, so it's worth it. The trouble is, he has to dream up enough bits of news, for they will go on asking questions, they will want to know details, not just how many kilometres; he must invent the answers. He hoped his brain would be equal to it, not everyone is good at inventing; so far he has invented something only once in his life, that was years ago, a new recipe for potato pancakes with cottage cheese and onions and caraway seed, you can hardly compare that.

'And besides, it's important that they're advancing at all,' says Kowalski reflectively. 'I mean, better to advance slowly than to retreat quickly. . . .'

We're late enough coming to Lina, inexcusably late, for she is of some importance to all this. It is she who rounds it out, if one can say such a thing. Jakob goes to her every day, but we have only come now.

Lina is eight years old, long black hair and brown eyes, just the way they should be, a strikingly beautiful child, most people say. She can look at you so that you feel like sharing your last mouthful with her, but only Jakob does that; sometimes he even gives her everything. That's because he has never had children of his own.

For two years Lina has had no parents: they went away, they got into a freight train and went away, leaving behind their only child, alone. Barely two years ago Lina's father was walking along the street;

no one had pointed out to him that he was wearing the wrong jacket, the jacket without the yellow stars. It was early autumn, and he was walking along with nothing bad in mind; they would certainly have noticed on the job, but he never got there. Half-way to work he met a patrol; one sharp look was enough, but Nuriel didn't know how to interpret it.

'Are you married?' one of the two men asked him.

'Yes,' Nuriel said, never suspecting what they wanted of him with their strange question.

'Where does your wife work?'

In such and such a place, Nuriel replied. So off they went with him to the factory and hauled her out of the building. The moment she saw him with the two men she noticed the bare places on the front and back of Nuriel's jacket. She looked at him in horror, and Nuriel said to her: 'I don't know what's going on either.'

'Your stars,' she whispered.

Nuriel looked down at himself: only then did he realize that this was the end, the end or shortly before it; a much lesser reason would have sufficed for the end, according to the rules of the ghetto. The men accompanied Nuriel and his wife to their home, telling them on the way what they would be allowed to take with them. Lina wasn't playing in front of the building, nor was she in the hallway; her mother had given her strict instructions to leave their room as little as possible. But we can't know, can we, what children get up to all day while their parents are at work: a fervent prayer that this one time she may have been disobedient. She wasn't in the room either, so she couldn't be surprised and ask what was the matter, why Papa and Mama were coming home so early, and the men would have known that Nuriel had more than a wife. They packed their few things, the two men standing beside them to make sure everything was being done correctly. Nuriel moved like a sleep-walker until his wife nudged him and told him to hurry up. Now he hurried too, he had caught her meaning: at any moment Lina might come into the room.

Going down the stairs he had seen through a landing window that Lina was playing in the yard (all this without witnesses, but perhaps that's exactly how it was and not otherwise). She was balancing on the low wall between the two yards: God knows how many times he had forbidden her to do this, but that's the way children are. A neighbour who happened to be on night shift that week met them on the stairs, and she heard Nuriel's wife telling him that he shouldn't keep looking out of the window but should watch his step or he'd fall. So he did

56

that, he didn't fall, without incident they emerged into the street, and since then Lina has had no parents. Shortly afterwards, a new family was allocated to the Nuriels' room: at that time there was still a stream of new arrivals.

What to do with Lina became a problem; no one could take her in permanently, and not only because of insufficient space or lack of kindness. All it needed was a spot check: What is this child doing here? For weeks everyone waited for a search to be made for Lina: someone in some office somewhere, in going through some papers, could have noticed that instead of three Nuriels only two went on that transport, but nothing of the kind occurred. Eventually a few women in the building cleaned up the little attic, her bed was moved upstairs together with a chest of drawers containing her belongings – which of course were still there – and Lina lived on the top floor. Only a stove was lacking: not one was to be found. During the coldest nights, when even two blankets are not enough, Jakob, who never had any children of his own, risked taking her secretly into his bed. The natural result of this was that she belongs to him more than to anyone else; she has had two years to twist him round her little finger, more than enough time.

Tonight is not a cold night, let alone the coldest; Lina will have to sleep alone. Herschel Schtamm has been sweating profusely all day. Jakob goes up to her room; he does this every evening. Lina is lying there with her eyes closed. Jakob knows quite well that she isn't asleep, and she knows quite well that he knows, which results every evening in some new little joke. He takes a paper bag from his pocket, in the bag is a carrot, which he puts down on the chest of drawers beside the bed; then he performs today's joke. He blows up the paper bag and bursts it by clapping his hands, but Lina is already laughing while her eyes are still closed: something is about to happen. So what happens is the bang. Lina sits up, gives him the kiss he has earned, and insists that she is already feeling much better. She intends to get up tomorrow, this silly old whooping cough can't last for ever, but Jakob can't make that decision himself. He puts his hand on her forehead.

'Do I still have a temperature?' Lina asks.

'Maybe just a little, if my thermometer is working properly.'

She picks up the carrot, asks him what that actually means, a temperature, and starts to eat.

'I'll explain that some other time,' says Jakob. 'Has the professor been to see you today?'

No, not yet, but he said yesterday that there was some improvement, and Jakob shouldn't always put her off with 'some other time': he still had to explain to her about gas masks, epidemics, balloons, martial law, she's forgotten what else, and now he also owes her about temperatures.

Jakob lets her talk; she seems quite cheerful. Perhaps he thinks a bit wistfully of the three cigarettes the carrot had cost him, he must get the next one more cheaply. In the end everything turns into pure conversation, of which Lina is a master; she must have been born with that gift.

'How's work going?' she asks.

'Couldn't be better,' replies Jakob. 'Nice of you to ask.'

'Was it also so hot where you were today? Here it was frightfully hot.'

'Not too bad.'

'So what did you do today? Did you ride the engine again?'

'What gave you that idea?'

'The other day you rode it as far as Rudpol and back again – don't you remember?'

'Oh yes, of course. But not today, the engine has been out of commission for the last few days.'

'What's wrong with it?'

'It's lost a wheel, and there aren't any new ones.'

'What a shame. How's Mischa, by the way? He hasn't been to see me for ages.'

'He's very busy. But I'm glad you reminded me, he sends you his love.'

'Thank you,' says Lina. 'Give him mine too.'

'I will.'

It could go on like this for hours, via twenty carrots. It doesn't matter what they chat about; they keep talking until the door opens, until Kirschbaum comes in.

If I hadn't made up my mind from the start to deal with something else, I would tell Kirschbaum's story. Maybe I will some day, the temptation is great, although we only met briefly two or three times, and he never even knew my name. I really only know him from Jakob's sparse comments; he mentioned him almost marginally, but he made me curious. Kirschbaum plays no major role in this particular context: the main thing is that he cured Lina. Years ago Kirschbaum was a celebrity, nothing like Rosa's father but a genuine, bona fide celebrity heaped with honours, head of a Cracow hospital, in great demand as a heart specialist. Lectures at universities all over the world, fluent in French, Spanish and German, said to have been in intermittent correspondence with Albert Schweitzer. Anyone wanting to be cured by him had to go to a good deal of trouble; to this day he continues to exude the dignity of an eminent personage, with no effort on his part. His suits, too, made of the best English cloth, a little worn at elbows and knees, but still beautifully cut; all of them dark in colour as an effective contrast to his snow-white hair.

Kirschbaum has never given a thought to being a Jew; his father before him was a surgeon, what does it mean, of Jewish origin, they force you to be a Jew while you yourself have no idea what that really is. Now he is surrounded only by Jews, for the first time in his life nothing but Jews. He has racked his brains about them, wanting to find out what it is that they all have in common: in vain, they have nothing recognizably in common, and he most emphatically nothing whatever.

For most of them he is something of a wizard. Kirschbaum doesn't feel comfortable with that; he'd prefer warmth to respect. He tries to adjust but goes about it awkwardly, while everyone expects something special from him, and he is so totally lacking in the humour that might help.

He comes into the attic bringing a pot of soup for Lina, his step as springy as a thirty-year-old's; the tennis club has kept him young.

'Good evening, everyone,' he says.

'Good evening, Professor.'

Jakob gets up from the bed, making room for Kirschbaum, who wants to listen to Lina's chest. She is already taking off her nightgown; the soup is still too hot, she is always examined first. Jakob goes to the window, which is open, a little attic window, yet from it one can see half the town. Perhaps a sunset, the buildings grey and gold, and much peace. The Russians will march along all the streets, not omitting a single one, those damned stars will be removed from the doors and leave behind light patches, like ugly pictures that have hung too long on the wall and go to their well-deserved end on the rubbish heap. At last one has, like the others, a little time for rosy thoughts, as if it were Kowalski who had reported the miracle. That somewhere down there the future lies hidden, no more great adventures, let the younger generation plunge into those; no doubt the shop will need a new coat of paint, perhaps a few new tables as well; he might even get a licence to serve schnapps, of which in former days there had been virtually no prospect. We shall see. A place for Lina could be fixed up in the storage room; he just hoped no distant relatives would come barging in wanting to take her away. Only her parents can have her, but who knows whether they are still alive? Next year she'll start school: ridiculous, a young lady of nine in the lowest grade. The lowest grade will be full of overgrown children; perhaps someone will come up with an idea so they won't have to waste too much time. It wouldn't be a bad idea to teach her a few things in advance, at least reading and a bit of arithmetic – why hadn't he ever thought of that before? But first she must get well.

'Well, now I can tell you,' says Kirschbaum. 'Things looked rather bad for this young lady. But when young ladies do as they are told it is usually possible to achieve something. We have pretty well repaired the damage. Take a deep breath and hold it!'

In the cupboard, right at the bottom, is an old book, a travel description of Africa or America that would do quite nicely for learning to read; it even has a few illustrations. Somehow the idea must be made appealing to her, for if she doesn't feel like it one might as well give up. As soon as it's possible I'll adopt her, after searching for her parents first of course, without her knowing about it. They say adoption is not so simple, there are a whole lot of formalities and authorities if someone at an advanced age comes by a child. The Germans have their share of responsibility, and the Russians have theirs, who has the greater? I shall tell her that we're finished now with forever telling fairy tales, that there's more to life than princes and witches and magicians and robbers; reality looks quite different, you're old enough now, this is an A. She is bound to ask what that means, an A, she will want to know what it's for, she has a very practical mind, at her age questions are half of life. He can see difficult times ahead. As a child she is already eight years old, and as a father I am barely two.

Kirschbaum is holding the stethoscope to her chest and listening intently. Suddenly he registers mock surprise, looks at Lina with wide eyes, and asks: 'Dear me, what have we here? Do I hear some whistling in there?'

Lina throws an amused glance at Jakob, who doesn't stop; he hadn't realized he'd started, but now he carries on, not wanting to spoil Kirschbaum's meagre joke, and Lina laughs at the silly professor who is quite unaware that the whistling comes not from her chest but from Uncle Jakob.

W hy was it said, one wonders, that coming events cast their shadows before them? Far and wide no shadows, a few uneventful days pass, uneventful for the historian. No new decrees, nothing visibly happening, nothing you can put your finger on, nothing that would seem to indicate change. Some say they have noticed that the Germans have become more restrained; some say that, because nothing at all is happening, it is the calm before the storm. But I say the calm before the storm is a lie, that nothing at all is a lie, the storm, or part of it, is already there: the whispering in the rooms, the fears and speculations, the hopes and prayers. The great day of the prophets has arrived. When people argue, they argue about plans, mine is better than yours; they have all packed their belongings, all are aware of the inconceivable. Anyone who is not must be a hermit. Not everyone knows the source of the report, the ghetto is too big for that, but the Russians are on everybody's mind. Old debts raise their heads again, diffidently the debtors are reminded, daughters turn into brides, weddings are planned for the week before the new year feast, people have gone stark staring mad, suicide figures have dropped to zero.

Anyone executed now, so shortly before the end, will have suddenly lost a future, for heaven's sake give no cause now for Majdenek or Auschwitz (if causes can be said to have any meaning), use caution, Jews, the utmost caution and make no thoughtless move.

Two parties quickly formed, dividing every building, not every one is Jakob's friend: two parties without statutes but with weighty arguments and a platform and the art of persuasion. One lot is feverish for news, what happened last night, how high are the losses on each side, no report is so trivial that one conclusion or another can't be drawn from it. And the others have heard enough, Frankfurter's party; for them this radio is a source of constant danger – Jakob could so easily reassure them; I hear their misgivings at the station and on the way home and in the building. In your naïvety you'll be the death of us all, they warn, the Germans are not deaf or blind. And the ghetto regulations are not merely suggestions for good behaviour; it says right there in black and white what it means to listen to a radio, as well as what happens to those who know that someone is listening and don't report it. So calm down and wait quietly in your corner, when the Russians show up they'll show up, no amount of talking will get them here. And above all stop talking abut that wretched radio, about that potential cause of a thousand deaths; the sooner it's destroyed the better.

That's the situation, so not everyone is Jakob's friend, but he is not aware of this, nor has he any way of finding out.

Those who crowd round him, those greedy for news, the hundred Kowalskis, they'll be sure not to tell him because Jakob might have second thoughts, change his mind, and suddenly decide to say nothing; they'd rather say nothing themselves. And the admonishers would be the last to tell him, they're not going to send any warning delegation to him, that would be far too risky. They give Jakob a wide berth: no one must be able to testify that they'd been seen in his company.

The ringleted Herschel Schtamm, for example, is one of the others, those who don't want to hear and see any more and don't wish to be accessories. At the freight yard, when, our hands held to our mouths, we evaluate the latest Russian successes, fresh from Jakob's lips, he moves a few steps away, but not too far, I'd say within earshot. As long as it's not a conversation in which he is seen to be involved: that's obviously what he is worried about. Herschel's gaze wanders aimlessly over the tracks, or lands on one of us with disapproving severity, yet it is quite possible that under the sweat-inducing fur hat he pricks up his ears like a rabbit.

The power failure that turns Jakob's radio for days into a life-threatening dust-gatherer is, Herschel feels, his personal achievement. Not that he makes any such claim in public: Herschel is not given to boasting, but we heard about this from his twin brother Roman, who spends every evening and every morning in the same room with him and every night in the same bed. He must know, after all. When we ask Herschel how he brought off such a feat – cutting off the power in several streets for several days isn't exactly child's play – his expression becomes benign, almost a smile as after surviving a great ordeal, but he refuses to say a word.

And then we ask: 'How was it, Roman? How did he manage it?' The last few minutes before going to bed, Roman tells us, are filled with prayer, quietly in a corner, an old habit established well before the radio. Roman waits patiently in bed until their shared blanket can be drawn over their heads. He has long ceased urging Herschel to hurry up and come to bed, having been enlightened as to the incompatibility of prayer and haste. He disregards the monotonous

62

murmuring, the chanting; to listen would be a waste of time since Roman doesn't understand a word of Hebrew. But recently some familiar sounds have been penetrating his ear. Ever since Herschel has had concrete petitions to send up to God, no longer the usual pious stuff about protecting and making everything turn out for the best, he resorts more and more often to the vernacular. In a fragmentary way, Roman can now listen to what is preoccupying and tormenting his brother: nothing extraordinary – if one were to pray oneself, one wouldn't have anything very different to say. Night after night God is informed about hunger, about the fear of deportation or being beaten by sentries, all of which cannot possibly be happening with His approval; would He please see what could be done about this, soon, if possible, it is urgent, and could He also give a sign that one has been heard? The sign is slow to appear, a test of constancy passed with flying colours by Herschel: each succeeding day has been scanned in vain for some modifying intervention. Until at last it did appear, that longed-for sign, unheralded like all divine action, and so potent that any word of doubt could not but die away on the lips of even the most hardened unbeliever.

That night Herschel's topic was the radio, at present the most overriding of all worries. He explains to God in minute detail the incalculable consequences that will result if thoughtlessness and carelessness allow the gossips to overlook a German ear and, before you know it, it's happened: the gossips are called to account, in line with the present law, together with their silent accessories. And it will be claimed that we are all accessories, that the news has not circumvented a single person, and actually they will be right. Besides, it need not even be a German ear that happens to be near by; there are also camouflaged German ears, and only You know how many informers are at large among us. Or someone wants to save his own skin and betrays on his own initiative the existence of the radio, there are scoundrels everywhere, You know that too, without Your consent they would not be in this world. Don't permit the great disaster to overwhelm us, so close to the end, seeing that all these years You have held Your sheltering hand over us and saved us from the worst: for Your own sake, don't permit it. Don't let the Germans find out anything about the radio; You know what they are capable of. Or better still, if I may make a suggestion: destroy that cursed radio, that would be the most satisfactory solution.

At this point the light bulb below the ceiling suddenly begins to flicker. At first Herschel ignores it, but then he looks up with wide eyes: in a flash the significance of this is revealed to him. God has granted his request, his prayers have not been in vain; at the appropriate moment He sends His sign, the acknowledgement of receipt, truly a sign that could not be more practical: that proves He is God! Without power the radio will be doomed to shut up; the more ardently Herschel prays, the more the light flickers. 'Don't stop now!' Roman spurs him on, but there's no need for him to say that, Herschel knows what is at stake: advice from scoffers is not asked for when bliss beckons as a reward. Fervently he exploits his contact until the crowning success: the light finally goes out, the ultimate word has been spoken. Herschel rushes to the window and scans the other side of the street: not a single curtain shows a glimmer of light, not even in Jakob Heym's building. We have silenced you, my friend, heavenly silence will reign, take your terrible box and give it to the devil, it's of no further use to you. And don't imagine that the power, the loss of which you innocently assume to be a breakdown, will be restored tomorrow: short circuits instigated by the Supreme Being take their time.

Proud and moderately happy, as far as circumstances permit, Herschel, his day's labours over, goes to bed and serenely accepts Roman's congratulations.

Worried faces wherever Jakob looks: what's going to happen? Here they sit, high and dry, with no idea of what is going on in the outside world. These intolerable conditions are already in their third day; this is no longer a power failure, this is a natural disaster. Must we really be the victims of this catastrophe too? They had been rash enough to take the joyful reports for granted; they had become addicted to the advance of a few kilometres every morning, and all day long there was something to hope for and to discuss. And now this dismal silence. Our first step each morning has led us to the light switch; some of us even got up in the middle of the night. We have pressed the switch and obtained the dreaded response that for yet another day Jakob will be no wiser than we are. Only the current will make him all knowing again, only the current that the powers of darkness have turned off, only when the lights go on again in all the rooms: only then will his light shine with a special brilliance, but when will that be?

The one person for whom the new reason for anxiety is no reason is Jakob. For once, Jakob is not affected by this calamity. His connection with the outside world has not broken off; what does not exist cannot break off. The connection is as tenuous as it had ever been, only that at last he can admit this. Sheer madness the way

Fortune chooses its little cooking vessels, even though it be a very modest Fortune disguised as a power failure. May it last until the first Russian faces take the sentries at the outskirts of the town by surprise. At least Jakob can breathe more freely now, can revert to being just one among many; nobody forces him to know more than all the others, but he must keep up the pretence, a constant pretence, he must feign regret where there is none: regret over the power failure – no easy task considering his relief. You have seen, my friends, that I was doing my best; as long as it was possible I supplied you with the latest and the best, there hasn't been a day when you have been deprived of comforting reports. How I would love to go on reporting until that longed-for hour arrives, but my hands are tied, you can see for yourselves.

Next morning Kowalski has won the race again: he is hauling with Jakob, except that this time it was no longer really a race. Overnight Jakob has become just another worker, an elderly person with two undeniably weak hands that are no longer in great demand. Kowalski has paired off with Jakob more from habit, or out of friendship; in any case they are hauling together. It is a long time since things have been so quiet between them. To Jakob the crates seem a shade lighter since Kowalski and the others have stopped plying him with questions; to Kowalski no doubt heavier now that answers are no longer forthcoming. Weight, as can be seen, is not an absolute quantity. The last question was whether in Jakob's building the light – God forbid – had also failed, to which Jakob answered simply and truthfully with a Yes. After such a long time he was quite happy to be able to speak the unadulterated truth, and since then it has been as quiet round him as round anybody else. That's how it will remain until the current is restored, and no one should be surprised at Jakob's composure.

When the whistle blows for soup, they sit down side by side in the sunshine. Kowalski sighs and spoons and sighs; this is not due to the soup, which tastes neither better nor worse than on any other day. Recently Jakob has learned to dread Kowalski's presence. Kowalski was the most avid among the curious, letting Jakob neither eat nor sleep and using him simply as a vehicle for his curiosity, relentlessly. But today his presence cannot alarm Jakob; questions would be a waste of words. The sun is shining, they are sitting side by side, peacefully and silently eating, and somewhere in the distance Stalin's soldiers are approaching at an unknown speed.

'How long do you think this power failure can go on?' Kowalski asks.

'For twenty years, I hope,' says Jakob.

Kowalski looks up from his bowl with an injured expression: that's no kind of answer between friends. Of course the last few days haven't been easy for Jakob, the sole connection with the outside world that everybody wanted to take advantage of, we've been assaulting and peppering you, and there's been some risk too, but can one in our situation object to that little extra effort? Who in your position would have acted otherwise? Look for him among us and you will not find him, and then in reply to our modest question we have to listen to such harsh words.

'Why are you so mean?' Kowalski asks.

'You'll never find out,' says Jakob.

Kowalski shrugs and goes on eating; there's no talking to Jakob today, maybe he's in a bad mood – as a matter of fact, there have always been days when he was strangely quarrelsome. When one came into his cheerless shop, in the old days, after entering in the best of moods and sitting down at one of the many empty tables and asking Jakob a perfectly normal question, such as How's business, the way anyone would, it sometimes happened that, instead of giving a normal answer, like Business is thus and so, as might be expected from an adult person, he would snap back: 'What a stupid question – can't you see for yourself?'

Not entirely by chance, Kowalski and Jakob are joined by two others. Mischa sits down beside them: he's brought along Schwoch, junior partner of Lifschitz & Schwoch, wholesale and retail stamp pads. At first Jakob assumes that they've sat down simply because there is still room here, a little, unobserved spot in the sunshine, until he notices that they keep exchanging looks, Mischa's being encouraging and Schwoch's undecided. Now he realizes that it's no coincidence, some unknown factor is involved; he has learned to pay attention to the minutest nuances. Mischa's looks mean 'Go ahead and say it,' and Schwoch's mean 'No, I'd rather you said it,' and when all these looks threaten to go on for ever, Jakob says between two spoonfuls: 'I'm listening.'

'We have sort of an idea,' says Schwoch.

So far so good, there's always room for a decent idea, good ideas are like air for breathing, let's hear what you've come up with, then we'll see.

66

But Schwoch seems tongue-tied after his tentative opening. He looks at Mischa again, and his eyes convey: 'I'd rather you said it.'

'The thing is this,' says Mischa. 'We've been thinking: if the power won't come to the radio, then the radio must go to the power.'

'Is this some kind of a riddle?' Jakob asks uneasily, though there's no mystery about Mischa's words. They mean no more and no less than that somewhere in some street in this ghetto the lights are still on, he'll soon hear in which street; any normal intelligence can put two and two together.

'In Kowalski's street the power is on,' says Schwoch.

These propitious words, uttered for Jakob's benefit, reach Kowalski's ears just as he is scraping out his bowl. His hands stop in mid-air, for a brief moment he closes his eyes, his lips whisper bitterly, may Schwoch be struck by lightning, and he moves aside. Not far, just a few symbolic centimetres. He hasn't heard a thing, let these madmen go on saying what they like, all this has nothing to do with him.

Jakob has observed this minor revelation; a pity one mustn't smile. There are important things to do before their break is over and Mischa's and Schwoch's plan begins to circulate and is judged worthy of at least some consideration. That with Kowalski they'll find themselves up against a brick wall is as clear as day to Jakob; there's no danger from that quarter. Anyone who has lived within earshot of Kowalski all these years knows what a hero does not look like. Trimming your beard in the latest fashion and arranging your hair artistically so that people in the street turn round to look at you – this may be within his scope; but listening to broadcasts on pain of death and passing on their contents – he's not that stupid. The problem certainly doesn't lie with Kowalski; the real worry is that someone else will be found – Kowalski's street is a long one. Someone else may come and say, Hand over the set, we'll let it play and sing and proclaim heaven on earth.

They must be totally persuaded to drop their plan if nothing is to come of it, and nothing will come of it: it must be the plan's fault, not Kowalski's. He must emerge from the affair as a perfectly honourable man; words must be found that disparage the very idea itself and prove its complete uselessness. So, lets have such proof, but where to find it in a hurry? Maybe Kowalski will come up with the right thing. For once he is Jakob's ally; they are sitting in the same uncomfortable boat. Kowalski, too, will gnaw away with all his strength at Mischa's and Schwoch's idea; he'll say anything except that he is too scared. He has to be shoved into the water up to his neck, then he'll talk; all one can hope is that in this short time he will be able to grow the appropriate angel's tongue.

'Did you hear what they want you do to?' Jakob asks.

Kowalski turns his head towards him, pretending that his thoughts were far away, and asks with perfect innocence: 'Who, me?' And then he asks Schwoch: 'What is it?'

'We're talking about the power,' Schwoch explains patiently. 'One could take the radio to your place, couldn't one?'

Kowalski acts as if he has heard a bad joke. 'To my place?'

'Yes.'

'The radio?'

'Yes.'

'Wonderful!'

These idiots want to kill me, he must be thinking; they want to ruin me, as if I don't have enough to worry about, and they talk about my doom as if it were the most natural thing in the world.

'How about you, Jakob? What do you say?'

'Why not?' says Jakob. 'It's up to you, it's fine with me.'

He merely appears to be playing with fire; he knows exactly what to expect from Kowalski, and besides, if Kowalski were suddenly to turn into a hero, one could always change one's mind later. But it's safe to assume that that won't be necessary. Kowalski is an arithmetic problem for six-year-olds.

'Don't you realize the risk you're running? Kowalski asks, utterly astonished at such recklessness. 'And what does that mean, anyway, one could take the radio to my place? Who is *one*? Me? You? He? Who is *one*? Do you intend to carry the radio through the ghetto in broad daylight? Or better still, at night, after eight o'clock maybe?'

He leans back, indignant; it verges on the comical, what they're suggesting, and they claim to be intelligent people.

'They're planning on a procession! The patrols and sentries will go to bed during that time, and when it's over we'll go and wake them up and say, You can carry on now, the radio is safely at Kowalski's!'

Schwoch and Mischa exchange worried looks; taken apart, their plan no longer seems quite so brilliant, and Jakob also contributes a few significant looks, serious and full of doubt. Kowalski's outburst seems to have given even him food for thought.

'Besides, there's another important point,' Kowalski goes on. 'By this time many people know there is a radio in the ghetto, but who has any idea that it's at Jakob's? We four here at the freight yard and maybe his neighbours. If so far nothing has gone wrong, that's to say, if so far the Germans haven't the slightest suspicion, we can assume that there are reliable people living in Jakob's building. But what makes you think it's like that in my building? I share with three men: who can guarantee that there isn't a traitor or a coward above me or beside me or below me? And that he will have nothing more urgent to do than run to the Gestapo and tell them what he knows?'

A long pause, Kowalski's words are assessed and weighed, and in a low voice Schwoch says: 'Shit, he's right.' Mischa shrugs, undecided, and Jakob stands up, saying: 'If that's how you feel . . .'

'Why be in such a hurry and run a risk, fellows?' Kowalski says. 'The power is bound to come back on again, if not tomorrow then the day after. Then it still won't be too late for Jakob to tell us how far they've got.'

By the time the Whistle summons them back to work, Mischa's and Schwoch's plan is dead and buried. It has been discussed in detail, as is only proper among people endowed with intelligence; its weak points have been brought to light, and it could not withstand the light. It would have been wonderful, what a shame, but clear thinking has opened our eyes. Schwoch and Mischa put their empty bowls back on the handcart – they are almost the last, the sentry is already casting impatient and threatening looks their way.

Once again Jakob and Kowalski form a solitary pair, each relieved of an anxiety, each having survived an ordeal.

'The ideas they come up with!' says Kowalski with a grin, more to himself than to Jakob, thus closing this chapter.

Lina is standing idly in the doorway, watching Rafael and Siegfried sitting on the kerb and whispering together, whispering with exaggerated caution, it seems to her. As soon as someone walks by they stop, and squint innocently into the sun. Lina pricks up her ears in vain, her restraint quickly melts away, and she crosses the street to find out what the two show-offs are whispering about. She picks up Siegfried maintaining that there's not much time left, and Rafael saying that at home they claim it can't last more than a few days.

Then she is discovered. The two boys look at her nonchalantly and wait with deadpan expressions for the interruption to end. But they can wait for ever, Lina doesn't walk on; she stays where she is and smiles brightly. Until Rafael finally gets up.

'Come on. No need for her to listen to what we have to discuss,' he says.

That's just what Siegfried thinks too. Drawing himself up to his full height in front of Lina he gives her to understand that they would beat the daylights out of her if she weren't just a runt of a girl. Lina accepts the threat impassively, since anyway the two boys turn and disappear into their own building. Lina waits for a few moments; Jakob, who has strictly forbidden her to go into strange buildings, is far away, and Lina follows them in. Carefully sticking her head through the door to the inner courtyard, she catches sight of Siegfried and Rafael going into the shed where, in happier days, Panno the carpenter used to have his workshop; to this day it still reeks of glue. There is no glass in the window of the shed, Lina knows that without checking; she was there herself when Rafael managed to hit the last-remaining pane with his first throw. So the nefarious thoughts of the two boys won't remain hidden for long, not from her. She tiptoes to the dark window and quietly crouches down on the ground. She is ready, they can fire away now.

'What we could do is blow up the military office,' she hears Siegfried say.

'What if they catch us?' asks Rafael.

'Don't wet your pants. You know the Russians will be here soon. Besides, they can't catch us if we blow them up because then they'll all be dead. Only we mustn't let them spot us first.'

Siegfried has always been a loudmouth; Lina could bet then and there that nothing will come of it.

'D'you s'pose the Russians' top man will give us something if we bring it off?' asks greedy Rafael.

'What a silly question! A decoration, or a real pistol, or something to eat!'

'Or all three?'

'Of course! Wouldn't that be something? And we wouldn't tell anybody at home.'

For a second or two there was silence. No doubt the two idiots were imagining all the things the Russians would fish out of their over-flowing pockets to reward them for their heroic deeds.

Suddenly Rafael says disconsolately: 'Siegfried – it won't work.'

'Why?'

'Where are we going to get hold of some dynamite? Even if I empty my two cartridges, that'll never be enough.'

'You're right. Haven't you got any more at home?'

'No.'

'Nor have we.'

Lina laughs and puts her hands over her mouth, which almost lets out a shriek; it's incredible how stupid two ten-year-old boys can be.

Rafael has another idea: 'You know what? We'll lock them up!'

'Who?'

'The Gestapos of course! We'll simply lock up the military office. At night they're all asleep, and then we'll lock them up. The doors are at least that thick, and they themselves put bars on all the windows – they'll never get out! And then when the Russkies arrive we've got the lot!' Rafael is panting with excitement.

'But we haven't got a key!'

'We'll find one,' says Rafael confidently. 'In my dad's drawer there's a bunch with at least twenty keys on it. One of them is sure to fit, you'll see.'

'Not bad at all,' Siegfried grumbles, audibly annoyed at not having thought of this brilliant idea himself. He'd be only too glad to find fault with Rafi's plan, but there's nothing wrong with it.

Just then the door to the courtyard opens and little Mrs Bujok appears, looking for her wayward son, but she can't see him. She sees only Lina sitting on her heels and smiling. 'Have you seen Siegfried?'

Lina is startled out of her absorption; she looks up at Mrs Bujok and regains her smile. That 'runt of a girl' still echoes in her ear – one might as well make hay while the sun shines: Lina gestures with her thumb to the shed behind her. Mrs Bujok looks menacingly at the shed, pauses for a moment to take a deep breath, then marches in. Lina hears a none-too-gentle slap, then 'Ow!' and 'How often do I have to tell you to stay close to my window!', and finally one more slap and 'You go home too, you rascal!'

As silence settles over the yard, Lina gets up and brushes off her skirt; the performance is over. Mrs Bujok emerges from the shed; anger has made her red in the face. Siegfried is hanging on to her with one hand while holding the other against his cheek. At least he's not howling. They quickly leave the yard: Siegfried doesn't notice Lina.

Lina also goes towards the courtyard door. She is in no hurry. She could stay, actually, but since Rafael is alone her listening post has lost its value. He might even deign to make do with her now, but she couldn't care less about that, she no longer feels like it. Let him sit there by himself and stew over which of the twenty keys will fit, nothing's going to come of it anyway.

So she leaves, turning back once more in the doorway. Rafael is taking his time.

'You're both pretty stupid!' she shouts across the yard towards the shed, which doesn't make her exactly popular.

And the resistance, I will be asked: where is the resistance? Could it be that the heroes are gathering in the shoe factory or in the freight yard, at least a few? Is it possible that at the ghetto's southern limits, which are the least clearly defined and hence the hardest to keep under surveillance, dark passages have been discovered through which weapons can be smuggled into the ghetto? Or are there in this wretched town only hands that do exactly what Hardtloff and his sentries demand of them?

Condemn them, go ahead and condemn us; those were the only hands there were. Not a single righteous shot was fired, law and order were strictly maintained, never a trace of resistance. I suppose I should say that I believe there was no resistance. I am not omniscient, but I base this assertion on what is called probability bordering on certainty. Had there been anything of the kind, I would have been bound to notice it.

I would have participated, I can swear to that; they need only have asked me, if only for Chana's sake. Unfortunately I am not one of those rare individuals who raise the battle cry; I cannot inspire others, but I would have participated. And not only myself: why didn't the man emerge who could cry 'Follow me!'? The last few hundred kilometres would not necessarily have been so long and so hard. The worst that could have happened to us would have been a meaningful death.

I can tell you that I have since read with awe about Warsaw and Buchenwald, another world but comparable. I have read much about heroism, probably too much, I have been gripped by senseless envy, but I don't ask anyone to believe me. Be that as it may, we remained passive until the last second, and there's nothing I can do about it. I am not unaware that an oppressed people can only be truly liberated if it contributes towards its liberation, if it goes at least a little bit of the way to meet the Messiah. We did not do this, I did not take a single step, I learned the rules by heart and adhered strictly to them, and only asked poor Jakob from time to time what new reports had come in. I will probably never come to terms with this, I haven't deserved any better; my whole thing about the trees no doubt has something to do with it, as well as my fatal sentimentality and the generosity of my tear ducts. Where I was, there was no resistance.

They say that what is good for your enemies is bad for you. I don't intend to argue about this; anyway, it only makes sense with concrete examples, such as the one I now have, but I don't want to argue about it. My example is the electric current. Jakob doesn't mind in the least doing without it, in fact he manages splendidly without it. Doing without? No one would ever have thought how good no current can be. Apart from the Russians and good health for Lina, there is nothing Jakob wishes for as much as no current. But Jakob is only one, and we are many. We want current, we are at the mercy of our imaginations: if it can't be our deliverers, then let it at least be electric current.

The Germans, to return to the example, also want current, and not only because at the military office they are ruining their eyes with candlelight. The fine-tuned plans have been thrown into disarray; not a chair, not a sideboard, leaves the furniture factory, there are no pliers or hammers or screws coming out of the tool factory, no shoes, no trousers: the Jews are sitting around twiddling their thumbs. Two groups of hurriedly assembled electricians swarm out in search of the damage, double rations of bread and cigarettes, day and night they test fuses and whatever else can be tested, dig up streets, expose cables, accompanied by our good wishes. After five fruitless days Hardtloff has them shot; there is talk of sabotage, which is sheer madness: the electricians were all in one way or another Jakob's customers and had a personal interest in eliminating the problem. They are executed on the square in front of the military office; anyone is free to watch: let this be a warning, and do what is demanded of you

Then a German special detachment arrives on a truck, like men from Mars. Equipped like divers, they are seen to laugh and relish their importance, we'll take care of it all right, let's see what's stumped these Jewish bunglers. Two days, and the trouble spot is exposed: a swarm of rats has been gnawing at a cable and succumbed to their greed. A new cable is lowered into the ground, and once again there are chairs, shoes, pliers, screws, Jakob's radio.

We want to know whether it is true that they intended to sell us for ransom. If so, where's the money? We want to know whether it is a fact that a Jewish state is to be founded. If so, when? If not, who is obstructing it? Above all we want to know what's taking the Russians so long, for three weeks you've been making our mouths water the way you never managed to do with your pancakes. Tell us how they are breaking through the front, what tactics they are employing, whether they are treating prisoners as prisoners or as convicts, whether the Japanese are being a big nuisance to them in the east, whether the Americans can't at least relieve them of that burden if they aren't landing in Europe. And we also want to know what kind of a career Jan Kiepura is having, how he's getting along in America. By this time a whole lot of news must have accumulated. Fair enough, so they won't broadcast a special news summary for us, they've no idea how we've been suffering from the power failure, but there are a few things one could find out about other than the latest news. Please don't leave out anything, do you hear, nothing, please.

Jakob deserves our sympathy. He should have a well-equipped office, headquarters with three secretaries, better still with five. A few contacts in all the important capitals who punctually and reliably relay to headquarters every little detail they have managed to ferret out; where secretaries are slaving away at sorting those details, scanning all the leading newspapers, listening to all the radio stations and extracting from all this a summary which they submit to Jakob as the person ultimately responsible. Only then could he truthfully answer roughly a third of the questions – to the extent that newspapers and radio stations and contracts are to be trusted.

A newspaper is tucked into the Whistle's pocket. The Whistle emerges from the red brick building and, dragging his wooden leg, walks past the freight cars and right through all the Jews, who are not even aware of what is limping past them, why care about newspapers, we have Jakob. Only Jakob sees and cares, the magnifying glass in his eye is glued to the precious object in the railwayman's pocket, some pieces of paper containing truthful or fabricated reports on actual events – at any rate, infinitely more valuable than a non-existent radio. Respite for his exhausted powers of invention, if he could bring off a bold exchange of ownership.

Beyond the last track the Whistle reaches his goal, a wooden privy for Germans only: it says so on the door, right under the little heart-shaped opening they had carved into it, as is the custom in their own country, I imagine.

Jakob refuses to be distracted by his job with Kowalski and keeps one eye firmly on the privy. If the newspaper is intact so far, as appeared to be the case, and the railwayman is not too wasteful, there should be some left over. If the railwayman isn't stingy, he should leave some of it behind. He mustn't be wasteful, he mustn't be stingy, there's nothing to show one way or the other; when Jakob gets a chance he will go and take what's left. Yet whatever the chance it would inevitably mean risking his life, what business has a Jew using a German privy, for you, my brothers, I'll risk life and limb. I don't intend to steal potatoes like Mischa, who is a more practical type and thinks realistically; if all goes well I'll carry off a few grams of news and turn them into a ton of hope for you. If my mother had endowed me with a smarter brain, gifted with as much imagination as Sholom Aleichem – what am I saying, half that much would be enough – I wouldn't need to resort to such petty theft, I could dream up ten times as much as they can write in their newspapers, and better too. But I can't, I can't, I am so empty it almost frightens me, I'll do it for you, my brothers, for you and for myself, I'll do it for myself too, for one thing is certain: I can't survive as an individual, only together with you. That's what a liar looks like from behind, I'll go into their privy and take what's left, hoping there is something left.

At last the Whistle emerges into God's sunshine, takes a few deep breaths, and lights a cigarette, for which in that wind he needs four matches. He takes enough time for Jakob to want to throttle him, but the pocket, the all-important pocket, is empty. What were newspapers like in the old days? Ours usually had eight pages, four sheets; let's assume his also had four, that would be normal. You tear one sheet in half, then once again, then a third time, that means per page – let's see – eight small pieces per page. You can also tear it four times, but then the pieces turn out rather small, so let's stay with three times, he has plenty of paper after all. Four sheets times eight, that makes thirty-two small pieces, no healthy person needs that many; you tear up only one page and put the others aside for reading. But even if he has torn them all up, there's bound to be something left over, unless in his ignorance he has tossed the remainder down the hole.

'What do you keep mumbling about?' Kowalski asks.

'Me, mumbling?' says Jakob.

'All the time. Four and sixteen should make so and so much – what are you working out?'

The Whistle at last disappears into the brick building. Jakob looks at the sentries: one is standing by the gate, looking bored, another is sitting on the footboard of a freight car, reassuringly far away, the third is nowhere in sight, presumably he's inside the building or he's hidden himself away somewhere for a nap since nothing ever happens, and there are no more than three.

'Go on working and don't look round at me,' Jakob says.

'Why?' asks Kowalski. 'What's going on?'

'I'm going to use their privy.'

Kowalski assumes his surprised expression and does not go on working: the next thing will be that this madman goes into the red brick building for schnapps and tobacco, tries to borrow money from a sentry, and they'll put him up against the wall for that just as they will for what he's about to do now.

'Are you crazy? Can't you wait till soup-time and then go behind the fence?'

'No, I can't.'

Jakob ducks and runs off like a professional; the stacked crates shield him almost all the way from eyes in the brick building, except for the last few metres, but they're part of it and he manages them too: Jakob closes the privy door behind him. Not a word about the smell, or about the graffiti on the walls: beside the hole lies the rich booty. But first a glance out through the little heart: no one has noticed anything, in the freight yard framed by a heart everything looks normal. The booty consists of the expected remainder, the German has not been wasteful, there are a good number of neatly torn squares of paper, as if cut with a knife, and under the squares a double sheet, intact. Jakob stuffs the squares under his shirt, as flat as he can so they won't rustle while he is working, better on his back than on his stomach. The double page is worth nothing, or rather, it *is* worth something: four pages, filled from top to bottom with death announcements bordered in black, gratifying in one way but short on information. Killed in action . . . killed in action . . . We'll leave those behind, we don't want to carry around any ballast, we'll easily memorize them, four pages of the dead, let the next visitor enjoy them too. But we'd better not linger, as if we were on our own WC, we won't risk spending too much time in here, we want to return to work, impatient to get through it. Then we'll go to our unobserved

76

room, free our back of its burden, and play our new radio. And tomorrow you can come again and ask as long as the supply lasts.

Jakob looks outside once more to see whether the coast is clear, it's not clear at all, far from it, the way back is strewn with mines, a soldier is walking towards the privy, purposefully one might say. His fingers are already fumbling with his belt buckle, in his mind's eye he is already sitting down and feeling better. It's too late for anyone to leave the privy without his noticing, what do you do now? Jakob's knees remind him emphatically that he is no longer young, no matter how speedily he had covered the ground to get here, one always finds this out too late. The door can't be fastened, some idiot has ripped off the loop for the hook; if you try to keep it closed, one shove of the shoulder and the man will be inside and gape and do God knows what to you. Theoretically one should keep a cool head, remain calm, the advantage of surprise is on our side, and he still has eight whole steps to go. The planks of the back wall will take at least five minutes and make far too much noise, five steps to go, and all that's left for you is the little oval hole, down into their crap. To which you can't bring yourself, though you're skinny enough.

The soldier opens the door, which offers resistance; to his dismay he sees before him an opened double sheet of newspaper, trembling moderately, although at such an embarrassing moment this doesn't particularly strike him.

'Oh, excuse me!' he says, quickly closing the door, without having seen the disintegrating Jewish shoes beneath the newspaper or the want of a display of lowered trousers that would have rounded out the picture, a manoeuvre, however, for which the head had been not cool enough and the time too short. Perhaps just as well, too much camouflage can be damaging too, the main things being that the soldier has shut the door devoid of any suspicion: he prepares for a brief wait, his belt is already looped over his arm, and he walks up and down, that being less uncomfortable than standing.

For how long a wait should Jakob prepare? Over the edge of the newspaper and through the little heart he sees the grey uniform walking up and down. The only thing that can help now is a miracle, any old miracle will do, no need to cudgel one's brains, true miracles are not calculable. There are at most two more minutes for the unexpected to materialize, and if it fails to do so, which would be reasonable enough, then the proverbial last hour will look this ridiculous.

'Hurry up, comrade, I've got the trots,' he hears the soldier pleading.

The squares of paper on his back are beginning to stick, they will have to be dried before use, if by some miracle everything turns out well. And Jakob tells me that suddenly he is tired, suddenly fear and hope slip away, everything becomes strangely heavy and light at the same time, his legs, his eyelids, his hands, from which the four pages of heroes fallen for the Fatherland slide to the ground.

'Did you hear that Marotzke is getting home leave again? It smells fishy to me! He must know some people right at the top, eh? He's forever going off, while chaps like us have to wait and wait and hang around with these garlic-eaters.'

Heavens above, garlic, if a fellow could have just one clove, spread very thin on warm bread, you idiot, some Schulz or Müller is presumed to be in the privy, no well-wisher of Marotzke's, which is correct in a way, whoever Marotzke is. Jakob leans back against the back wall and closes his eyes; if they expect some heroic resistance from him they can wait a long time, he is beyond that. It's up to the comrade outside, he has to keep the action going. He's welcome to leave or stay, tormented by stomach cramps he can fling open the door, gasp, and shoot, the man he hits will not be taken by surprise. What follows is his business.

Who could possibly suspect that the miracle is already in the works, the rough outline already designed? There is still Kowalski, Kowalski with two horrified eyes in his head, he knows what's going on, he's aware of the situation. He sees the soldier in dire need and the door still presenting a barrier, he knows who is inside and cannot be set free without his help, assuming he hasn't already died of fear. Salvation lies in distracting the German, not merely by throwing a pebble against the wall to make him turn round to see who threw it: something must happen that requires his immediate intervention. The first thing that comes to mind is the stack of crates, some two metres high and rather wobbly. If two crates are pulled out from below, the stack will cease to stand there all proud and ready for transport, its balance will be destroyed, and that could provide a fine distraction. But what will happen to the numskull who is responsible for such clumsiness, what will happen to Jakob if there is no clumsy oaf far and wide, what are forty years of friendship worth? Calculations facing Kowalski.

Jakob hears a low rumbling in the distance, the ears can't be closed as the eyes can, then he hears military boots hurrying away. Reason enough to open the eyes wide again: that's exactly what a miracle sounds like. Arms and legs reassuringly regain their former weight, things are on the move again. The glance through the heart tells him that the coast seems clear; the Jews visible through the opening in the door have halted in their work and are all staring in one direction, towards the spot where the miracle is presumably happening.

Kowalski has successfully infiltrated the stack of crates. His strength was only just sufficient, and one crate fell on his head. The soldier rushes blindly from the privy into the trap and flings himself upon the bait, Kowalski. It may be said that rarely has sleight of hand been more successfully performed. Although the blows find their mark – the crate falling on his head was nothing in comparison – Kowalski merely whimpers as he tries to protect his face with his hands and apologizes profusely for his unforgivable blunder.

The rest of us stand as if rooted to the spot and grind our teeth; one man beside me claims he saw Kowalski toppling the stack deliberately. The soldier goes on punching and beating, Marotzke has been given home leave again and he hasn't, maybe he is genuinely outraged over such clumsiness, but suddenly he stops in the midst of his task. Something is moving inside him, not pity and not exhaustion: it is his diarrhoea demanding its rights, as is plain for all to see. He grimaces and runs in long strides to the privy that has meanwhile been vacated for his benefit, or rather, first he calls out: 'I want to see it all properly stacked up again when I come out, d'you hear?' Only then does he perform his long leaps, which, in spite of everything, look very comical. The matter permits no delay: now he would insist that any newspaper-reader vacate the position, immediately, instantly, other-wise there'll be a minor disaster. But he can save himself the trouble: he flings open the door onto an empty latrine, the minor disaster was prevented in the very nick of time.

Not one of us looking on dares help Kowalski or comfort him. The place is for work, not for comforting. He wipes the blood from his face and tests his teeth, which are still there except for one; all things considered, it could have turned out considerably worse. The pain will pass, Jakob has been preserved for us, after the war we'll present him with his own private WC where he can sit for hours to his heart's content and think about his good friend Kowalski. The man so miraculously rescued comes round what remains of the stack of crates, behind Kowalski, who is still feeling himself all over. Jakob plucks up the courage to face him, for Kowalski must not find out the true reason for the daring expedition. He of all people; he has deserved not to be bothered with this reason; for him it must remain an inexplicable whim of Jakob's, a whim that came within an ace of costing him his life.

'Thank you,' Jakob says in an emotional voice. Emotional is the right word, emotional for the first time in forty years; one doesn't have one's life saved every day, and then by someone one has known for such a long time and of whom, to be quite honest, one wouldn't have expected it.

Kowalski doesn't deign to glance at him; getting up with a groan he sets to work on the crates, which had better be stacked up before the soldier returns from his urgent business and checks to see how much his word is worth here. They could all still be standing in neat rows, like the few teeth in Kowalski's mouth, if Jakob were a normal person, if he hadn't yielded so irresponsibly to some wondrous yearnings for which others must pay bitterly.

Jakob makes his hands fly, one crate by Kowalski is matched by three of his, which in Kowalski's case is due partly to the question of guilt, partly to fury, and no doubt also to pain. 'Did you at least have a good shit?' Kowalski inquires, making an effort not to shout. 'Have a look at my face, have a good look, I bet it's a beaut! It wasn't him, it was you! But why am I getting excited, the main thing is you had a high-class shit, that's all that matters. There's just one thing I'll swear, Heym, just try that again! Go ahead, try it, then you'll find out who helps you!'

Jakob takes shelter behind work; Kowalski is right, of course, from his point of view. The words that would calm him down, Jakob mustn't say, and any others would lead to a new outburst. Later, Kowalski, when all this is behind us, when we two are sitting quietly over a glass of schnapps, when the pancakes are sizzling in the pan, then I'll tell you everything. At our leisure, Kowalski, you'll hear the whole truth, we'll laugh and shake our heads to think how crazy the times once were. You'll ask why I didn't tell you right away, tell you, at least, my best friend, and I'll answer that I couldn't because you would have told all the others, and they would have taken me for one of those thousands of liars and rumourmongers and would have been without hope again. And then you'll put your hand on my arm, because maybe you'll have understood, and you'll say: 'Come, Jakob my friend, let's have another vodka.'

When, after quite some time, the privy door opens again, the stack of crates rears up proudly, as if no one had ever brought about its collapse. The soldier strolls over, his hands clasped behind his back, uniform all adjusted; he has been expected. Not exactly with longing, merely to have the matter finally over and done with. But the way he approaches and then stops and holds his head, his whole manner, is

80

enough to make one uneasy, for he looks more benign than critical. Somehow he is looking at the world with different eyes; how a few good minutes can change a person. The crates, he's completely forgotten about the crates, he has eyes only for Kowalski's swollen face, which for the time being is red but on which one can already seem to divine blue and green and purple, and the soldier looks concerned. If Jakob can trust his eyes, he looks concerned, what's one to make of that? Without a word he turns round and walks away. Jakob is thinking, lucky he didn't discover his soft heart until now and wasn't a good person from the beginning or he would never have dashed away from the privy door, he would have stayed there and very soon his goodness of heart would have undergone much too severe a test.

In passing, the comrade drops two cigarettes, Junos, without tips. He drops them either by mistake or on purpose, a question that will never be resolved, any more than his motives, assuming it was deliberate. Anyway the cigarettes belong to Kowalski; he has paid for them, after all.

A few minutes later the Whistle emerges from the brick building and trills for the midday break: the railwayman whom up to this hour none of us has heard say a word, but who nevertheless is the most informative among our Germans because he left behind a half-way useful radio. It all started with the Whistle today, and he suspects nothing, whistles as usual for soup-time, and has no way of knowing how shamelessly his forgetfulness, or whatever it had been, was exploited. Only Jakob knows, reminded by the little squares of paper under his shirt, and the double page that meanwhile has suffered an uncertain fate and shouldn't really have been left behind unused.

'By the way, did I tell you that the Germans are suffering huge losses?' Jakob asks.

They are already queuing up; Kowalski turns round to him, and, in the midst of his bruises, a hint of a grateful smile – grateful in spite of everything – blooms fleetingly.

The radio turns out to be not particularly fruitful. Jakob arranges the squares side by side on his table, nine of them altogether, and Piwowa and Rosenblatt refrain from disturbing him. Today they are what they are, long since dead, due to cat meat and a guard; today they don't interfere in Jakob's business, for he has to concentrate on his game of patience.

The name of the newspaper appears nowhere, nor does the date; blind chance has seen to that. The nine squares of newspaper yield not a single coherent page, the Whistle having picked up squares at random, which means extra work for Jakob. He tries this way and that but can find scarcely two places that match, that fit together. At the end of all his effort he is faced with two extremely patchy pages, the gaps revealing the colour of the tablecloth: two pages that look as if a circumspect censor had cut out everything worth knowing and taken care that only items of no consequence find their way into the hands of unauthorized persons. The sports section, for instance, has been perfectly preserved: how happy the Jews will be that the Luftwaffe boxing team has defeated a Navy team by ten to six. Or that once again the Berlin footballers, as so often in the past, didn't have a chance against the Hamburg eleven. Then the uncommunicative page divulges the further earth-shattering news that a *Gauleiter*, whose name has been torn off, has made some favourable comments about an art exhibition somewhere, that His Excellency the Spanish Ambassador would like to see a further expansion of mutual friendly relations, and that, in a People's Court trial of two agents in the pay of Jewish world capitalism, justice has prevailed.

You sit there looking disappointed; you hadn't ever expected much, a little favourable wind for your poor brain, the occasional hidden allusion from which with a bit of skill a feast could be prepared, but you hadn't counted on quite so little. Not a word about Bezanika, through which the Russians must long since have advanced; not so much as a hint that the Germans are encountering difficulties. Instead, those nitwits are playing football and putting on exhibitions and meting out justice.

Let us at least try to be fair and leave open the possibility that the newspaper is old or that the best part of it was used by the Whistle, but, one way or another, it was idiotic to have such high hopes. One should have guessed what to expect, if one had given merely five seconds' thought to it. The kind of newspapers those people can produce is only too well known; years ago there was a German paper in our area, the *Völkischer Kurier*, and don't ask me what that was worth. No one ever bought it, throwing away money is a sin, but sometimes you did run across it, whether you wanted to or not. At the market they wrapped fish in it, at the dentist's there was a copy in the waiting-room, at the insurance office of course, and occasionally at Kowalski's barber shop, because he wanted to make a cosmopolitan impression. He was told, Kowalski, if you leave that filthy rag lying around here any longer you'll ruin your business. Or do you really think some German customer will happen to stray into your place so that your Yiddish fingers can fiddle around with his Kaiser Wilhelm moustache? That's none of your business, Kowalski replied in an offended tone, do I tell you how much sawdust to mix into your potato pancakes? That's how Kowalski was, and may my hands fall off right here and now if this slander is true. Anyway, a glance at the paper was enough to show what kind of a rag it was. The Germans constantly felt threatened and humiliated and discriminated against by God and the world; it wasn't they who humiliated us, but we them. The question of how long Germany was to go on suffering from the shameful consequences of the last war obsessed them in every issue, three times a week. And the back page contained, beside a picture puzzle, poems so unintelligible that you almost thought you had forgotten their language.

Only the classified advertisements weren't so bad, they had a certain flair for that section. Every other Wednesday or Tuesday the two middle pages were closely printed with classified ads, and if you needed something that was hard or impossible to find on the market, say a few nice-looking chairs, with woven rattan seats perhaps, or a modern standard lamp or a sizeable lot of plates because dishes never lasted long in the shop, then a glance at the *Kurier* wouldn't do any harm. Of course, it was essential to pay attention to the name of the person offering the goods; if it was Hagedorn or Leineweber one didn't even bother to go there, if it was Skrzypczak or Bartosiewicz one went with great reluctance, and if it was Silberstreif one simply went. For when it came to advertising, the *Kurier* people weren't choosy. They took from anyone, what counted was the ability to pay. But, as I said, that was only the classified section, every other Wednesday or Tuesday; the rest was sheer unadulterated rubbish.

All this might have been remembered in time to avoid sticking one's head in the noose to no avail and only getting it out again through a miracle wrought by a friend. That's how they used to produce newspapers, and that's how they produce newspapers to this day; so far nobody has shown them a better way. Only the talent for successful classified sections has apparently stayed with them, and the four abandoned pages filled with casualty lists would seem to indicate that there are still people on the job who know their business.

Jakob turns over each square, one by one, all is not yet lost, there is still an unread reverse side that has as many gaps as the front but may tell us a little more. There is an item about a hero such as only our nation can produce, a pilot with a French name who shoots down enemy planes like sparrows out of the African sky. The Führer has replied to a message from the Duce, and in Munich a lorry collided with a tram, causing a traffic jam lasting several hours. A cartoon. A man holding a lighted match over a sandwich. Question: What does this mean? Answer: Sandwich under fire. And a fat headline claiming, Victories on All Fronts! One can believe it or not, we'd rather not, the lower half is missing. As a claim it hangs in the air, so to speak, and we know they have been trying to tell us that they were already not far from Moscow. It was the Germans who claimed that, not us, but we heard with our own ears that there is fighting near Bezanika. There's quite some distance between the two; if that's what a victory looks like, you're welcome to hundreds more of the same.

That's all very well, Jakob can figure out for himself that they tell a few fibs, but how is he to answer the questions that will rain down upon him first thing tomorrow morning? His notion of what it would be like, he told me with a sigh, had been far too naïve: one reads their slanted reports, he had thought, sees through them with no effort, or very little effort, simply turns everything round and right away one's mouth is bursting with news ready to be released at the appropriate time. But now try just turning things round. The Luftwaffe boxers didn't win against the Navy, they lost, the *Gauleiter* with the torn-off name declared the art exhibition to have been atrocious, the German hero didn't shoot down a single plane in Africa, the tram in Munich skilfully avoided the lorry, and the Führer didn't reply to the Duce's message because he never received one. I tell you, nothing but rubbish. Perhaps I can make something out of the cartoon, I think; Sandwich under fire means they're firing at Sandwich,

84

and Sandwich, if I'm not mistaken, is a town in England, and if they're firing at England, then England will be firing back, that seems reasonable. Wonderful, they'll tell me tomorrow morning, so England is defending itself, but England is far away and what about us? Perhaps I could turn the victories on all fronts into defeats, but what do I know about fronts, where they are or how many there are? Defeats must be substantiated with details, and I don't know any – what would you have done in my place?

Jakob comes to a crucial decision. The power failure was a divine respite, the only drawback being that one had no influence on its duration. We'll gain another respite for ourselves, but without the drawback, because the interruption we have in mind has no end. When they ask us, what's the latest, Jakob, our shoulders will droop and we'll put on our saddest expression and whisper in a despairing voice: Just imagine, Jews, last night I sit down with expectant ears at my set and turn the knob, like I always do, but not a sound! Not one! Yesterday it was still singing like a little bird, and today not a murmur. It's no use wringing our hands, Jews, you know how temperamental a radio can be, and now it's dead.

The radio is dead. Jakob scrunches up the squares of newspaper, all nine of them, into a little heap; he is able to contain his annoyance at not having had this brilliant idea earlier. It is far surpassed by the joy of discovery: if the toilet paper had been of no other use than to enlighten him, then, in spite of everything, it was worth while, then the price paid by Kowalski was not too high. No longer will one be lying night after night with wide-open eyes, racking one's brain over what lies to tell them next morning. Now one can spend night after night with wide-open ears, listening, like everybody else, for whether the longed-for distant rumble of cannon has finally broken its silence. The radio is dead, the scraps of newspaper are tossed into the stove, Jakob will set a match to them when it becomes necessary to heat the room, the lid is firmly closed.

Just in time, for in his haste Jakob has forgotten to lock his door: it opens, and a smiling Lina enters without knocking.

'Did you forget about me today?' she asks.

'Of course not,' says Jakob, giving her a kiss, and at least now he locks the door. 'I was just about to come up to you, but I had something to do first.'

'What was that?'

'Nothing you need to know about. Have you had your supper?'

'Yes, what you put out for me.'

Lina looks round the room, not in search of anything special but just to make sure everything is tidy and not dusty. She draws her finger across the cupboard, inspects it, the result is not that fantastic.

'I'll tidy up your room tomorrow,' she says. 'I don't feel like it today.'

'No, you won't,' Jakob says sternly. 'The professor said you weren't supposed to move around too much yet.'

Lina doesn't reply. With a smile she sits down at the table; Jakob knows as well as she does that she is going to tidy his room. For some time it has been quite clear who sets the tone here, it's no longer a subject for discussion. Jakob's job is to provide the food and clothing and in winter the heating; she is responsible for everything else, even though occasionally he still makes a bit of a fuss. She hasn't come into the room to argue about matters long since settled, or out of fear he might have forgotten her; she knew he wouldn't have. The reason for her coming goes back a few days, when she heard a lot and understood little; there was something that was rather unclear to her.

'Have you heard what they're all talking about?' Lina asks.

'About what?'

'That the Russians will soon be here?'

'You don't say!'

Jakob goes to the cupboard, takes out his weekly bread ration, breaks off enough for his supper, and starts eating.

'Who's talking about that?'

'Oh, Siegfried and Rafael and Mrs Sonschein and Mrs London – everybody. Haven't you heard anything?'

'No.'

Jakob sits down opposite her, sees the disappointment in her face; she had hoped for enlightenment, and he knows nothing. He divides his bread and holds out one half of it to Lina as compensation. She accepts it, even starts eating, but the bread is not nearly as good as his lack of knowledge is bad.

'That's to say, I did hear something,' says Jakob. 'But nothing definite. What's so important about it?'

Her eyes gradually grow resentful, how stupid does he think she is, as if she was a baby, and she takes care of all the housework. Everybody is talking about something tremendous, and what's so important about it?

'What's it going to be like when the Russkies are here?'

'How should I know?' says Jakob.

'Better or worse?'

Jakob is ready to groan. You've managed to escape the hyenas at the freight yard for today, even for ever if the idea of the broken-down radio stands the test. But already you have to look for some other means of escape, for within your own four walls a new tormentor is taking shape, albeit a much-loved one, but she can ask more questions than you have hairs on your head. Or you don't look for one, you submit to your fate: a child of less than nine, surely you can cope with her. You'll tell her, as best you can, something about the world of tomorrow, after all that interests you too, and to have a rough idea of what is in store for her certainly won't do her any harm.

'Will it be better or worse?'

'Better, of course,' says Jakob.

'But how better? What will be different?'

'We won't have to wear stars any more. Lina can wear whatever she likes, and no one will stop her in the street and ask where she has left her yellow star.'

'Is that all?'

'Of course not. You'll get enough to eat. . . .'

'As much as I like?'

'As much as you like. Just imagine, there's all kinds of food on the table, you take whatever you happen to fancy, and when you can't eat any more the table is cleared, and at the next meal it's all there again.'

'You're pulling my leg,' she says, because it would be quite nice if he confirmed it to her all over again.

'That's the solemn truth. And you'll have pretty dresses, we'll go shopping together and. . . .'

'Wait a moment. What kind of food will there be on the table?'

'Whatever you like best. Meat paste with butter and *Challah* and hard-boiled eggs and fish, you can choose.'

'Will you be making potato pancakes again?'

'I certainly will.'

'In your shop?'

'In my shop.'

'You haven't forgotten your promise, have you? That I'll be allowed to help you in the shop?'

'Of course not.'

'You'll stand behind the counter making the pancakes, and I'll be allowed to take them to the customers, in my white apron. And in summer I'll take them ice-cream.'

'That's how it'll be.'

'I can hardly wait.'

Lina can hardly wait, and whenever she is in that mood she hunches her shoulders up to her ears. At last Jakob can get on with his supper, starting with the dry bread, until after some thought she frowns because she has suddenly foreseen a snag.

'But what's going to happen about school? You've also told me that later on I'll have to go to school. And if that's true I won't have any time for the shop, will I?'

'School is more important,' Jakob decides. 'While you're there I'll be able to handle the customers by myself. After school you can come and help me, if you still feel like it.'

'But I'd rather help right away!'

'What have you got against school, then? Has some idiot been telling you bad things about it?'

She shakes her head.

'There you are then. School is a wonderful, wonderful place, where all kinds of stupid kids go in and all kinds of clever kids come out. But if you think I like you better stupid. . . .'

'Will Siegfried and Rafael have to go to school too?'

'Of course.'

After this reassurance there is a knock at the door. Lina jumps up to run to the door and unlock it, but Jakob holds her back and places his finger on his lips. A knock is always suspicious, not every suspicion is confirmed. It might be Kirschbaum, for instance, come to discuss Lina's recovery, or his neighbour Horowitz would like to borrow a spoonful of malt coffee till the next distribution, word of honour. It may be quite an ordinary knock, we'll soon find out, but even so there's no need for Lina to be seen, she doesn't concern anyone. Jakob puts his arm round her shoulder, draws her to the window, points behind the bed.

'Hide behind there,' he whispers. 'Don't move till I tell you. Right?'

Right. Lina crouches down and doesn't move, and Jakob opens the door. Who should be outside but Kowalski, standing there with his swollen face, trying to smile.

'Can't get rid of me, can you!'

Jakob would gladly dispatch him right there at the door, tell me quickly what's up and then goodbye, but Kowalski clearly gives the impression of having all the time in the world. Walking past Jakob, who is still holding the door handle, he sits down at the table and says: 'Aren't you going to close the door?'

Jakob closes the door rather loudly; Lina, as ordered, makes no sound. He has no choice but to sit down on the other chair, and he tries hard to look pressed for time.

'I see you're just having supper,' Kowalski observes. 'I hope I'm not disturbing you?'

'Aren't you ever going to tell me why you're here?'

'Is that the way to treat a guest?' Kowalski asks amiably.

'No, it isn't, I'll rush down and bring up some wine from the cellar!'

'Why so impatient? That always was your problem, Jakob, you weren't pleasant enough with your customers, they often used to tell me that while I was cutting their hair. That's why you were getting fewer and fewer customers.'

'Thanks for the advice. But did you come here to tell me that?'

Behind the bed there is a soundless giggle, audible only to someone who knows there is another person in the room.

'Believe it or not, I've nothing special in mind. At home the walls are closing in on me, a man can't spend evening after evening in the same room. I'll go and have a chat with Jakob, I thought, he'll be in the same boat, I thought, he'll be glad. In the old days people used to meet after work, didn't they? Everybody found that quite normal. Shouldn't we gradually start getting used to something normal again?'

Before Jakob can reply that the old days were the old days and today is today, and that he wants to be left in peace and go to bed because the work at the freight yard is becoming too much for him, Kowalski digs into his pocket, brings out the two cigarettes, and puts them on the table, one in front of himself and one in front of Jakob, and thus momentarily silences him.

'That's kind of you,' says Jakob. Kowalski may believe that Jakob is referring to the visit, but Jakob is looking at the cigarettes, perhaps he actually means both.

'Besides, you've told me very little today,' Kowalski says after a suitable pause. 'The news about the losses was pretty encouraging, but you can imagine that other things interest me just as much. And there hasn't been a word about those today.'

'For crying out loud, Kowalski, why do you keep badgering me? Aren't things difficult enough, do you have to keep harping on that? I can't take it any more! When I know something I'll tell you, but surely in my own room at least you can leave me in peace!'

Kowalski nods a few times thoughtfully, rolling his cigarette between his fingers, and pushes out his lower lip, the swollen one. He has come with a suspicion that seems to contain some truth. 'You know, Jakob,' he says, 'I've noticed that you always get impatient with me, you even lose your temper, when I ask you for news. You never volunteer anything, so I have to ask, and the moment I do, you get furious. I simply don't understand that, I can't see any logic in it. Imagine if it was the other way round, Jakob, if I had the radio and you didn't, wouldn't you also be asking me then?'

'Are you mad? In front of the child!'

Jakob jumps from his chair and turns towards the window. Lina has been crouching and listening long enough, and, as agreed, she emerges from her uncomfortable hiding place; after all, in a way he did call her. She is grinning from ear to ear.

'Good God!' stammers Kowalski in a shocked voice as he claps his hands together. But no one pays any attention to him, this is a matter between Jakob and Lina. They exchange glances, Lina winks, now you're in the soup, I bet you weren't counting on that! Jakob abandons his faint hope that she might not have heard anything, children are often God knows where with their thoughts, or that at least that she hadn't understood. She is a wide-awake young rascal, she winks, and everything is crystal clear. That'll give him a nice big load to think about before straightening out this new disaster, every day a fresh one, once again he can forget about listening for the rumble of cannon in the night. But night has yet to come, and Lina is still standing there, enjoying the little triumph which that fool of a Kowalski has so unthinkingly handed her. One can't take root and sweat blood and water for ever, one has to give some kind of sign of life.

'Run upstairs now, Lina. I'll be up to see you later,' says Jakob wearily.

First, though, she goes over to him and pulls down his head. Jakob thinks this is for the kiss that is part of even the briefest separation. But he can think what he likes, Lina's mind is not on kissing, not now; she pulls down his head because his ears are attached to it, and into one of them she whispers: 'So they've all heard it from you! You *were* pulling my leg!'

Then she is out of the room, Jakob and Kowalski are again seated at the table, Kowalski expecting a flood of reproaches while feeling completely innocent. For nothing would have happened if Jakob hadn't hidden his child from him, from his best friend. And if he did have to hide her because he couldn't be sure who was knocking at the door, he should have let her out when he saw who it was. But no, he leaves her there in her corner, probably he's forgotten her, I ask you, how can anybody forget a child? One isn't clairvoyant, after all, and now he's angry and about to let loose his accusations.

'A fine job you've made of it! It's not enough that the whole ghetto is yacking about it, now she knows about it too!' Jakob does in fact say.

'I'm sorry, I'm sure, but I couldn't possibly see her. With this eye. . . .'

Kowalski points to his eyes, Jakob can take his pick, both are orientally narrow, impressively framed in dark blue. Yes, Kowalski is pointing to his eyes, a discreet reminder of this morning's life-saving operation, no need to press the point; if reproaches are in order here, the question is by whom to whom. Or we can both be a bit generous and forget about what happened, that is water under the bridge anyway. And the ploy is successful, the eyes are superbly effective. Instantly the mood at the table changes, becomes a few degrees warmer, instantly Jakob responds to the demand made on his pity; he shifts a little closer and looks with new eyes at the damage he has caused.

'Doesn't look too good.'

Kowalski makes a dismissive gesture, it'll soon heal up; if Jakob wants to be conciliatory, Kowalski won't be petty either, he's in a generous mood. There lie the cigarettes, still cold, but Kowalski has thought of everything, even matches. As a final surprise he takes some out of his pocket and lights one on the worn striking surface, now the time has come for a smoke, brother. Come on, lean back and close your eyes, let's not spoil the pleasure by talking, let's take a few puffs and dream of old times, which will soon be back again. Come on, let's think of Chaim Balabusne with his thick steel-rimmed spectacles and the tiny shop where we always bought our cigarettes, or rather the tobacco to roll our own. His shop was closer to yours than mine was, and closer to mine than yours was, it was between our two shops, yet we never became real friends with him, but that was his fault. Because he wasn't interested in pancakes and ice-cream, or in a haircut or a shave. Many people said he let his red hair grow so long out of religious piety, but I know better, it was out of stinginess, nothing else. Ah well, never mind, mustn't speak ill of the dead, Balabusne always had a good selection, cigars, pipes, cigarette cases with little flowers, gold-tipped cigarettes for the rich, always tried to persuade us to take a more expensive brand but we stuck with 'Excelsior'. And the stand with the little gas flame and the cigar cutter on the counter, the brass stand he was always polishing when one went into his shop, it's that brass stand one always remembers in thinking back to the old days, though we only bought tobacco from him once a week at most and never used the stand.

'Are you thinking about Chaim Balabusne too?'

'Why bring up Chaim Balabusne all of a sudden?'

'No special reason. Maybe the smoking.'

'I'm not thinking of anything.'

The last pull, one more would burn the lips. The smoke has tickled the lungs gloriously and made one quite woozy, like after a few little glasses too many; the world is circling leisurely, but one is firmly seated, hands on the table. A bit of sighing, a bit of groaning, the smoke is still floating round the room. 'And now let's get to the point, Jakob,' says Kowalski. 'How do things look out there? What news about the Russians?'

Jakob remains calm, it had been only a matter of time anyway before Kowalski brought up the real reason for his visit; the cigarette couldn't deceive anyone. Now there's no Lina hiding in the background, now it's possible to speak freely, we've already concocted an answer for you and your kind, brace yourself. So, bring on the despairing expression, bring on the sad, drooping shoulders, now comes the last act in our question-and-answer game, Kowalski, and you won't like it. But I can't worry about that any more, I've been doing it long enough, I'm just another tormented human being.

'I didn't want to tell you. . . .'

'They're being pushed back!' cries Kowalski.

'No, no, it's not that bad!'

'What then? for God's sake tell me!'

'Can you imagine,' says Jakob in a low voice, offering a perfect picture of distress, 'a while ago I sit down at my set and turn the knob like I always do, but not a single sound comes out. I mean, yesterday it was still working perfectly, and today it's completely silent! It's hopeless, my friend, a radio is a miraculous object, and now it's broken down.'

'Good God!' exclaims Kowalski in horror; for the second time tonight Kowalski exclaims 'Good God!' and even claps his hands together, probably because for him one is not possible without the other.

f only we could have a smoke!' Jakob says longingly, for it is the next day, and the cigarette, the Juno without a tip, lives on only in his memory. He is standing in a boxcar, doing a *yontev* job, a holiday job, as it may well be called, which consists of taking from us Jews the bags that we are privileged to carry today. We carry the hundred-pound bags to him across a distance of fifty metres or more; all he has to do is move them along in the freight car and stack them up neatly against the walls, hence holiday job, also because there are two of them to do it, Jakob and Leonard Schmidt. The day, incidentally, had started out surprisingly enough when we were shown what we were to do today; we had looked at each other in amazement and thought, they don't know what they want. Well over two weeks ago a whole trainload of bags of cement arrived as if they were planning to put up some buildings; we unloaded every last one and covered them with tarpaulins, and today we are suddenly told to load the bags back on to the cars. Well, it's their business, we obediently reload the bags, just the way they want them, we lug them over to the cars, in one of which Jakob is standing doing his *yontev* job and saying 'If only we could have a smoke!' and Schmidt answers him half-amused: 'If that's all you've got to worry about, Mr Heym. . . .'

Leonard Schmidt. The fluke that had brought him to this ghetto transcended anything he could ever have imagined, since Schmidt could look back on a life that deserved to have continued on the other side of the fence. His presence in our midst was, for him, one of the few mysteries on this earth.

Born in 1895, in the town of Brandenburg, the son of a wealthy father and a monarchist mother, attended an excellent high school in Berlin where his father had moved two years after Leonard's birth for business reasons (acquisition of a textile factory); on completing school immediately joined the army, Flanders offensive, Verdun, occupation of the Crimea and later Champagne when the army was short of men: such was Schmidt's war. Then he received an honourable discharge from the defeated army, a proud lieutenant decorated for bravery in the face of the enemy and whatever else, and turned his attention to his future career. University was the next step, as was expected of privileged sons: reading law at Heidelberg with the final semesters in Berlin. The results couldn't have been better, all his exams passed with flying colours, most of them even with honours. Three obligatory years of articling, then the professional card 'Leonard Schmidt, D.L.L.', and finally the longed-for moment, the opening of his own law practice in the best part of town. Good clients were quick to show up; his father's connections more or less propelled them there. Soon he had to engage two juniors for the less important cases, and he made a name for himself ten times as fast as many another lawyer. A love match, two beautiful fair-haired daughters, the world respectfully doffed its hat to him every day, until an envious fellow-member of the bar association conceived the fateful idea of looking into his family tree, then to chop away at it and allow everything to reach its disastrous conclusion. His wife, his two daughters, and his bank account made it safely to Switzerland because good friends had warned Schmidt, but he was too late. He was still busy settling his most urgent affairs when there came a peremptory knock on his door.

In Schmidt's mind the whole thing persists like some idiotic joke; perhaps he'll wake up one morning to find clients once more sitting in his waiting-room. He had been well on the way to becoming a German nationalist. But they didn't let him, they knocked on his door and told him not to make a fuss, the maid's horrified face between the white-shrouded, plush-covered armchairs. They brought him here because his great-grandfather attended the synagogue and his parents had been stupid enough to have him circumcised, although by now they had forgotten why. Joke or no joke, he suffers doubly and triply in the first few days. When he was still a newcomer he told me his life story, and added miserably: 'Can you understand that?'

And a short time later – it was possible, in so far as one thought about him at all, to imagine that he was gradually getting used to life in the ghetto – he turns up at the freight yard, and what we see makes our hearts stand still. On his left breast is a pin from which hangs a small object, black and white, that on closer inspection proves to be an Iron Cross. 'Have some sense!' someone tells him. 'Take that cross off and hide it or they'll shoot you down for it like a mad dog!' But Schmidt turns away and starts working as if nothing were wrong. We all give him a wide berth, no one wants to be involved, he's beyond help, and from a safe distance we don't take our eyes off him. It is a good hour before a sentry notices the enormity, swallows a few times, stands mutely before Schmidt, and Schmidt stands pale faced before him. After an eternity the sentry turns on his heel; it really looks as if he had been rendered speechless. He goes into the red brick building, returns immediately with his superior, and points at Schmidt, the only person to have resumed work. The superior beckons Schmidt over, no one will give two cents for his life now; the superior bends down to the pin and carefully inspects the object like a watchmaker examining a tiny damaged part.

'Where did you get that?' he asks.

'Verdun,' says Schmidt in a shaky voice.

'We can't have that here. It's against regulations,' says the superior. He removes the decoration from Schmidt's chest, puts it in his pocket, doesn't make a note of any name, doesn't shoot any malefactor. Treats the incident like a nice diversion that will cause general mirth in the bar that night. He returns cheerfully to the brick building, the sentry has his eyes elsewhere again, nothing more is said about it, Schmidt has had his fun and we have had our spectacle. Thus, not long after arriving, he achieved an odd notoriety; so much for the life story of Leonard Schmidt.

'Never in my life have I had anything to do with a court case,' says Jakob.

'I see,' says Schmidt.

They make an easy day of it, picking up each bag together after we have lifted it onto the edge of the car, then hoisting it with a 'One, two!' onto the right spot. Even the rain doesn't bother them since their boxcar has a roof. In the brief intervals that occur they lean against the wall, wipe from their brows the sweat that has inexplicably appeared there, and chat just like in peace-time. When Kowalski or the Schtamms or Mischa pantingly unload their bags, look at them enviously, and snidely remark that if they don't watch out they'll work themselves to death, they smile. 'Don't worry about us!'

'What I mean is, I once was a witness,' says Jakob.

'I see.'

'But not in court. Only in the office of the public prosecutor who was handling the case.'

'What case?'

'It had to do with whether Kowalski owed money to Porfir the usurer or not. Porfir had miraculously mislaid the promissory note, and I merely had to testify that Kowalski had paid him back the money.'

'Were you actually there at the time?' asks Schmidt.

'Oh no! But Kowalski had already explained the whole thing to me in detail.'

'But if you were not there and thus knew the facts merely from hearsay, you should not have appeared as a witness at all. How could you be certain that Kowalski had actually returned the money? I don't wish to insinuate anything, but after all it is conceivable, isn't it, that Kowalski might have lied to you so that you would testify in his favour?'

'I don't think so,' Jakob says without hesitation. 'He has many faults, nobody knows them as well as I do, but he's not a liar. He told me right away that he hadn't paid back the money to Porfir. Where would he have got it from?'

'And although you knew that, you testified before the public prosecutor that he had paid it back in your presence?'

'Naturally!'

'Well, it's hardly that natural, is it, Mr Heym?' Schmidt says with a smile; he is undoubtedly wondering about the remarkable notions of justice harboured by these quaint people to whom he is supposed to belong.

'Anyway, it helped quite a bit,' Jakob went on, bringing his story to a close. 'That cutthroat Porfir had no luck with his accusation. His money was gone, but what am I saying, *his* money! Over the years he had gradually managed to fleece every one of us small businessmen. Thirty per cent interest, can you believe it? The whole street broke into cheers as Porfir and Kowalski came out of the court house after the verdict, Porfir seething with rage and Kowalski beaming with joy!'

Kowalski of the many-hued eyes tips his bag onto the floor of the car; with half an ear he has caught something about Kowalski beaming with joy, and he asks: 'What kind of stories are you telling about me?'

'That old business of Porfir's mislaid promissory note.'

'Don't believe a word he says,' Kowalski tells Schmidt. 'He gives me a bad name whenever he gets a chance.'

Kowalski pads back for the next bag, wet to the skin, after giving Jakob a come-off-it look. Schmidt and Jakob, both comfortably dry, also bestir themselves – without chatting, for a change – to see how many bags will fit into one car. Until the next interval, until Schmidt remembers something important, until he asks: 'I hope you don't mind my curiosity, Mr Heym, but what has Mr Churchill to say about the present situation?'

'Who?'

'Winston Churchill, the British Prime Minister.'

'I've no idea what he has to say. Haven't you heard? My radio's on the blink.'

'You must be joking!'

'What do you take me for?' Jakob says seriously.

Schmidt seems stunned and looks narrowly at Jakob, just like the others who that very morning had had to be told, with drooping shoulders and despairing voice, the only real news of the day. Schmidt, who is a bit stuck up and whom some wit has dubbed Leonard Assimilinski – this same Schmidt seems to feel a stab to the heart like all the others; suddenly he is no different from the rest.

'How did it happen?' he asks in a low voice.

The answer to this question had been reworded that morning; there hadn't been time to present it to each one as it had been handed to Kowalski, wrapped in tissue paper. Jakob had to settle for some major deletions. How did it happen? 'Well, how? The way a radio like that does go on the blink. Yesterday it was still working, and today it isn't.'

Reactions had been mixed; some cursed an unjust God, others prayed to Him, and some consoled themselves with the thought that radio and Russians were two entirely different things. One man had wept like a child, his tears blending with the raindrops running down his cheeks. One of them said: 'Let's hope that isn't a bad omen.'

Jakob couldn't say Yes and couldn't say No; he had to leave them to their minor anguish rather than expose them to the whole truth. Nor has he any words of comfort now to whisper to the disconsolate Schmidt. His store of comfort is exhausted. At this point we should remind ourselves briefly that Jakob is just as much in need of consolation as all the poor souls round him, just as cut off from all further supply of news, that he is tormented by the same hopes. Only a freak coincidence has turned an equal person into a special person and prevented him thus far from laying all his cards on the table. But only thus far: today I have let you glance up my sleeve, you have seen how empty it is, there is no trump card inside. Now we are all equally informed, there is no difference between us any more, except for your belief that I was once a special person.

'There's nothing to be done, Mr Schmidt, we have to carry on. Right now in fact!'

Across the freight yard, through the rain that has abated somewhat, booms an unfamiliar voice: 'Keep your hands off that!'

Jakob and Schmidt hurry to the door to see what is happening outside. Herschel Schtamm, one of the twins, is standing on the siding beside an ordinary-looking boxcar that is still closed. Thinking no doubt that this was the next one to be loaded, he hears the unfamiliar voice that can mean only him, and he snatches his hand away from the bolt, which he had been just about to raise. The only remarkable thing about the incident so far is the voice, but that is very remarkable: it is the Whistle's, hence unfamiliar. The Whistle in his railwayman's uniform advances, as quickly as his wooden leg allows, on Herschel Schtamm, who backs away in fear. The Whistle stops beside the boxcar and checks the bolt, which is still firmly closed.

'Didn't you hear before? This car is not to be touched, goddammit!'

'Yessir!' says Herschel Schtamm.

Then the Whistle turns towards all the Jews, who have paused in their work to enjoy the thrill of a totally new sound. Raising his voice he turns towards them and shouts: 'Have you all got it into your heads now, you vermin? This car is not to be touched! Next time there will be a bullet!'

So that's what his voice sounds like, not a very impressive premiere I'd say, a weak baritone I'd say, one could have wished for a pleasanter sound. The Whistle stalks back to the brick building, Herschel Schtamm resumes work as fast as he can so as to get out of the limelight, and we do the same. The incident, which wasn't a genuine one, has come to its temporary conclusion.

'What kind of a boxcar do you suppose that is?' asks Schmidt.

'How should I know?' Jakob replies.

'Mr Schtamm can count himself lucky to have got away with it. Actually the sentry did order us this morning to leave that boxcar alone. You must have heard that too.'

'Yes, of course.'

'So why did he go over there?'

'How in the world am I supposed to know!'

Schmidt has no instinct for when a conversation has come to an end. He expresses his views on the advisability of strictly obeying orders, on the increased chances of survival resulting from such adherence, then delivers a brief lecture on the factual legal situation deriving from the present power configuration. Jakob listens with only half an ear. Frankly, he doesn't find Schmidt particularly likeable; without ever actually saying so, Schmidt considers himself superior and more intelligent and more cultured – he probably wouldn't have the slightest objection to the entire ghetto if they hadn't picked on him to be put in there. When he makes an effort to gloss over social differences, which he usually does, the impression is inescapable that he is pretending, look how nice of me, I'm just behaving as if we

98

were all of the same kind. The differences are there, he can't fight them: if only in the way he looks at a person or speaks or eats or talks about the Germans or the past, but above all in the way he thinks. One can't choose one's fellow-sufferers, and a fellow-sufferer he undoubtedly is; he trembles no differently from anyone else for his portion of life – well, yes, a bit differently perhaps, in his special way, a way that our kind don't happen to find all that pleasant.

Soon Herschel Schtamm appears lugging a sack, wearing the soaked fur cap under which he hides his piety, and Jakob asks him: 'What was all that about, Herschel?'

'You won't believe it, but I heard voices in that car,' Herschel says.

'Voices?'

'Voices,' says Herschel. 'As true as I'm standing here, human voices.'

He may be feeling a cold shiver down his spine, especially since he is always much too hot under his fur cap. He puffs out his cheeks and nods anxiously a few times: you can imagine what that must mean. Jakob can; he accompanies Herschel's performance with despairing sighs and by closing his eyes and raising his eyebrows. They are carrying on an inaudible little dialogue, and Schmidt stands beside them without understanding a single syllable.

Mischa comes up to them, sets down his bag of cement, and says quietly: 'You'd better go on working, the sentry's already looking this way.'

Suddenly Jakob has two left hands, the bag slips from him, and Schmidt says in annoyance: 'Watch what you're doing!'

Jakob must watch himself. He feels, as he remembers later, like a person who has just been dreaming of happiness and quiet little places when someone comes and pulls away your warm blanket, and you lie there naked and trembling from the impact of cold reality.

'You're very silent,' says Schmidt after a while.

Jakob persists in his silence; deeply distressed, he picks up the bags as they are handed to him, merely casting an occasional furtive glance at the innocuous-looking boxcar on its siding, behind whose walls human voices have been heard. Ventilation holes right up under the roof, no one is tall enough to look out, and no one is screaming, neither from inside nor outside, why isn't anyone screaming, the bags need to be carefully stacked. Standing there reddish-brown on its siding as if forgotten, but they won't forget it, in some ways they can be relied upon. Yesterday it wasn't here yet, tomorrow it'll be gone again, just a brief stop on its way to somewhere. A car like that – loaded and unloaded and loaded by us a hundred times, crates, coal, potatoes under strict surveillance, machinery, stones, boxcars exactly like that, but this one mustn't be touched, or they'll shoot.

'D'you think it's true?' asks Schmidt.

'Think what's true?'

'About those voices.'

'Don't ask such stupid questions. D'you think Herschel Schtamm is trying to impress us?'

'But who can possibly be inside that car?'

'Who d'you think?'

Schmidt's mouth opens; suddenly he is seized by a dreadful suspicion. 'You mean . . . ,' he breathes.

'Yes, I mean!'

'You mean, they're still sending people to the camps?'

Unfortunately that's how it is, Schmidt is not at home in the game of hints where certain things aren't mentioned and yet are said; he'll never be at home, in his heart he is and always will be an outsider. He needs to be told everything in blunt, unequivocal terms.

'No, they're not sending any more! The war is long since over, we could all go home if we wanted to, but we don't want to because we're having such a good time here!' says Jakob, rolling his eyes. 'Are they still sending people! Do you imagine there are none left? I'm left, you're left, all of us here are left. Just don't get the idea it's as good as over!'

Schmidt interrupts the well-deserved lecture with a quick gesture, pointing outside in alarm and exclaiming: 'Look! Schtamm!'

Herschel had never attracted much attention, except for his praying, which at the time he was convinced had led to the power failure. Now he's making up for it: he is standing on the siding beside the boxcar. The sentries haven't noticed him yet. Herschel is pressing his ear to the wall of the car and speaking: I can clearly see his lips moving, see him listening and then speaking again, our pious Herschel. His brother Roman happens to be standing next to me, his eyes like cartwheels: he makes a move to dash over to Herschel and bring him back before it's too late. Two men have to restrain him by force, and one of them has to whisper: 'Calm down, you idiot, you'll only draw their attention to him!'

I can't hear what Herschel is saying or what the people inside are telling him, it's much too far away, but I can imagine it, and this is not a case of vague conjectures. The longer I think about it, the surer I am of his words, even though he never confirmed them to me.

'Hello! Can you hear me?' Herschel begins.

'We can hear you,' a voice from inside must surely answer. 'Who are you?'

'I'm from the ghetto,' Herschel says. 'You must hang on, only for a short time, you must hang on. The Russians have already advanced past Bezanika!'

'How do you know?' they ask from inside, all quite logical and predictable.

'You can believe me. We have a secret radio. I have to get back now!'

The people locked up inside thank him, utterly bewildered; a little white dove has strayed into their darkness. What they say is of no consequence, maybe they wish him happiness and riches and a hundred and twenty years of life before they hear his footsteps moving away.

Everyone is watching spellbound as Herschel starts on his way back. Crazy fools that we are, we stand there gaping instead of getting on with our work and behaving as if everything were normal. First we keep Roman from committing a stupid blunder, then we commit one ourselves; perhaps Herschel wouldn't have escaped them anyway, who can tell in retrospect, in any event we do nothing to distract their attention from him. Only now does he seem to have discovered fear; so far everything had gone as if of its own volition, according to the unfathomable laws obeyed by sleep-walkers. Cover is pitifully inadequate, almost non-existent. Herschel has good reason to be afraid. A stack of crates, another empty boxcar, otherwise nothing along his path where he would need the protection of a convoy. I see him sticking his head round the corner of the boxcar, centimetre by centimetre; with his eyes he has already reached us, I can already hear him telling us about his great journey.

So far the opposition is quiet. The sentry by the gate is standing with his back to the railway tracks; there is no sound to rouse his attention. The other two sentries have disappeared, are inside the building presumably, driven in by the rain. I see Herschel making his final preparations for the great sprint, I see him pray. Although he is still standing beside the boxcar and moving his lips, it is obvious that he is not talking to the people inside but conversing with his God. And then I turn my head towards the brick building: it has a little window in the gable. The window is open, and on the sill lies a rifle being aimed, very calmly and deliberately. I can't make out the man behind it, it is too dark in the room; I see only two hands adjusting the aim of the barrel until they are satisfied: then they are still, as in a painting. What should I have done, I who have never been a hero, what should I have done if I were a hero – given a shout, that's all, but what good would that have been? I don't shout, I close my eyes, an eternity passes, Roman says to me: 'Why are you closing your eyes? Look, he's going to make it, that crazy fool!'

I don't know why, but at this moment I think of Chana, executed in front of a tree whose name I don't know. I'm still thinking of her after the shot is fired, until the men round me are all talking at the same time. A single dry shot; the two hands had, as I said, plenty of time to prepare everything all the while Herschel was praying. It is a strange sound – I have never heard a single shot before, always several at a time – like a naughty child stamping its foot in a tantrum, or a toy balloon being blown up too hard and bursting, or even, since I am already indulging in images, as if God had coughed, a cough of dismissal for Herschel.

Those locked behind the reddish-brown walls of the boxcar may be asking: 'Hey, you there, what's happened?'

Herschel is lying on his stomach, across the track and between two ties. His clenched right hand has fallen into a black puddle; his face, of which at first I can see only one half, has a surprised look with its open eye. We stand silently round him; they allow us this little respite. Roman bends down to him, pulls him off the track, and turns him over on his back. Then he removes the fur cap, his fingers fumbling awkwardly with the flaps under the chin. He thrusts the cap into his pocket and walks away. For the first time in this freight yard, Herschel's ringlets are allowed to wave freely in the wind; many of us have never seen them before, have merely been told about them. So this is what Herschel Schtamm really looks like, without disguise. For the last time his face, darkly framed by wet earth and black hair; someone has closed his eyes. I won't lie, why should I, he was no beauty, he was very pious, wanted to pass on hope, and in doing so he died.

Unnoticed, the sentry from the gate has come up behind us; it is time to divert our thoughts, and he says: 'You've been gawking long enough, or haven't you ever seen a dead man before? Come on, back to work – on the double!'

At the end of the day we will take him with us and bury him; that's permitted, without its being printed in black and white in one of the many regulations: it has simply become accepted. I look once more up to the window, which is now closed again: no rifle, no hands, and no one emerges from the building, they pay no further attention to us; for them the incident is closed.

Life goes on; Schmidt and Jakob start moving the bags again. By this time Schmidt has understood enough to hold his tongue and not let on why Herschel insisted on dashing over to the boxcar although the railwayman had emphatically and specifically warned him earlier.

In Jakob's head, self-reproaches follow one upon the other; the part he has played in this drama is frighteningly clear. You construct some scanty consolation for yourself; you visualize a huge scale with two trays, on one you place Herschel while on the other you pile up all the hope you have been spreading among the people. Which side will go down? The problem is, you don't know how much hope weighs, and no one is going to tell you. You must find the formula by yourself and complete the calculation alone. But you calculate in vain, the problems mount, here's another, who can divulge to you how much harm was prevented by your inventions? Ten disasters or twenty or only a single one: what has been prevented will remain hidden from you for ever. Only the one you caused is visible: there it lies beside the tracks in the rain.

Even later, during the lunch break, Jakob hasn't come one bit closer to the solution of the problem with all its unknown factors. He sits apart as he swallows his soup; today everyone leaves everyone else in peace. He has avoided Roman Schtamm. Roman hasn't sought him out; only beside the cart where the empty tin bowls are always deposited do they find themselves suddenly face to face. They look each other in the eye, especially Roman. Jakob tells me: 'He looked at me as if I had shot his brother.'

The evenings belong to Lina.

A long time ago, Jakob stopped with her in the corridor outside his door and said: 'Listen carefully, Lina, so that, if anything should happen, you'll be able to find the key to my room,' is what he said. 'Here behind the door frame is a little hole in the wall, see? I'll put the key in here now, then wedge this stone in front of it. It's quite easy to remove – if you stand on tiptoe you'll be tall enough. Try.' Lina tried; she stretched up, removed the stone, barely managed to grasp the key, and held it out proudly to Jakob. 'Wonderful,' Jakob said. 'Remember the place carefully. I don't really know why, but maybe someday it'll be important. And one more thing – never tell anyone about this place.'

By now Lina no longer has to stand on tiptoe; for two years she has been tirelessly growing up towards the little hole behind the door frame. If anything should happen, Jakob had said, today something had happened: Lina retrieves the key, unlocks the door, and stands with bated breath in the empty room. She is a bit nervous, but that will pass; if Jakob comes in unexpectedly she'll simply tell him she's tidying up. The motives driving her are adventurous, he would hardly approve of them, and what he doesn't know won't hurt him.

In her path lie two obstacles: she is under no illusions. The first is the hiding place, still unknown; the second is that she doesn't know what a radio looks like. Hiding places are not unlimited in this room, in a few minutes it could be turned upside down; the second obstacle seems much more difficult to her. There are all kinds of things that Jakob has explained to her. She would have no difficulty, for instance, in describing a bus, although she has never been face to face with one; she could talk about bananas, aeroplanes, teddy bears that start to growl when you lay them on their backs. During the recent power failure, Jakob even traced with her the highly mysterious path travelled by the light from the coal mine to the little bulb under the ceiling, but not a single word has he ever uttered about a radio. There are a few scanty clues: everyone is talking about it, it is forbidden to own one, it reveals things not known before, it is small enough to be easily hidden.

'Will you show me your radio tomorrow?' she asked him the previous evening, when he came up to the attic to see her after Kowalski's futile visit.

'No,' he said.

'And the day after tomorrow?'

'No!'

'And the day after the day after tomorrow?'

'No, I said! And that's enough!'

Even her normally infallible look of wide-eyed entreaty had no effect; Jakob didn't even notice it. Hence her new attempt after a resentful pause: 'Are you ever going to show it to me?'

'No.'

'Why not?'

'Because.'

'Will you at least tell me what it looks like?' she asked then, her plan already half-formed in her mind. But he refused to answer this either, so her half-formed plan became a whole one.

In a nutshell: Lina must look for an object of which all she knows is that Jakob keeps it hidden away, an object without colour, shape, or weight, the only good thing being that Jakob can't have that many unfamiliar objects in his room. The first one she finds and has never seen before can confidently be assumed to be called a radio.

Lina starts with the obvious hiding places: under the bed, on top of the cupboard, in the table drawer. Quite possibly a radio is too big to fit into a table drawer – perhaps anyone watching would laugh out loud to see Lina looking in there for a radio. But it's not her fault that Jakob remains so obstinately silent, and besides, no one is watching. It's not in the drawer, there's nothing in it; all she finds under the bed and on top of the cupboard is dust. All that's left is the inside of the cupboard, there's no other hiding place. The cupboard has two doors, one at the top and one at the bottom. She can forget about the top one; behind it are the two soup plates and two flat plates, the two cups of which one lost its handle when Lina dropped it on the floor while washing up, also a knife and two spoons, the ever-empty sugar jar, and behind all that the food, when there is any. Behind this door Lina is at home; she often lays the table, serves the meal and clears it away, she could forget about that one, but her project must not fail for want of thoroughness. She looks: the four plates, two cups, sugar jar, knife and spoons, plus some bread and a small bag of dried beans, no surprises.

Now for the bottom door. Lina hesitates: her fingers are already round the key and can't make up their mind. If what she is looking for isn't in there, then it's nowhere. So far she'd never had any reason to look inside. 'That's where I keep my stuff,' Jakob had said. Nothing could sound more harmless. His stuff: only now is it clear what is concealed behind two such innocent words.

There is a limit to her hesitation, and Lina finally opens up; outside in the corridor footsteps hurry by. Locking the door won't do: if Jakob comes he won't ask what she's doing here, he'll ask why she has locked herself in, and there's no answer for that. Lina takes everything out: a pair of trousers and a shirt, a needle and thread, a saucepan – why isn't that in the top section? – a box of nails and screws, an empty picture frame, the book about Africa. She allows herself a brief pause, the book has more to offer than the words and letters to which Jakob has recently been attaching such strange importance. The pictures do deserve a few moments' attention, regardless.

The woman with those amazingly long breasts, so flat and dried-up looking, and the ring stuck through her nose – Jakob has promised to explain the meaning of that later. The naked men who have painted their faces all over, carry long spears, and on their heads wear enormous structures of feathers, hair and ribbons. Or the skinny children, with round, protruding stomachs, animals with horns and stripes and endless noses and even longer necks: all this can certainly cause delay, but not enough to make one forget one's real purpose.

Lina crawls waist-deep into the cupboard; a final obstacle is removed, a modest pile of underwear with a green towel on top, and then. . . . The path has been cleared to that as yet unseen object, a proud smile of triumph, there it stands, inconspicuously in the corner, mysterious and forbidden. She brings it out to the light, some delicate latticework, a little screw, glass, and round; she places it reverently on the table and sits down facing it. Now something will happen. His stuff, Jakob had said; while she is staring at it the minutes tick away: what will be revealed now that one didn't know before? Does this thing speak like an ordinary person, or does it deliver up its secrets in some other way, in some miraculous way? After a prolonged, expectant silence, Lina realizes that, left to itself, it will reveal nothing, it must be made to speak; maybe one simply has to ask it something. If so, then not, she hopes, by means of some prearranged formula like with Ali Baba outside the cave of Sesame.

'What is my name?' Lina starts off with the simplest words she can think of, but already this seems to be too much for the thing. Lina allows it plenty of time: in vain. Her disappointment makes way for the thought that she must ask for something unknown, for something she doesn't already know – after all, she does know her own name. 'How much is thirty times two million?' she asks. When this evokes no reply either, she takes a new approach; she remembers the light that can be switched on and off according to one's fancy. Perhaps this thing can be switched on in the same way, let's try the little screw. It has rusted, can hardly be moved; after much effort, just a tiny squeak, and already her fingers are sore. At that moment Jakob appears in the doorway and asks, as predicted: 'What are you doing here?'

'I,' says Lina, 'I wanted . . . ,' she says, having to recover from the shock, 'I wanted to tidy up your room. Don't you remember?'

Jakob remembers; he looks at the Sodom and Gomorrah in front of the cupboard, then back at Lina, who had wanted to tidy up; before he can open his mouth she knows it won't be all that bad. 'But I hope you haven't finished yet?' asks Jakob.

Of course she hasn't finished yet, she's only just begun. She jumps up and stuffs saucepan and book and underwear back into the cupboard, in such a hurry that his eyes can scarcely follow her. Next, the picture frame, in her haste the nails fall out of the box, in no time they're gathered up, then come the needle and thread, where are the needle and thread, she'll find them next time, the cupboard door is slammed shut, and already the mess is forgotten. Only that thing remains on the table, he has seen it anyway; there stands his only secret, and he is still not giving vent to his anger.

'You're not cross with me, are you?'

'No, no!'

Jakob takes off his jacket, then washes the station dirt off his hands. Lina grows uneasy: the thing is standing there being ignored.

'And what did you really mean to do here?'

'Nothing. I was tidying up,' she says, knowing that it's hopeless.

'What were you looking for?'

Now he does begin to raise his voice, but she finds the question too silly for words: he's sitting in front of the thing, asking in pretended innocence what she has been looking for, and to that we refuse to give the obvious reply.

'What's the lamp doing here?'

'What lamp?'

'This one. Do you see any other?'

When Lina remains silent and wide eyed, staring at the alleged lamp, and the wide eyes gradually fill with tears, Jakob draws her close and asks in a much gentler voice: 'What's the matter?'

'Nothing.'

He pulls her onto his knee; she doesn't often cry, who is to know what's going on in a little mind like that, a mind that has all day to brood alone? 'Come on, tell me what's the matter. Does it have anything to do with the lamp?'

'No.'

'Have you ever seen it before?'

'No.'

'Would you like me to explain how it works?'

Lina stops her tears: after all, Jakob can't be blamed for her mistake, and besides, tomorrow is another day, somehow she'll find the hiding place that she overlooked today. She attends to eyes and nose with her sleeve, which is not quite adequate: Jakob's handkerchief hurries to her aid.

'Would you like me to explain?'

'Yes.'

'Well, then. This thing is a kerosene lamp. In the old days all the lamps were like this, before there was any electric light. This is where you pour in the kerosene, into this little bowl. This is the wick, it sucks up the kerosene, and only its tip sticks out. It can be made longer or shorter, with this screw here. You hold a match to the wick, and then the room is lighted up.'

'Could you do it for me?'

'I'm sorry, I don't have any kerosene.'

Lina slips off Jakob's knee; she picks up the lamp in both hands and looks at it from all sides: so that's why it was no use waiting for an answer. At home, in the Nuriel family, there had been no kerosene lamp and no radio; mistakes arise from lack of experience. After one last look she puts the thing back in the cupboard. Order is completely restored, also with Lina. She even discovers a funny side to her unsuccessful voyage of discovery.

'D'you know what I thought it was?'

'Well?'

'But you won't laugh at me?'

'I wouldn't dream of it.'

'I thought it was your radio.'

Jakob smiles; he remembers how, as a very little boy, he had believed an old woman who lived next door, a hunchback, to be a witch, a similar mistaken conclusion, but soon his smile gradually fades. Lina was looking for the radio, she admits that. It wouldn't have been a bad idea to leave her to her belief: what difference does it make to a lamp to be taken for a radio? He would have sworn her to secrecy, now at last you've found it, now you know what it looks like, now not another word about it, above all not to strangers. And for weeks there would have been peace for him, at least at home. But he had let the opportunity slip by; Lina hadn't betrayed herself until it was too late, and he hadn't had enough presence of mind correctly to size up the situation in the room and the lamp on the table and the significance of her tears. Any minute now she will ask, all right, so that was a lamp, now where's the radio? Any minute now, or in an hour, or tomorrow at latest, she's already itching with impatience. Telling her it's broken won't satisfy her, then show me the broken one, and unfortunately he's not one of those who can answer awkward questions with the occasional slap. There is still, of course, one way out, a very simple one: Jakob could claim to have burned it, a damaged radio, if found, being no less dangerous than an intact one.

He could say that, then he'd be happily rid of the radio, for Lina and all the world, but it so happens that the day just past at the freight yard also plays a certain role. The dead Herschel Schtamm, his brother Roman with the tormenting gaze, the unknown people locked up on the siding: they all have a right to speak before the radio is finally destroyed. And the individual Jews who arrived hopefully in the early morning with their questions and left again in dismay, without the news to which they are entitled. By this time they will already be home, relatives and friends will be knocking on their doors, what's the latest news at the freight yard? Nothing, they'll be told, the radio says nothing any more, it's broken, yesterday it was still working, and today not a sound. The relatives and friends leave, spread the latest news throughout all the buildings and streets, which soon will once again seem as wretched as they did before that night when the searchlight picked up Jakob about seven-thirty on the Kurländischer Damm. There's a lot to be considered before making frivolous decisions, before buying the peace that is no peace.

'Will you show me the radio now?'

'I already said No yesterday. Has anything changed since then?'

'I'll find it anyway,' says Lina.

'Then go on looking.'

'Want to bet that I'll find it?'

She is switching to open attack, let her search rather than ask questions, Jakob is not going to talk her out of the next radio she finds. And the radio that she'll never find will for the time being be saved from the fire, for many reasons, the first being Herschel of the ringlets: that very morning, as he lay in the rain between the railway ties, he had as good as repaired it.

Jakob goes to work with a light heart. Anyone observing his posture and his brisk walk and drawing comparisons with yesterday or the last few days is struck by changes: there goes a man of poise. With a light heart, for the hours in bed had been rich in important decisions; contact with the outer world has been restored. The radio had been on half the night, right after Lina had been shaken off it went on and stayed on until sleep came unbidden, and by that time his ear had picked up a number of reports, and not to be sneezed at either. With a light heart, for the little flame of expectation must not go out. Thus Jakob's resolve; he had spent half the night looking for wood and kindling to keep it going. He has succeeded in achieving a substantial advance, he and the Russians; he has quietly let them win a great battle on the banks of a little river, the Rudna, which, although it doesn't babble along right outside the front door, is gratifyingly closer than the town of Bezanika.

In reviewing the news items supplied thus far, Jakob noticed that, when looked at more closely, these had consisted only of extended trifles; except for the very first item about Bezanika, nothing substantial. He had turned every notion into a tremendous story, often transparent and lacking in credibility. Doubts had so far not arisen merely because hope had made the people blind and stupid. But during the night before the battle of the Rudna an insight was gained: Jakob has at last discovered the source of his difficulties. In other words, hardly had he turned out the light when it came to him in a flash why his inventions had become so laborious and eventually failed him almost entirely. He was too modest, he suspected; he had always tried to keep his news items within a sphere which at some later date, after life has resumed its normal course, cannot be verified. With each news item some inhibition had stood in his way, some pang of conscience; the lies had come stumbling and reluctantly from his lips as if looking for a hiding place they could crawl away to in a hurry before anyone took a closer look at them.

But this procedure was fundamentally wrong, as he came to realize last night; a liar with pangs of conscience will always remain a bungler. In this type of activity, restraint and false modesty are inappropriate; you must go the whole hog, you must exude conviction, you must demonstrate how a person should look who is already aware of what they are going to hear from you the very next moment. You must throw out figures and names and dates right and left; the battle of the Rudna is merely a modest beginning. It will never go down in history, but in our history it will be given a place of honour. And when all these tribulations are over, when anyone who is interested can look up the true events of the war in books, they are free to come and ask: 'Hey, you, what kind of nonsense did you tell us back in those days? When was there ever a battle of the Rudna?' 'Wasn't there?' will be the surprised answer. 'Let's have a look at that book . . . You're right, there never was. It's not in here. So I suppose I must have misheard at the time, I'm sorry.' They will probably forgive you, at worst they'll shrug and walk off, and perhaps there will even be some among them who will thank you for the error.

As regards the progress of the fighting, Jakob has done some preliminary work, and for this his local knowledge had come in very handy. The battle of the Rudna and its aftermath are to suffice for the next three days, we mustn't go overboard, for the crossing of the river isn't altogether without its problems. We're not going to make it that easy for the Russians: the Germans have blown up the only bridge, Jakob has thought it all out. Before the advance can be continued, a temporary pontoon bridge has to be built, and this will take three or four days. When that's been taken care of, the Russians will march on the little town of Tobolin, which the Germans have turned into a kind of fortress. Tobolin in turn resists for three days; it is surrounded, softened up by the artillery, and stormed by the infantry. In a hopeless situation Major Karthäuser, a splendid name with a credible rank, signs the document of surrender: Tobolin is liberated. Incidentally that will please Mischa – he has an aunt living there who, it is hoped, will live to see this victory. The aunt, Lea Malamut, owned a haberdashery and, when Mischa was a boy, always used to send him a little box of coloured buttons and threads for his birthday. But let's not linger in Tobolin, it's a long way from there to the district town of Pry, the next town in our direction. Some seventy kilometres; they have already been planned in rough outline but aren't yet ready in every detail. That will be Jakob's night-work for the next little while. As far as Tobolin everything is clear, and today at the freight yard the result of the glorious battle of the Rudna will be announced.

With a light heart Jakob goes off to work, and a nice little highlight occurs to him that he could apply to events at the Rudna. Might not secret German plans have fallen into Russian hands, thus revealing all the enemy's actions on this front for weeks to come and rendering them ineffectual? That would be a few raisins in Jakob's cake, but immediately doubts arise in terms of probability, for would secret plans be kept in such an insecure place? After all, the Germans are no fools. Nor are the Russians: even if they did capture plans of that kind, they're not going to broadcast the fact to the world over the radio. They'll keep it carefully to themselves and discreetly make their preparations. So we'll dispense with the little highlight: what we already have is enough to give the Jews a bit of the poise with which Jakob continues on his way to work, a light heart.

At the corner of Tismenizer-Strasse he sees Kowalski waiting for him, nothing special about that, Kowalski often waits for him here, he lives here. As he approaches, though, it turns out that Kowalski is not alone; with him is a young man, that *is* somewhat unusual, especially since Jakob has never seen the young man before.

From some way off, Kowalski points at Jakob; the young stranger follows the finger with his eyes, as if Kowalski were explaining: that's the man, the one in the dark-grey jacket.

Jakob comes up to them, they shake hands, and all three walk on; there have been no introductions yet. 'You're late today,' Kowalski says. 'We've been waiting quite a while for you.'

'Had we arranged to meet?' Jakob asks. He looks out of the corner of his eye at the young man, who doesn't say a word and seems a bit awkward and embarrassed, staring straight ahead. A blind man would be aware that there is some special significance to his presence. Kowalski has said, 'we've been waiting', so the young man is not here by chance. Kowalski has a hand in this, he must have told him to come.

'Won't you introduce us?' says Jakob.

'You've never met?' asks Kowalski with a show of surprise. 'This is Josef Najdorf.'

'I'm Jakob Heym.'

'I know,' says the shy young man. So his name is Najdorf. His first words convey nothing.

'You don't work at the freight yard?' asks Jakob.

'No.'

'Where, then?'

'At the tool factory.'

'But then you're heading the wrong way. You should be going in exactly the opposite direction.'

'We start later than you do,' Najdorf says, and it is obvious that he is not comfortable with his explanation.

'I see. And since you have some time to spare, you choose to accompany us all the way to the station. Stands to reason.'

Najdorf suddenly stops, the way one does before running away; he looks haunted and says in a low voice to Kowalski: 'Can't you really manage without me? You see, I don't want to have anything to do with this whole business. I'm scared, you see.'

'Oh, don't start that again! Didn't I already explain it all to you till I was blue in the face?' Kowalski says impatiently, taking him by the arm before he can get away. 'Can't you get it into your head? He won't say a word, *I* won't say a word, and *you* won't say a word. Apart from us three, not a soul will ever find out about it. So what can happen?'

Najdorf still looks most unhappy, but he stays when Kowalski cautiously lets go of him.

'What won't I say a word about?' asks Jakob, who by now has become curious. Kowalski gestures to him to be patient, the gesture means many things: that you can see what a state the boy's in, that we must allow him a moment or two to come to terms with himself and his fear, for Kowalski's gestures can be highly expressive. He gives Najdorf an encouraging wink, which with his swollen eyes isn't that easy, and says: 'Now you can tell him what you are.'

Najdorf still hesitates. Jakob is quite intrigued, a surprise early in the morning that makes a young man afraid and about which they must – although so far for unknown reasons – keep silent: Kowalski can't bring off one like that every day.

'Actually I'm a radio mechanic,' Najdorf finally says in an agonized voice.

A radio mechanic.

There is no chair waiting for Jakob: looks fly back and forth, pleased ones and withering ones. An insane rage towards Kowalski almost chokes Jakob. Trying to play God, this cretin of a friend, arranges for repairs without the vaguest idea of their extent, and, what's more, undoubtedly expects one to feel grateful to him for his enterprising efforts. It couldn't have been easy, after all, in a single short evening that is already over by eight o'clock, to dig up someone who knows something about radios, but not too difficult for a friend like Kowalski. There he stands, beaming expectantly, haven't I done a good job, magnificent of course; any more help like that and one might as well go and hang oneself right away. And it is for him that one has just helped to win the battle of the Rudna; one is tempted to burn the radio after all. Right after they had parted yesterday evening, he must have dashed off and driven the whole ghetto frantic. He hadn't known this Najdorf before, one would have known if he had, for unfortunately Kowalski's friends are also one's own. He must have sidled up to one person after another, asking confidently in his penetrating voice: 'D'you happen to know anybody who can repair a radio?' 'A radio? Why on earth do you need someone to repair a radio?' 'Why do you think?'

Someone or other must have then put him onto this poor fellow Najdorf, who has more intelligence in his little finger than Kowalski has in his whole head; the boy's fear is the best proof. Kowalski has told him God knows what to reassure him, then dragged him here and contrived this highly embarrassing situation, and now one is confronted with a radio mechanic in the flesh.

'What a splendid profession!' says Jakob.

'Yes, isn't it?'

Kowalski is as pleased as Punch, there is simply no end to his deeds of friendship – the other day the miraculous rescue from the privy, today the second noble deed. He dares anyone to match that, in a place where there is so little room for kind actions. But he's not looking for any special gratitude; among true friends such things are taken for granted: they don't waste much time on talk, they act. And because time is getting on, and because so far no visible signs of joy or comprehension are noticeable in Jakob, Kowalski explains to him: 'He's going to fix your radio, you see. And don't worry, the lad's reliable.'

'I'm glad to know that,' says Jakob.

'Of course, I can't guarantee anything,' Najdorf says with modest eagerness. 'If, say, a tube's gone, there's nothing I can do about it. I have no spare parts – I told Mr Kowalski that right away.'

'Just go there and have a look at it,' says Kowalski.

Jakob has only minutes to find a way out; one would imagine that it gets easier from one time to the next, seeing that practice makes perfect, but actually it always remains just as difficult. Ruefully he remembers all the decisions he had reached last night, more easily made than carried out when obstacles of this kind show up, but Jakob pulls himself together. Happy news requires a happy face, but Jakob can't manage one: the sight of Kowalski the demon helper precludes all possibility of a smile. With a great effort, Jakob stretches his lips from side to side and forces a look of grim affability into his eyes as he tries to convey that something of immense importance has just occurred to him.

'Of course, you couldn't know!' he says. 'You've gone to all that trouble for nothing. The radio is working again!'

'You don't say!'

'But I appreciate your efforts all the same.'

'How did it happen? Did you fix it yourself?' Kowalski asks, and it's impossible to tell whether he is genuinely glad or whether he is disappointed at his helpfulness having gone for nothing.

'It's working again. Isn't that enough?'

'But how?' asks Kowalski. 'A radio can't repair itself, can it?'

If Najdorf weren't with them, Jakob could tell Kowalski anything, a tube had come loose, or he had banged it a few times with his fist and it came on again: Kowalski knows as little about radios as he does. But unfortunately this Najdorf with his expert knowledge is still there, not only does he look relieved because his help isn't needed after all, but there is also a gleam of professional interest in his eye. And now it's up to you to improvise a suitable explanation that will satisfy nitwit and expert alike. You must know, after all, how you repaired your radio: tell them quickly and look cheerful about it.

'It was only the wire in the electrical cord. I just made it a bit shorter.'

So everything has worked out splendidly, Jakob is quite proud of himself, all three parties are satisfied. As he leaves, Najdorf shakes hands with Jakob, many thanks again for your trouble, he walks off in the direction of the tool factory and doesn't have to be scared any more.

Kowalski and Jakob continue on their way to the station: Jakob is thinking up a revenge for the ruined morning that had started out so well: namely, the battle of the Rudna will be withheld from Kowalski, let others bring him the joyful news. Friends who never miss a chance to torture a person nearly to death don't deserve battles won during sleepless nights of torment. Even if no harm was intended, what Kowalski has inflicted on one today, the difficulties he lands one in with no harm intended, are getting alarmingly out of hand; one can't stand idly by watching this trend. Two days ago Kowalski had forced him to cope with Lina, today with Najdorf, and among all the questioners Kowalski is the most tireless, so the counter-measure of a single suppressed battle is surely appropriate.

'Was there any news last night?' asks Kowalski.

'Nothing.'

A few men they know say good morning as they pass, the street is the only one leading to the freight yard, and it gradually becomes crowded. Jakob notices people looking at him narrowly, at Kowalski apparently too. Kowalski is basking a little in Jakob's glory and whispers to someone: 'The radio is working again!' As if he had been instrumental, and the other fellow quickens his step and whispers it to others. Soon many are turning to look at Jakob and seem to perk up. Jakob nods imperceptibly, that's right, you heard correctly, and the repaired radio will probably arrive at the freight yard before its owner.

'I meant to ask you,' Kowalski says, 'I've been wondering whether the time hasn't come to think of some other things.'

'Such as?'

'Such as business.'

'Business? What kind of business?'

'I'm a businessman,' Kowalski says. 'Isn't this the best time to prepare at least mentally for the future?'

'What d'you mean, business? And what d'you want to prepare? Isn't your barber shop standing there waiting for you?'

'That's what I'm wondering about. I've been thinking for a long time that maybe I should try something different in the future.'

'Something different, at your age?'

'Why not? Just between ourselves, I've got some money tucked away. Not exactly a fortune, mind you, but mightn't there be some better way to invest it than in my old shop, which I've never really liked? If you're honest, you haven't either, have you? And if I go ahead with something like that, I want to be sure I'm not throwing my money away.'

'And where do I come in?'

'From time to time there must surely be some business news on the radio?'

'There is.'

'Hasn't there been anything that could be taken as a guideline? Some hint or other?'

'I'm not interested in such things.'

'Not interested in such things – look who's talking!' says Kowalski. 'I'm sure you must have heard something!'

'What is it you want to know, then? So far I haven't understood a single word.'

'I simply want to know which line of business has the best prospects.'

'Sometimes you're positively childish, Kowalski. Do you seriously think that they announce over the radio: We advise you to invest your money after the war in such and such businesses?'

This makes sense to Kowalski, and he says: 'Well, all right, then I'll simply ask you as a friend. If you had some money, where would you be most likely to invest it?'

So Jakob considers it too; an investment like that deserves a lot of consideration: where would he be most likely to invest it? 'Luxury foods perhaps? If you remember, after the last war no one could get enough of them. And David Gedalje, you must have known him too, built himself a magnificent house in those days from schnapps.'

'He did, he did,' says Kowalski, 'but where to find the raw materials? Do you really think that, right after the war, there'll be enough potatoes to make schnapps?'

'That's not the way to look at it. There'll be no raw materials for anything. What you need for post-war business is not logic but a good nose.'

Kowalski is still doubtful, his nose doesn't favour schnapps, his money's too good for that.

'Actually, textiles shouldn't do too badly. There's always a need for clothing,' he says.

'You may be right. For years they only made clothing for soldiers, soldiers' trousers, soldiers' socks, soldiers' tunics, soldiers' greatcoats – ordinary people went on wearing their old clothes. And what does that mean?'

'Well?'

'There'll be a demand.'

'That's only half the truth, Jakob. Don't forget that during the same period a lot of clothing has been lying unused in cupboards – I mean, all the soldiers' clothes. And today they're as good as new.'

'Hm,' Jakob says pensively.

And so on, while they consider two or three other possibilities, and Kowalski even toys with the idea of joining forces with Jakob and establishing a large restaurant with all the frills. But Jakob thinks this is too big a risk; besides, he is sure Kowalski isn't really serious. Jakob reverts to his first suggestion, which is that Kowalski is to remain in his old shop and, if he doesn't know what else to do with that bit of money tucked away, he can have the place modernized, and for heaven's sake get some new chairs – demand or no demand, hair and beards will go on growing. By the time they reach the freight yard, Kowalski is almost back to being a barber again.

L ina wins her bet, for in the long run Jakob is no match in the unequal battle: he shows her the radio.

After some days of fruitless search – there was nothing left she didn't already know – she resorted to pleading. No one can plead like Lina, and she particularly knows how to plead with Jakob, with flattery, tears, hurt looks of a special kind, more tears, and all this with incredible perseverance. Jakob has held out for a few days, then his strength is exhausted: one predictable evening Lina wins her bet.

For me, probably the only one who is still alive and able to reflect on the matter, that evening is the most incomprehensible of the whole story. Even when Jakob explained it to me, as best he could, I didn't fully understand it; I asked him: 'Didn't you go a bit too far? Mightn't she have betrayed you and everything would have been over?' 'Of course not,' Jakob replied with a smile, 'Lina would never betray me.' I said: 'I mean without the slightest intention. Children so easily let fall a thoughtless remark, and someone or other picks it up and builds a whole house out of it.' 'Lina is always very careful about what she says,' Jakob replied, and I had to believe him.

But there was also something else that I found almost impossible to understand. 'There's something else, Jakob. How could you be sure that she didn't see through the whole thing? She could so easily have noticed what was actually going on – she's a clever girl, you've said so yourself. Wasn't it an outrageous stroke of luck that she didn't see through it?' 'She did see through it,' Jakob said, his eyes lighting up with pride. 'You know, I really didn't care whether she noticed or not. I simply wanted to give her pleasure, regardless of the consequences: that's why I went down into the cellar with her.' And after a pause, which was much too short to allow me to understand that evening, he added: 'Or rather, I did care. I believe that at the time I wanted her to know about everything. I had reached a point where I simply had to show my radio to someone, and I would rather it was Lina than anyone else: with her it was like a game. Anyone else would have been horrified by the truth, but she was happy afterwards. So that evening I said to her, come down now into the cellar, we'll listen to the radio together.'

And at this point I suddenly smiled and said: 'If I'd known at the time all the things you're capable of, I would have come to you and asked you to show me a tree.' Which in turn Jakob couldn't understand. Let's listen to that evening.

Considerable suspense, Lina hangs on to Jakob's jacket, the cellar passage is long and dim. The metal doors that are passed on tiptoe are all locked, as if to hide riches of incalculable worth. The air is damp and cold, although it's August outside. With anxious foresight, Jakob has insisted on a winter dress, stockings and a scarf for Lina; from ceiling and walls hang droplets that glisten like tiny, feeble lamps.

'Are you scared?'

'No,' she whispers firmly, and it's not that much of a lie, her curiosity will make her forget everything else. After all, at the end of the passage waits the thing she has been searching for in vain for days and that she has almost given up as a lost cause, and who is she to say now, I'm scared, let's go back?

At last Jakob stops, at almost the last locker in the long row. Taking the key from his pocket, he unlocks the door and turns on the light, which is only slightly brighter than no light at all.

The locker room has to be described: four metres square with no window. Its most noticeable feature is a partition built right across it, making almost two out of it and leaving only a narrow passage: the builders must have had a coal cellar in mind. The inventory is quickly listed: an iron bedstead with rusty springs, the remains of an old stove with some left-over tiles, green and brown, and a few stove pipes, including an elbow. And in the corner by the door, the only treasure worth locking up: a small, carefully stacked pile of fire-wood in which Piwowa, the demanding poacher, had been sleeping some months ago while it still represented a piece of furniture. Then a glance behind the partition, more stove debris, bricks, a spade, a bucket with holes in it and an axe. That's all: I'm being so accurate not because these items are of any significance but because later I was there, during my search for witnesses and traces and non-existent trees. Just as I have measured the distance between the military office and the next corner with my tape measure, just as I went into Jakob's room where by that time an old woman was living by herself who knew nothing about the fate of any former tenants – the housing authorities had allocated the room to her on a temporary basis – I have also been in this locker; it still belongs to that room. Mrs Domnik handed me the key without demur, saying merely that she had never been down there, she didn't own anything that needed to be kept in the cellar, so I mustn't be surprised at the dust or at any mess I might find there, she wasn't responsible for that. And indeed it was dusty, with cobwebs everywhere, that is the truth, but I didn't notice any mess, I found everything just as Jakob had described it to me. The bedstead, stove debris, axe and bucket, even the chopped-up wood was still by the door.

Jakob locks the door from the inside; Jakob says: 'So nobody will disturb us.' Then he goes on: 'And now sit down here,' pointing to the iron bedstead.

Lina has already looked round a bit, so far without any result, yet she sits down without protest; under these circumstances he could demand a much greater display of obedience from her.

'Where do you keep the radio?'

'It won't hurt you to wait.'

He squats down in front of her, takes her chin in one hand, turns her face towards him, forcing her to look at him, and starts off with the necessary preparation: 'Now listen carefully to what I have to say. First of all you must promise me you'll be good and do everything that I'm now going to ask of you. Sacred word of honour?'

The sacred word of honour, intended only for occasions of the utmost importance, is given impatiently; her eyes demand that he cut short the preliminaries.

'You'll sit here keeping perfectly still. The radio is behind that partition. 'I'll go behind there now and turn it on, then we'll both hear it play. But if I notice you getting up, I'll shut it off again immediately.'

'Mayn't I see it?'

'Absolutely not!' says Jakob firmly. 'Actually little girls like you aren't even allowed to hear it either, it's strictly forbidden. But I'm making an exception with you. Agreed?'

What can she do, she's being blackmailed and must submit. Hearing is better than nothing, although she had been looking forward to actually seeing it. Besides, she still might, she might, you never know.

'What is your radio going to play?'

'I don't know in advance, I have to switch it on first.'

The preparations are completed, nothing more can be done for self-protection. Jakob stands up. He goes to the partition, pauses in the little passage, and looks once more at Lina, with an expression intended, if it were possible, to chain her to the bedstead; then he finally disappears. Jakob's eyes must first get used to the unfamiliar light, which hardly reaches beyond the partition, and he knocks the bucket with his foot.

'Was that the radio?'

'No, not yet. It'll be another moment or two.'

Something is needed to sit on, for the stunt may take a while once it gets started. Jakob turns the bucket bottom-side up and settles down on it. At this late stage he is faced with the question of what kind of a programme the radio has to offer, Lina having already touched briefly on this, and the time is ripe for an answer. He should have thought about this earlier – all the things he should have done, perhaps even practise a bit, but as things are the radio will have to play whatever comes to mind, whether it be music or talk. Jakob remembers how, aeons ago, his father could imitate an entire brass band, with tuba, trumpets, trombones and big drum, enough to send the family into fits of laughter. After supper, if the day had passed without any major annoyance, he could sometimes be persuaded. But

Jakob wondered whether he could manage to produce an orchestra like that the very first time; his father had spent hours polishing his act. Lina is waiting silently in her winter dress, and Jakob is already sweating, although the performance hasn't even begun yet.

'Here we go,' says Jakob, ready for whatever suggests itself.

A fingernail flicks against the bucket, that's how radios are switched on, then the air is filled with buzzing and whistling. He skips the warming-up period, a detail for connoisseurs, Jakob's radio has the correct temperature right away, and the station is also quickly selected. An announcer with a high voice – the first thing to suggest itself, as has been said – comes on the air: 'Good evening, ladies and gentlemen far and near, you are about to hear an interview with the British prime minister Mr Winston Churchill.' Then the announcer releases the microphone and a man with a mid-level voice is heard, the reporter: 'Good evening, Mr Churchill.'

Then Churchill himself, in a very deep voice and with a noticeable foreign accent: 'Good evening one and all!'

Reporter: 'I am delighted to welcome you to our studio. And here is my first question: Would you please tell our listeners how from your vantage point you assess the present situation?'

Churchill: 'That's not too difficult. I am firmly convinced that the whole mess will soon be over, in another few weeks at most.'

Reporter: 'And may one ask the source of this reassuring conviction?'

Churchill (somewhat embarrassed): 'Oh well, things are progressing nicely on all fronts. It is fairly obvious that the Germans won't be able to hold out much longer.'

Reporter: 'Wonderful! And what is the situation in the area of Bezanika specifically?'

There is a minor interruption; either it's the sweating and the cold air in the cellar, or something has got into Jakob's nose: whatever the cause, reporter, announcer and Mr Churchill all have to sneeze at the same time.

Reporter (the first to recover himself): '*Gesundheit*, Mr Prime Minister!'

Churchill (after blowing his nose): 'Thanks. But back to your question. In the Bezanika area, things are looking particularly bad for the Germans. The Russians are having it all their own way, and Bezanika has been in their hands for some time. Only yesterday they won an important battle on the River Rudna, if you know where that is.'

Reporter: 'Yes, I'm familiar with that river.'

Churchill: 'Then you also know where the front is now. I'm certain it can't last much longer.'

Reporter (delighted): 'That will please our listeners very much, if they don't happen to be Germans. Thank you very much, Mr Churchill, for this enlightening conversation.'

Churchill: 'Don't mention it.'

Announcer (after a brief pause): 'That, ladies and gentlemen, was the promised interview with the British minister Mr Winston Churchill. Goodnight.'

A fingernail flicks against the bucket, that's how radios are switched off, and Jakob wipes the sweat from his forehead. A bit thin, that interview, he thinks, and also a bit above Lina's head, but – unfortunately this will never change – he hasn't the inventive gifts of a Sholom Aleichem, don't ask too much of a harassed man, that should be enough for today. Jakob reappears; the situation proves highly satisfactory not only in the area of Bezanika but no less so here in the cellar. At last Lina's own ears have heard a radio, strictly forbidden for children, and she is thrilled. It might have turned out differently, disguising his voice had been a step onto virgin soil, and in three variations too: Lina might have icily demanded that he stop this nonsense and turn on the radio. Jakob would have died of heart failure, the mere thought of it, but Lina wouldn't dream of saying anything of the kind. The situation couldn't be better, he sees that at once.

'Did you like that?'

'Oh yes!'

Satisfaction on both sides. Jakob stands in front of her and is about to suggest they leave, we've had our fun, bed is waiting, but Lina says: 'You don't mean it's all over?'

'What else?'

'I'd like to hear some more.'

'No, no, that's enough,' he says, but without much conviction. A brief verbal skirmish, it's already too late, she would like to hear more, some other time perhaps, anything, can't get enough, all he has to do is turn the radio on again, she'll be happy with anything. Jakob sneezes again, this evening the whole world has to sneeze. As he blows his nose he studies her expression and finds no suspicion reflected in it. That settles it.

'What do you want to hear?'

So Jakob is again sitting on the bucket, in complete silence, now seized by ambition. Ambition in terms of the brass band: he can't get it out of his head, although it has been silent for a good forty years, covered with dust, the instruments all rusty. Jakob is ready to take a chance, so determined is he today.

First there is the flicking, then the buzzing and whistling; the second time it already sounds more convincing, and then the music starts in a rush, with drum and cymbals taking the first bar. Drum and cymbals are followed by a solitary trombone, which needs a few notes to get on to the right track. The tune is uncertain, Jakob tells me, an improvised series of notes, interspersed with a variety of familiar themes but with no particular pattern; the only certainty is that it is a march. Tentatively the feet take over the percussion, supported by the fingers using the bucket, thus releasing the mouth for the remaining instruments. For one trombone does not a make a brass band; it must be relieved by the trumpet, and that in turn by the falsetto of the clarinet, and from time to time a tuba note from the back of the throat. Jakob loses, as one says, all inhibitions. The only constraint he submits to: despite his haste his ear has not forgotten a certain rule, strictly observed by his father, namely that vowels be used sparingly, if possible avoided altogether. Since instruments give voice only in consonants or, to be more precise, only in sounds that can be approximated by consonants and are remotely similar but not identical to them. So his lips don't produce a simple ta-ta-ra-ta or la-li-la; he has to shape sounds not be found in any alphabet. The cellar reverberates with sounds never yet heard. Maybe too much effort for the sake of a child like Lina, who would be satisfied with less polish, but let us remember that ambition is involved, a self-imposed test, and virtuosity thrives best without compulsion. Soon the key is maintained without difficulty, trumpets and trombones toss phrases back and forth, experiment with antiphony and almost always bring things to a happy conclusion. The clarinet, too uncomfortably high in pitch, perforce retreats farther and farther into the background: instead the tuba makes itself heard more often, now and then even venturing a little extra flourish, a run in the lower regions, to escape, when breath runs short, into two or three bars of bucket thumping.

In a word, a piece of musical history is being written, Jakob has brought off a triumph, and Lina can't bear to stay where she is any longer. Without a sound she gets up, all sacred words of honour forgotten, and her legs move irresistibly towards the partition. She must see this thing that sounds so much like Jakob and yet so different, that can speak with various voices, sneeze like he does, and make such strange noises. Just one look, even at the cost of the discovery of a breach of confidence; there's no resisting her legs, which have a will of their own. Actually such great caution isn't necessary; the racket made by that thing drowns out all else. Nevertheless she moves stealthily. As far as the narrow passage, just as the trombone is finishing a masterly solo and making way for the trumpet. Lina cautiously pokes her head round the corner, invisible to Jakob. He is not only sitting sideways, he is also keeping his eyes firmly closed, a sign of extreme physical and mental concentration, the world forgotten as he rends the air according to rules known only to himself. No, Jakob isn't aware that for a few seconds he is sitting there totally exposed. Later, Lina's cryptic allusions will rouse his suspicions, and only much later will she tell him to his face what actually happened down there in that cellar. For the time being, a brief glance and a few seconds' surprise are enough for her, she set out for India and has discovered America; the purpose of this expedition had been to find out what the thing looked like, and now she knows: it looks exactly like Jakob. There remains only one question: one day she will ask him whether he has another radio besides this one – presumably not, where could he keep it hidden if not here? Lina knows something that no one else knows. Quietly she returns to her place; her pleasure in listening has not been diminished, only mixed with a few thoughts that are of no concern to anybody.

Then the march comes to an end, but not the performance. When Jakob emerges, exhausted and relieved and with a parched mouth, Lina clamours for an encore: all good things come in threes, now especially. This proves to him that she had not become suspicious, and such was her intention. If this march went well, he thinks, nothing can go wrong now.

'But this will be the very last,' says Jakob.

He goes back to his post, the next broadcast already in mind, and flicks. Lina is in luck, Jakob soon finds the station where fairy tales are being told by a kindly uncle who says: 'For all the children listening to us, your fairy-tale uncle will tell you the story of the sick princess.'

He has a voice similar to Winston Churchill's, just as deep, only a little softer and, of course, without a foreign accent.

'Do you know that one?' Jakob asks as Jakob.

'No. But how can there be a fairy-tale uncle on the radio?'

'What d'you mean, how? There is, that's all.'

'But you said radio was forbidden for children. And fairy tales are only for children, aren't they?'

'True. But what I meant was that it's forbidden here in the ghetto. Where there's no ghetto, children are allowed to listen. And there are radios everywhere. Right?'

'Right.'

The fairy-tale uncle, a bit put out by the interruption but fair enough to look for the reasons in himself, takes off his jacket and puts it under him, since the bucket is hard and sharp edged and the fairy-tale one of the longer ones – provided, that is, he can remember how it all goes. My God, how long ago that was, he has to think, now of all times. Fairy tales had not been his father's responsibility but his mother's. You used to lie in bed and wait and wait for her to be finished with her housework and come to you, and you almost always fell asleep while you were waiting. But sometimes she did sit down beside you, slip her warm hand under the cover on to your chest, and tell you stories. About Jaromir the robber with the three eyes who always had to sleep on the cold ground because there was no bed long enough for him; about Raschka the cat that wouldn't catch mice but only birds until one day it saw a bat; about Lake Schapun into which Dwojre the witch made all the children cry so many tears that it rose and rose and overflowed its banks and Dwojre drowned miserably in it; and sometimes about the sick princess.

'When's it going to start?' Lina asks.

'The tale of the sick princess,' the fairy-tale uncle begins.

About the good old king, who owned a vast country and a gloriously beautiful palace and a daughter as well, the old story, and how he got a terrible scare. Because, you see, he loved her more than anything in the world, his princess. He loved her so much that, whenever she fell and tears came into her eyes, he had to cry himself. And the scare came when one morning she didn't want to get out of bed and looked really sick. Then the most expensive doctor in all the land was summoned to make her well quickly and happy again. But the doctor tapped and listened to her from head to toe and then said in great perplexity: 'I'm terribly sorry, Mr King, I can't find anything. Your daughter must be suffering from a disease I have never come across during my entire lifetime.'

Now the good old king was even more scared, so he went to see the princess himself and asked her what on earth was the matter. And she told him she wanted a cloud: once she had that, she would immediately be well again. 'But a real one!' she said. What a shock that was, for, as anyone can imagine, it is far from easy to get hold of a real cloud, even for a king. All day long he was so worried that he couldn't rule, and that evening he had letters sent out to all the clever men in his kingdom ordering them to drop everything and come forthwith to the royal palace.

Next morning they were all assembled, the doctors and the ministers, the star-gazers and the weathermen, and the king stood up on his throne so that everyone in the hall could hear him properly and shouted: 'Si—lence!' Instantly you could have heard a pin drop, and the king announced: 'To the one among you wise men who brings my daughter a cloud from the sky I will give as much gold and silver as can be heaped on to the biggest waggon in all the land!' When the clever men heard that, they started then and there to study, to ponder, to scheme and to calculate. For they all wanted that heap of gold and silver, who wouldn't? One especially smart fellow even began building a tower that was to reach up to the clouds, the idea being that, when the tower was finished, he would climb up, grab a cloud, and then cash in the reward. But before the tower was even half-way up, it fell down. And none of the others had any luck either; not one of the wise men could get the princess the cloud she so badly wanted. She grew thinner and sicker, thinner and thinner, since from sheer misery she never touched a morsel, not even matzoth with butter.

One fine day the garden boy, who the princess sometimes used to play with outdoors before she got sick, looked into the palace to see whether any of the vases needed flowers. So it came about that he saw her lying in her bed, under a silken coverlet and pale as snow. All through the last few days he had been puzzling over why she never came out into the garden any more, but didn't know the reason. And that is why he asked her: 'What is the matter, little princess? Why don't you come out into the sunshine any more?' And so she told him, too, that she was sick and wouldn't get well again until someone brought her a cloud. The garden boy thought for a bit, then exclaimed: 'But that's quite easy, little princess!' 'Is it?' the princess asked in surprise. 'Is it quite easy? All the wise men in the land have been racking their brains in vain, and you claim that it's quite easy?' 'Yes,' the garden boy said, 'you just have to tell me what a cloud is made of.' That would have almost made the princess laugh if she hadn't been so weak. She replied: 'What silly questions you ask! Everybody knows that clouds are made of cotton wool!' 'I see, and will you also tell me how big a cloud is?' 'You don't even know *that*?' she said in surprise. 'A cloud is as big as my pillow. You can see that for yourself if you'll just pull the curtain aside and look up to the sky,' whereupon the garden boy went to the window, looked up to the sky, and exclaimed: 'You're right! Just as big as your pillow!' Then he went off and soon returned bringing the princess a piece of cotton wool as big as her pillow.

I needn't bother with the rest. Everyone can easily imagine how the princess's eyes lit up and her lips turned red and she got well again, how the good old king rejoiced, how the garden boy didn't want the promised reward but preferred to marry the princess, and they lived happily ever after, that's Jakob's story.

It is probably the same evening, or possibly one before or one after; lovely, gentle Rosa is lying beside Mischa listening to the battle of the Rudna. Mischa is telling her in a soft voice, but he is not whispering; there is a big difference between talking softly and whispering, and you may well ask, why isn't he whispering? And you may ask, why is the cupboard no longer in the middle of the room but standing quite normally against the wall, and why is the curtain covering the window again instead of dividing the room into two halves? What has happened to the screen, you may wonder, and above all, why is Rosa suddenly lying there naked although the light is still on, why is she no longer embarrassed? Then please be good enough to glance at the other bed, you will find it empty, and all those questions will boil down to one: Where is the deaf and dumb Isaak Fajngold of the sharp ears?

I don't know the answer any better than Mischa does, let alone Rosa. A week ago Fajngold left early in the morning to go to work, as he did every day, and has not been heard of since. The first evening it didn't seem too serious; Mischa thought he might have gone to visit a friend, that they got to talking and Fajngold suddenly noticed that it was past eight o'clock and too late to go home, so he had just lain down on the floor and spent the night there. 'What do you mean, got to talking?' Rosa asked suspiciously. 'He's deaf and dumb, isn't he?' 'What makes you think deaf and dumb people can't talk to each other?' Mischa answered quick as a flash. 'D'you think they're condemned to keep everything that's going round in their heads to themselves? They can communicate every bit as well as you and I, only in sign language, that's all.'

But the second evening Fajngold didn't come home either, nor the third, so on the fourth day Mischa went to see the only person with whom, as far as he knew, Fajngold was friendly, Hersch Praschker, who worked with Fajngold in the clean-up detail, clearing the streets of garbage and the bodies of those who had died of starvation. But Praschker had no idea either. 'I meant to go and look in at his place tomorrow,' he said, 'and find out why he wasn't turning up for work. They're sure to come for him, they've already got his name down.' 'When was the last time he was there?' 'Tuesday.' 'And Wednesday morning he left home as usual.'

He never arrived, never returned home; perhaps he escaped or died or was in an accident or was arrested off the street. Death or accident seems unlikely since he was never found: inquiries established this. A planned escape seems unlikely: none of his things are missing from the cupboard, not even the photograph of his grandson; he would never have left that behind, he guarded it like a treasure. So all that really remains is an arrest off the street. Why, is a mystery, for Fajngold has always been a reliable and law-abiding person, but we all know the saying, where there's a will there's a way. And all this makes it clear why Mischa is telling the story of the battle of the Rudna in a soft voice and not whispering.

Rosa is lying beside him for the second night in a row, something that has never happened before. Old Mr Frankfurter who, as a man of the theatre, is not known to be partial to ultra-strict morals, has uttered a word of warning: 'Very well, children, you love each other, that's understandable. But don't go overboard right away.' Because of that and because of Rosa's reserve, the number of nights they spent together remained within modest limits. Mischa had to persuade her each time almost as if it were the first, with few exceptions. And now the very next night again. Rosa imagines it must be something like this when one is married, but, frankly, she doesn't feel all that comfortable with it. This has nothing to do with Mischa, as if he were suddenly different from before, more uninhibited perhaps, or more demanding; Mischa's stock has not dropped by a single point, for she regards him with no less love than on the first day. Or let's say, the fifth. The reason for this, unaccountable though it may sound to some, is Isaak Fajngold; in some strange way she has become accustomed to him. But how can one become accustomed to a person who is only a distraction, deaf and dumb though he may be? In such a situation, in which privacy is taken for granted, how can one? One can, and one can't; we will try to get to the bottom of this.

In the first place, it was in this room that Rosa first made love, in Fajngold's presence; he was there from the very first instant, and keeping him in ignorance was a constant ingredient of all their caresses. In the second place, Fajngold's bed is not just an empty bed: no, Fajngold isn't lying in it, which makes a considerable difference. Each time she looks behind the screen, now superfluous and hence removed, she is reminded of his grim fate – uncertain, true, but, the longer she broods over it, only uncertain as to the manner of death. And in the third and final place, when Mischa told her that Fajngold had disappeared, her face showed dismay, as expected, but after a while not nearly as much dismay, and she caught herself thinking: At last. That wasn't directed at Fajngold, she wished him only the best; it simply had to do with herself and Mischa and implied: alone at last, at last undisturbed, at last a little nook for the two of us. That's what she caught herself thinking, and it bothered her quite a bit; she was ashamed of such thoughts yet kept on thinking: At last. Then she thought too, just as well Mischa doesn't know what selfish notions are being hatched in my head. And she also thought: Regardless of what happened to Fajngold, it's over and done with now, and the thoughts we keep to ourselves can't have any effect on people's lives.

But they did have an effect, it wasn't that simple. For several days she gave Mischa reasons why she couldn't go with him to his room, and he went off disappointed. Until yesterday, when she couldn't or wouldn't find any more reasons. 'And why aren't you coming today?' he asked her. 'But I am!' and then he said it: 'At last!' They went to his room. Mischa had already rearranged it, now that Fajngold's absence could be regarded as permanent. The cupboard stood, as noted before, against the wall, the curtain hung in front of the window. Rosa stopped short in the middle of the room and first had to get used to it, having never seen it like this. Of course she noticed Fajngold's neatly made bed, sensing right away that there would be a problem about that. 'What's that box there?' she asked.

'His things. In case someone comes for them,' Mischa replied. And that immediately set the mood.

At some point they lay down, but for a long time without speaking or moving and without joy. In the same way that everything else was different that evening, the light was still on. Mischa lay on his side and she on her back because the bed was too narrow for both to lie on their backs. With a glance at Fajngold's smooth bed he asked: 'What do you think, couldn't we . . . ?'

'Oh no, please!' she broke in nervously.

'All right then.'

He turned out the light, slid his arm under her head – that's how it usually began – and tried to kiss her, but she turned aside. Until he asked: 'What's the matter with you?'

'Nothing.'

He pondered for a while what nothing might mean, then said: 'But you didn't really know him at all, and even if you did, what can we do about it?'

Again he tried to kiss her, and this time she let him, but only just. He soon noticed that there was nothing doing, so he closed his eyes, tomorrow is another day, and fell asleep. That was the only thing that was as usual: he is always the first to fall asleep.

In the middle of the night she woke him up; he wasn't annoyed, he hoped she had finally changed her mind, and one is glad to be woken up for that.

'I have to tell you something, Mischa,' she whispered.

'Yes?'

Completely misinterpreting the ensuing silence, he drew her to him, and as he brushed his lips over her face he noticed that it was wet and salty, from the eyes down. This was a terrible shock to him because he was used to her seldom laughing and never crying; not even when her only friend had to board that train six months ago was she able to cry, although for days she didn't utter a word. And now suddenly her face was wet, it was enough to shock anyone, but she hadn't sobbed or moaned, it must have happened quite silently; he wouldn't even have woken up if she hadn't woken him. And besides, it seemed to be more or less over, to judge by her voice.

'I have a request, I'm sure you'll find it strange.'

'Tell me.'

'I'd like the room put back the way it was before.'

'What do you mean – the way it was before?'

'I'd like the cupboard back in the middle. And the curtain.'

'But why? Fajngold isn't there any more.'

'I'd like it that way,' she said.

He really did find it strange – first strange, then childish, then silly, then plain ridiculous. Then he remembered having heard or read something about the unfathomable moods of women and that it is advisable to nip them in the bud. The whole change that she wanted would have taken him no more than ten minutes, but he said: 'Only if you can give me a sensible reason.'

'I'd like it that way,' she said.

And that wasn't a sensible reason, not by any standards, and he steadfastly refused. He told her that, although it was to her credit to take Fajngold's disappearance so much to heart in spite of hardly knowing him, only his breathing and snoring, in the ghetto many people one knew just as little disappear every day, after all, and if one were to make such a fuss about every single one of those it would be unbearable. And she accused him of being an uncouth, insensitive clot. Their first quarrel was under way and, if it hadn't been for the eight o'clock curfew, she would undoubtedly have got up, dressed and goodbye. But as it was she merely turned her back to him to make him realize how much she despised him.

The next day – today, that is – he went to meet her right outside the factory because at her home, in the presence of her parents, a reconciliation would have been much more difficult. It was difficult enough anyway, not for any lack of good will but because they had no experience in ending quarrels. Finally they both admitted that they hadn't behaved all that well, a kiss in a doorway, and each could breathe more freely again. They dropped by her home to let them know where she would be spending the night. Mr Frankfurter did not seem enthusiastic; he could not know that last night had been practically a wash-out. Mischa heard Mrs Frankfurter murmuring to her husband: 'Let them be.'

So on to his room. Both did all in their power to be nice to each other, showing their best sides after the quarrel, but one could feel that a little more time must pass before everything was back to normal.

Mischa told her about the battle of the Rudna, or rather, since we have returned to the present, Mischa tells her about the battle of the Rudna in a low voice, and finally finishes it, as heard today from Jakob, the latest news, so to speak, from the ether. Rosa melts with bliss, she knows where the Rudna flows and how much progress since Bezanika this battle represents, and she's half inclined to start making new plans. But Mischa isn't interested in plans, not at the moment, they won't run away as this second night might, and he turns out the light to devote himself to Rosa. There is to be no more talk of victories; last night was practically a wash-out. The Rudna and Fajngold and words spoken in anger are forgotten, the two come closer together in the old familiar way, in so far as individual volition is in control. But it does not hold unlimited sway; they catch themselves making comparisons, that's how it is now, really no different from before. For a while they lie side by side looking at each other. And perhaps they are even conscious of there being no third person's breathing from the other half of the room to disturb them. Let's come right out with it: the attempt to make up for a lost night turns out rather woefully, even though they would never admit it, even though they pretend to be as content as young lovers.

We will leave them now, with some regret but in the hope that more carefree times will return; we are at liberty to hope this. Let us stop a moment to listen to Mischa, riding the wave of restored harmony, asking with a smile something he would have done better not to ask: 'Do you still want me to divide the room again with the cupboard and the curtain?' He says this with a smile, not doubting for a moment that Rosa sees things differently now, that in reply she'll say something about silly moods, that she didn't know what got into her yesterday, and that the whole tiresome incident would best be forgotten.

And, just before we leave, let us hear Rosa say: 'Yes, please.'

J akob has to hear with his own ears how distorted his stories become when they are passed on.

Jakob is on his way to the attic to see Lina; not that it's bedtime, but one has to do more with her than just to make sure she washes properly, cleans her teeth, and goes to bed at the right time. At the freight yard we were sent home two hours early; there was simply nothing left to be unloaded, and the sentries didn't feel like watching over idlers, so they told us to shove off. A few particularly bold theorists speculate that there is more than mere laziness behind this order: perhaps the sentries are trying to be friends, after all they could just as easily have kept us there another two hours, standing in line. But they sent us home. Perhaps this is a subtle indication that a new era is knocking at the door. Anyway, the two hours will be well spent with Lina, Jakob thinks. As he places his hand on the door handle he realizes that she is not alone. He hears Rafael's voice asking: 'What's it all about, then?'

'About a princess,' says Lina.

'Does she get abducted?'

'What makes you think that?'

'Of course she does. I know all that. She's abducted by a robber. He wants a lot of ransom money for her, but the prince kills him and sets her free. And afterwards they get married.'

'What rubbish you talk,' Lina retorts. 'It's quite a different story. Do you think there's only one story about a princess?'

'All right then, tell it!'

'Aren't we going to wait for Siegfried?'

'He won't come.'

Jakob can hear them waiting and the attic window being opened. Rafael shouts: 'Siegfried!'

Then he says Siegfried is nowhere in sight, and shortly afterwards Lina screams at Rafael to stop that nonsense. What nonsense she means isn't clear, but he doesn't seem to be stopping right away. Then he asks: 'Who told you the story anyway?'

'Uncle Jakob.'

That gives eavesdroppers pause for thought. Jakob has never told her a fairy-tale about a princess, he would be bound to remember that. It must have been the fairy-tale uncle, and without a tremor in her voice she turns two separate people into one man. That gives pause for thought; perhaps it was even Jakob who played the march music and asked the questions and gave the answers. Or it was a hasty slip of the tongue on Lina's part, or – and this would be best – she had resorted to a white lie so as not to reveal the existence of the radio. That remains to be seen; they will have to discuss it later.

'He won't be coming now, so you might as well start,' says Rafael.

And that's what happens. Lina clears her throat, Jakob pricks up his ears: he has never heard what his stories sound like when they are passed on.

'Once upon a time there was a king, a good old king, and he had a daughter, that was the princess,' Lina began.

'What was the king called?'

Lina is evidently trying to remember whether any names were mentioned at all. For Rafael this takes too long, and he says: 'Surely you must at least know what he was called?'

'His name was Benjamin,' Lina recalls. 'And the princess was called Magdalena.'

'*What* was he called? Benjamin? D'you know who's called Benjamin? My uncle in Tarnopol, he's called Benjamin. But never a king.'

'I don't care if you believe it or not, but the king in this fairy story was called Benjamin.'

'Oh, all right!' says Rafi generously, not about to spoil things for the sake of a name. Jakob is almost sure that he is standing there with folded arms in a patronizing manner.

Lina continues, but more hurriedly than at first, as if she had lost the thread, as if expecting further objections: 'One day the princess became ill. The doctor couldn't find anything because he didn't know what her illness was, but she wouldn't eat any more bread, and she wouldn't drink either. So the king went to her himself, he loved her so much, you see – I forgot that part. And he asked her what was the matter. Then she told him she wouldn't get well again till someone brought her some cotton wool as big as her pillow. And then the old king. . . .'

But that's as far as she gets, Rafael has had enough; he has tried hard and listened patiently, but too much is too much, his credulity can be stretched, but it has limits.

'What kind of an illness is your Magdalena supposed to have had?'

'You just heard.'

'And I'm telling you, there is no such illness! Not in the whole world!'

'How do you know?'

'If at least she had measles, or whooping cough, or typhoid,' Rafael protests. 'You know what the princess really had? A fart in her head!'

He laughs, much louder than Jakob, but Lina can find nothing funny about his explanation. 'D'you want to go on hearing the story or don't you?' she asks.

'I don't,' says Rafael, still amused; the best jokes are always one's own. 'Because she had a fart in her head. Because the whole story is a load of rubbish. First about the king, in the whole world you'll never find a king called Benjamin. And then princesses never eat bread, only cake. And the biggest rubbish of all is that illness. Or have you seriously ever heard of a person getting ill from not having any cotton wool?'

Lina appears to be impressed by Rafael's reasoning; at least she is silent, without tears, Jakob hopes. And he doesn't alter his opinion, she is a clever girl, anyone can make mistakes. The excitement in the cellar may have been responsible for the misunderstanding, or such flights of fancy are simply beyond a child of Lina's age. Jakob's hand is on the door handle again; one should intervene, console and explain, they might – God forbid – come to blows. One could go in quite innocently, hello Lina, hello Rafael, nice of you to come and see her, how's your mother? Then the conversation will automatically turn to the argument, which will be recounted by both parties, calm down, children, let's hear you each in turn. Then one will undoubtedly come up with conciliatory words that will make what is unclear appear in a fresh light, not a reason in the world, children, to be angry with each other, things actually look thus and so, and in the end it'll all be settled to everyone's satisfaction. So he is about to plunge into the fray when he hears Rafael's peaceable voice: 'If your uncle happens to tell you another story, ask him to think up something better than that rubbish. That princess just had a huge fart in her head.'

Jakob never gets to intervene; the door opens and, with his usual luck with doors, it opens outwards and provides a hiding place. Rafael is off to more rewarding pastimes; no doubt he is going to look for Siegfried and report. He can be heard running down the stairs and whistling, he is whistling 'Oranges and Lemons', and he goes on whistling as Lina shouts the meagre remainder of the story after him: 'But she did have that illness! And the garden boy got her the cotton wool! And that made her well again, and they got married!'

She has said everything, although to closed ears; down on the ground floor the little tune dies away, the front door clicks shut, and up in the attic a long, disappointed tongue is stuck out, and the attic door is slammed, with Jakob outside the door as at the beginning. Doubts arise as to whether the two bonus hours will be well spent with Lina after this. He tells me that, although it was quite amusing, those two children, he suddenly lost all desire to go in; he suddenly felt worn out. He would rather keep the two hours for himself after all. And he asks whether he is boring me with such details, if so I only have to tell him.

I tell him: 'No.'

Jakob goes for a walk with his two hours; there are other places to relax in besides cramped rooms or with children one has grown fond of. He still feels the urge to take a stroll, despite searchlight and military office. To take a stroll in a little town from which in your whole life you have never been farther away than a week; the sunshine is pleasant on your path, as pleasant as the memories that are after all the true reason for your having left the house, memories to which every second street builds a bridge, as we know. Round one corner, then another, and there you are in front of the building where it was so often decided how good your next winter would be, for here lived none other than Aaron Ehrlicher, the potato merchant. Much depended on the prices set by him: the price of potato pancakes and with that the turnover. Ehrlicher could never be persuaded to bargain, so-and-so much and not a penny less, if you think that's too high, Mr Heym, you're welcome to look round to see whether you can get potatoes cheaper somewhere else. If you do, please be kind enough to let me know, I'd like to buy there too. Never ever did he consent to bargain, and once Jakob said to him: 'Mr Ehrlicher, you don't deal in potatoes, you just sell potatoes.' Only in fun, of course, but Ehrlicher didn't burst out laughing. And it was hard to tell whether he was a poor soul, a humble tradesman, like oneself, or a businessman of a higher category. His wife used to wear a fine, brown fur piece, and his children were plump and round and stuck-up, yet his office smelled mouldy, it was small and shabby and consisted of a table, a chair, and blank walls. He would gesture at all this with a sigh and ask: 'How can I afford to reduce my prices?'

Now there are strangers living there, you turn the page of Aaron Ehrlicher and walk on, two free hours are a long time, head for Libauer-Gasse and stop in front of Number 38. There is no building you walk to as often as this one, when you're out for a stroll, none that you stand outside for so long, and there are good reasons for this. The fact that you even go into the dark inner courtyard – it all has its reasons; suspicious eyes inspect you through the windows, what is a stranger doing in their courtyard, but you aren't that much of a stranger here.

On the third floor, behind the door on the left of the corridor, is where, to put it grandly, you gambled away or won your life's happiness: at the crucial moment you couldn't make up your mind, and to this day you don't know how good or bad that was. Josefa Litwin asked you point-blank what your intentions were, and you couldn't think of anything better to do than cast your eyes down and stammer that you needed a bit more time to think about it.

A magnificent woman, if eyes are any judge. You saw her for the first time in the train and instantly you thought: Boyoboy! She was wearing a green velvet dress with a white lace collar, and a hat the size of an open umbrella. And she was at most in her mid-thirties and thus exactly right for the forty-year-old you were then, right as far as age was concerned. But there in the compartment you never dreamed that sitting opposite you was the greatest problem of your next few years. You just gaped at her, so you tell me, like a young idiot; she may not even have noticed. Coincidence or not, when you got off the train together and there was no porter in sight, she asked whether you would mind carrying her heavy suitcase, she lived only a few streets further on, at Number 38, Libauer-Gasse. But she didn't ask as if you were a man of inferior position, although even then you wouldn't have refused; she was helpless and smiled and asked you a favour in her capacity as a weak woman. In your capacity as a gentleman. Delighted you said: 'What a question!' Snatched up her suitcase as if you were afraid a porter might yet turn up and hurried after her as far as Number 38, as far as her own front door. There you set down the suitcase, and for a few seconds you smiled at each other in embarrassment. Then she thanked you nicely and said goodbye. And you stood there thinking: Too bad.

A few weeks later, and that was certainly a coincidence, she appeared in your shop one afternoon accompanied by a man. You recognized her at once, and quite unjustifiably felt annoyed about the man, but then you were pleased because she recognized you too. You didn't exchange a word, and the two of them had lemonade and raspberry ice-cream. You observed them and couldn't make out their relationship, and why should you?

But when she came back the very next day, this time alone, you knew that was no coincidence. For the first time you were glad your shop was empty; apart from her, there was no other customer in the place – and the very next day! You sat down beside her, you chatted and introduced yourselves; she was the widow of a watchmaker who had been dead four years. It goes without saying that you didn't allow her to pay for her ice-cream; she was to consider herself his guest, today and as often as she liked. The man yesterday was mentioned as a casual acquaintance, no reason for them not to meet often, no other reason either. So tomorrow in the shop, once again in the shop, then in another restaurant, in a neutral location so to speak, an innocent little dance. Then soon in your flat. Meanwhile, you had found out about her modest but by no means straitened circumstances, and that she had no children. Finally at Number 38 too. A cup of tea and some little homemade cakes, in the air a hint of delicate, flowery perfume; you spoke of mutual attraction, from the first moment really, and then another cup of tea, and there were more cakes in the kitchen.

That was an evening such as no poet ever described, my God, and a night, my God, ah well. What can one say, this story isn't about Jakob and Josefa, soon this page must be turned too. Just this: four whole years were the result, four years of living together as man and wife, though they never actually moved in together, though one subject was always avoided: rabbi or civil ceremony. Most carefully by Jakob, probably. There was ample opportunity to explore one another, Josefa's glitter wasn't always gold, some less precious metals were worked in with it. Sometimes Jakob found her domineering, sometimes too talkative, sometimes an indifferent housewife, and she in turn found the occasional flaw in him, without any of this immediately leading to a break-up. Quite the contrary, they got along very nicely together, and Jakob was beginning to think that things could go on like this indefinitely. But when she suddenly – what am I saying, suddenly! – suggested it might be better if she moved in with him and she could help in the shop, he was afraid he would become his own employee, and he replied: 'We'll discuss that later.'

Very well, later, Josefa was in no hurry, or so it seemed. Until, as noted, that particular evening came along, the one at Number 38, Libauer-Gasse, when Jakob gambled away or won his life's happiness, who knows. He arrived as usual and, as usual, took off his shoes and put his feet up on the sofa. Josefa stood at the window with her back to him.

'What's the matter with you today?' Jakob asked her. 'No tea?'

Josefa didn't turn round at once, but soon. With a forbidding expression she sat down, not beside him on the sofa but in the armchair opposite.

'Jakob Heym, I have to talk to you.'

'Go ahead,' he said, prepared for quite a lot but not for what came now.

'Do you know Awrom Minsch?'

'Should I know him?'

'Awrom Minsch is the man I came into your shop with on that very first day, if you happen to remember.'

'I remember all right. You told me at the time that he was a casual acquaintance.'

'This morning Awrom Minsch asked me to marry him.'

'And what did you tell him?'

'Jakob, this is serious! It's time you made up your mind!'

'Who, me?'

'Stop trying to be funny, Jakob. I'm now thirty-eight. I can't go on living like this for ever. He plans to join his brother in America, and he asked me whether I would go with him as his wife.'

What was Jakob supposed to answer? He didn't care for a pistol being held to his head, even less for the fact that Awrom Minsch had been kept a secret from him until this minute. No one proposes marriage to a casual acquaintance; for this purpose one must be more than slightly acquainted with her, and for four years he had imagined that Josefa and he knew each other inside out. The fact that Josefa was now offering him first refusal, as it were, could not dispel Jakob's disappointment, far from it. Silently he put on his shoes again, carefully avoided meeting her eyes until he reached the door, then by the open door said awkwardly: 'I need some time to think about it.'

One thinks about it and thinks about it, and to this very day is still thinking about it; even two bonus hours aren't long enough. A helpful person opens his window and calls softly across the courtyard: 'Hallo there!'

Jakob is startled and sees the moon coming up over the roof. He asks: 'What is it?'

'You don't live here, do you?'

'No.'

'It's way past seven.'

'Thanks.'

Jakob pulls himself together, not stopping as he walks home, while further memory-fraught buildings are ignored: it's already way past seven.

Lina is already in bed, and he has to explain why he is so late coming home from work: because there was much more to be loaded than usual. She chats away, not about personal worries such as fairy tales or tiresomely suspicious neighbours' sons, and Jakob can't very well ask. She knows how strenuous the days at the freight yard are, and now this extra work, he mustn't stay too long, just give her a quick kiss and go down to his room, love is entirely mutual.

Jakob leaves her, with a conscience that could be clearer. On the stairs he plans to make it up to Lina, tomorrow or quite soon. At his own table, meanwhile, as he is about to start on his supper of bread and malt coffee, he is not dissatisfied with the day just past, all in all: at the freight yard the Jews had been modest in their demands, the battle of the Rudna was still having its effects; then the bonus of two nostalgic hours, a diverting little fairy tale at the attic door, a less diverting Aaron Ehrlicher, but then Josefa. Josefa still there, between the few mouthfuls, between the sips, one simply can't get rid of the woman, what would have become of us two charmers if at Number 38 I had . . . ? Impossible to say, yet the question asked a thousand times over almost answers itself: a life half-way between heaven and hell, in other words, a perfectly ordinary life. How could it have turned out differently, and in what way, from those four familiar years? Years filled with variety, quarrels and misunderstandings, with moodiness, good times and some measure of contentment. And with a secret not discovered till the very last day. One simply can't get this woman out of one's head, until there's a knock at the door.

There is a knock, and Jakob is tempted to call out immediately: 'Come in, Kowalski!' That's to say, not exactly tempted, he merely assumes, but then he no longer assumes because it had been past seven over an hour ago, so it must be well past eight now, and even Kowalski isn't that crazy. Jakob calls out: 'Come in!'

Professor Kirschbaum is honouring Jakob at his supper, he trusts he's not disturbing him, no not at all, won't he please be seated, to what do we owe this rare pleasure?

Kirschbaum sits down, delays the start of the conversation with many and diverse looks, and succeeds in gaining Jakob's concerned attention, except that Jakob doesn't know for what.

'Can you not imagine why I have come to see you, Mr Heym?'

His first thought: 'Is it about Lina? Is she worse again?'

'I am not here about Lina. To come straight to the point: I am here to speak to you about your radio set.'

What a disappointment, what a shock, for a few hours the monster had been blissfully forgotten: now the battle of the Rudna will have to be dug out again. For your fellow citizens you are no longer a human being but the owner of the radio, the two being mutually exclusive, as has been clear for some time, and here it comes again. The right to the normal conversations of the old days has been forfeited. About the weather, or back pain, for which Kirschbaum would be an ideal partner, or gossip about mutual acquaintances. There is no talk of important nothings when you're around – you with your treasure are too good for that.

'You also want to hear the news,' says Jakob, more as a statement. Now he has Kirschbaum on his back too; never mind, one more or less.

'I do not wish to hear any news,' Kirschbaum says, however. 'I am here to express my disapproval. I should have done so long ago.'

'Disapproval?'

'I do not know, my dear Mr Heym, what motives led you to spread the information in question. But I find it difficult to imagine that you have given proper consideration to the danger to which you are thereby exposing us.'

Not news but disapproval, the ideas people have! No question, Kirschbaum is a very strange man. Do you, Professor, have to ruin my evening, my hard-earned free time? Do you have to make holier-than-thou speeches about matters over which my conscience was already struggling when for you my radio was an object hidden under seven seals? Do you have to tell *me*? Instead of patting me on the back and saying, Well done Mr Heym, carry on, there is no medicine people need as much as hope. Or rather, not coming at all, for we learned long ago not to expect a pat on the back, yet here you come knocking at my door, damn you, and interfering and trying to teach me how to survive. And to cap it all I have to look interested because your concern is a thoroughly worthy one, because some day I may need you again for Lina, and I must also provide you with some good reasons for my action, although I can think of nothing that concerns you less. Just so that, after lengthy explanations, your learned lips are able to say: I see, yes of course, I understand.

'I need not tell you where we are living, my dear Mr Heym,' says Kirschbaum.

'No, you need not,' says Jakob.

'And yet it seems to me essential. What would happen, for example, if this information were to come to the ears of the German Gestapo? Have you thought of that?'

'Yes.'

'I find that impossible to believe. Otherwise you would have acted differently.'

'I see,' says Jakob. 'Would I.'

Jakob gets up to take a walk, not the first one today, past table and bed and cupboard and Kirschbaum; his fury, since it cannot be put into words, has moved into his legs. But not all his fury, the room is too small for that; there remains for his voice an unmistakable residue that momentarily nettles Kirschbaum. When Jakob says: 'Have you ever once seen their eyes when they beg me for news? No? And do you know how badly they need some good news? Do you know that?'

'I can well imagine. Furthermore, I do not doubt that you are motivated by the best intentions. Nevertheless, I must. . . .'

'Oh, you make me sick with your "nevertheless"! Isn't it enough for you that we have almost nothing to eat, that in winter one in five of us freezes to death, that every day half a street gets taken away in transports? All that still isn't enough? And when I try to make use of the very last possibility that keeps them from just lying down and dying – with words, do you understand? I try to do that with words! Because that's all I have! – then you come and tell me it's prohibited!'

Oddly enough it is at this moment that Jakob thinks of a cigarette, so he tells me, of an untipped Juno. What Kirschbaum is thinking of is anybody's guess: whatever it is, he reaches into the pocket of his worn double-breasted suit and, hard though it is to believe, at this very moment pulls out a packet of cigarettes. And matches, and asks Jakob, with surprising politeness considering that barely concluded tirade: 'Care for one?'

A question, that's how civilized people behave, a tactful example perhaps, a good one, perhaps also a sign of some slight doubts arising, or neither. Silently they smoke and smooth their furrowed brows, whatever the explanation.

The greedily inhaled smoke not only creates a sense of well-being, it also tends to make a person more amenable. Let me tell you: as he smokes Jakob undergoes a change of mood, or something of the kind. Because a noble donor is sitting, intimidated, opposite him. Kirschbaum is helplessly twisting the cigarette between his thin fingers, scarcely daring to glance up, let alone open his mouth for anything but the next pull. Because uncontrolled outbursts are bound to follow: you make me sick with your 'nevertheless'. Or: Isn't that enough for you? And he had only come to have a talk with his neighbour: after all, a radio like that isn't private property in this town, like a chair or a shirt. He had come not to accuse but to discuss an important matter in quiet debate, and now this. Then you come and tell me it's prohibited. Kirschbaum did not leave, an indication of good will or excessive fear. He had stayed, put his hand in his pocket like a magician and fulfilled secret wishes, so surely he is entitled to a few neighbourly words.

'Of course I'm aware that the Russians won't arrive any quicker,' Jakob says half-way through his cigarette. 'And even if I tell people a thousand times, the Russians won't alter their route. But I would like to draw your attention to one further detail. Since the news has been passed round in the ghetto, I haven't heard of a single suicide. Have you?'

At that Kirschbaum looks astonished and says: 'You're right!'

'And before that there were many, nobody knows that better than you. I can remember your being called on many occasions, and usually it was too late.'

'Why did I not notice that?' Kirschbaum asks.

On one of the following days there is a sensation: a car drives through our little town, the only passenger car in our long story. A sensation, yes, but nothing to rouse hopes, not even in the most imaginative among those bold theorists: one is inclined to say, quite the contrary. It drives purposefully, unerringly; the exact route must have been studied in advance on a map of the town. The car is black; the streets empty out as it proceeds. In the back sit two men in civilian clothes; behind the steering wheel, a well-pressed uniform. The only ones who are of any importance are the two in the back. That's to say, they're not all that important either; in fact the whole car isn't important, in spite of its SS pennant, nor does it matter where it comes from or where it's going or whom it is conveying. Or just a little important, shall we say, or: not entirely unimportant in terms of the consequences.

The names of the two men are Preuss and Meyer. I know what they are talking about; I don't know what they are thinking about, although that is no insoluble riddle. I know their ranks, if necessary even their careers in outline, hence also their names. Later, when it comes to explaining, I shall unfortunately have to intervene clumsily and directly in the action to make sure no gap remains. The explanation will provide a stopgap, but that will come later; first the gap must be visible in its entirety.

The car stops beside Siegfried and Rafael who, as usual, are hanging round in the street, at the kerb, the only heroes far and wide who are not hiding. All the other Jews, neither blind nor crippled, are standing behind their windows or in sheltering corridors, trembling for two crazy children and for the as yet uncertain harm the German car can be expected to cause here. But many of those in the know will be thinking that the harm is not all that uncertain, since after all the car is not stopping at random: it is stopping outside Jakob Heym's building.

Preuss and Meyer get out of the car, on a special mission. Preuss is rather tall, with brown hair, slim, good looking, maybe a bit on the soft side; Meyer, as described to me, a head shorter, beefy, at first sight fiercely determined. Presumably a carefully chosen combination:

what one mans lacks, the other has, and vice versa, thus complementing each other nicely. They enter the building.

'Do you know which flat?' Preuss asks.

'One floor up,' says Meyer. 'The names are on the doors, I believe.'

One floor up, Jakob lives two floors up, yet they walk up only one floor, as far as Kirschbaum's door. After knocking politely they wait patiently outside the door, until a woman's voice, whose tone betrays that visitors are highly unwelcome, asks: 'Who is it?'

'Open up, please.'

Although this is not a very plausible reason for opening, a key is fumblingly inserted in the lock, then turned, and the door opens, first just a crack, then with no further hesitation. Quite unnecessarily, Meyer places his foot on the threshold. Facing them is Elisa Kirschbaum, old and severe, with well-concealed fear. Her much-mended apron does not deceive: Preuss and Meyer are not being scrutinized by some nonentity: the way she holds her head is enough to tell them that they are being scrutinized by a masterful woman. The fear is well concealed, the contempt not; a cool look into the faces of two tiresome visitors, then a glance at Meyer's foot making its crudely superfluous statement on the threshold. Meyer is doing his best to control himself.

'Yes?'

'Good morning,' says Preuss politely: perhaps he has no choice under such scrutiny. 'We wish to speak to Professor Kirschbaum.'

'He is not in.'

'Then we'll wait,' says Preuss firmly. He walks past her through the door, and at last Meyer can detach his unyielding foot from its position. He follows Preuss. They look round the room, what's all this talk, they don't seem so badly off here, sideboard with knick-knacks, sofa and two armchairs, a bit shabby, true, but still, bookcase crammed with books, like in the movies, a fancy ceiling light, almost a chandelier, these people are living in the lap of luxury here. Maybe only this fellow Kirschbaum, supposed to have been some kind of an authority, special rations and all that. They're certainly smart, these Ikeys, always managing to wriggle through and making themselves at home everywhere.

Meyer flops onto the sofa, but not Preuss, because Elisa Kirschbaum is still standing by the door with an air of a person awaiting an explanation.

'Are you Professor Kirschbaum's wife?' asks Preuss.

'I am his sister.'

'With your permission.' Preuss also sits down, in an armchair, crosses his legs, plenty of time, Elisa Kirschbaum remains standing. But eventually she has to ask: 'Kindly tell me what this is about.'

'None of your bloody business,' says Meyer. He can't remain silent any longer; what's going on here already seems weird enough to him, farce, pure farce, but he wants no part of it. In response to an insolent question he means to give more than an answer, he needs to straighten out the world a bit, or else where will it all end.

Well, Elisa Kirschbaum is hardly in a position to call the maid and tell her to show this boor the way out; her arsenal is as empty as can be. But at least she can punish Meyer by ignoring him, turning to Preuss and demanding frostily: 'Would you please tell this gentleman that he is not in his own home and that I am not accustomed to such behaviour?'

Meyer is ready to explode, is about to jump up, burst forth, cry out, but Preuss gives him an official look, special mission, then says: 'You are absolutely right. Please accept our apologies.'

'You were going to tell me why you are here.'

'I think I would prefer to tell that to Professor Kirschbaum personally. Do you know when he will be back?'

'No. Not later than eight o'clock.'

She sits down in the vacant armchair, very upright, and places her hands in her lap. They wait. I feel safe in saying that Kirschbaum arrives after about half an hour; the time is passed with trivialities. For example, Meyer lights a cigar and throws the match on the floor; Elisa Kirschbaum picks it up, brings him an ashtray, and opens the window. Meyer is a shade disconcerted.

Or: Preuss gets up after drumming a minute or two on the table; he is interested in the bookcase. Sliding open the glass panel, he tilts his head to one side, reads the titles on the spines, then picks out a book, leafs through it, then another, leafs through that one, all this for several minutes, then puts them back in their proper places.

'They are all medical books, every one of them,' says Elisa Kirschbaum.

'So I see.'

'We have a permit for them,' she says. And, since Preuss continues to study more titles: 'Perhaps you wish to see it?'

'No, thank you.'

He finds one that appeals to him especially, sits down, and has found something to occupy him. *Forensic Medicine*.

Or: suddenly Meyer jumps up, dashes to a door, flings it open, looks into an empty kitchen, is reassured, sits down.

'You never know,' he explains to Preuss, who goes on reading.

Or: again Meyer gets up, this time without haste, goes to the window, looks down. He sees two women dragging two children away from the car into the building opposite, sees in that building a face behind almost every window pane; the uniform is standing beside the car, bored.

'May be a while yet,' Meyer calls down, then seats himself again. As mentioned, half an hour.

Or: Elisa Kirschbaum goes into the kitchen, where she is heard moving about, and returns with a tray. Two supper plates, two cups, knives, forks, teaspoons, two linen napkins. She lays the table. Preuss hardly looks up from his book, whereas Meyer feels things are getting out of hand. Preuss hardly looks up from his book and says: 'Let her be.'

After about half an hour the professor arrives. He can be heard trying to insert his key in the lock, but there is another key in it, on the inside. Meyer stubs out his cigar, in the ashtray. Preuss puts the book down on the table, between the plates. Elisa Kirschbaum opens the door.

Alarmed, the professor pauses in the doorway, no use pretending, though he is not totally unprepared: the car down there outside the building. One would have hoped, of course, that it had something to do with Heym – that's to say, not hoped but assumed; one had merely hoped that it had nothing to do with oneself. In vain. Preuss stands up.

'We have visitors,' says Elisa Kirschbaum. She picks up *Forensic Medicine* from the table, puts it back in the bookcase, slides the panel shut. With a cloth taken from her apron pocket she wipes away any possible fingermarks.

'Professor Kirschbaum?' Preuss asks at last.

'Yes?'

'My name is Preuss.' Then a look towards Meyer.

'I'm Meyer,' growls Meyer.

They abstain from shaking hands. Preuss asks: 'Do you know Hardtloff?'

'You mean the head of the Gestapo?'

'I mean Stormtroop Leader Hardtloff. He requests your presence.'

'He requests my presence?'

Now Elisa Kirschbaum has to struggle to remain calm, as, incidentally, Meyer does too: requests his presence, the whole tone here, what a farce. Preuss says: 'Yes. He had a heart attack this morning.'

The professor sits down, looks helplessly at his sister who is now standing as stiffly as if turned to stone: Hardtloff had a heart attack this morning.

'I don't quite understand.'

'He wishes you to examine him,' said Preuss. 'Although I can imagine that you feel no particular grief at the sufferings of the Stormtroop Leader. You have no cause for alarm.'

'But. . . .'

'What do you mean, but?' Meyer asks.

More glances towards the sister: throughout his life she has removed all unpleasant situations from his path; with her cool head, her clear vision, her keen mind, she has kept all annoyances from him, hence one last look in her direction.

'Dis leurs que tu n'en as plus l'habitude,' she says.

'What's she saying?' Meyer asks Preuss and also stands up, to his full height.

'Please, you must realize,' says the professor. 'What you are asking of me is out of the question. Under no circumstances could I as a doctor take the responsibility, after so many years, my. . . . After all, it's four years since I treated a patient.'

Preuss remains admirably calm and places a soothing hand on the shoulder of the belligerent Meyer, special mission. Then he steps up to the professor, too close for comfort. His eyes express reproach, but not coldly, let alone angrily – compassionately rather, as if wishing to recall an impetuous person to his senses before it is too late. 'I am almost afraid, professor, that you have misunderstood me,' he says. 'We are not here to plead with you. Please don't make things difficult for us.'

'But I just told you. . . .'

'Do you need to take anything with you?' Preuss asks firmly.

With that the professor finally grasps that he need not look for further excuses; these two are not motivated by any desire to test their powers of persuasion. The relative courtesy of this man Preuss is his personal mark and does not entitle one to anything. So one must forget all the ifs and buts and strive to emulate one's sister. To be as aloof and dignified as she, at least this much, at least now, all one's life one has admired her for this, admired more than feared, some people say she is rather odd. One is not going to offer two German creatures the spectacle of collapse, did he need to take anything with him was the question, one is not going to fall on one's knees before them – look at the way Elisa stands there! That cannot be imitated at first shot, but normal, everyday gestures can be found, an impassive expression as if nothing out of the ordinary had occurred: a dignitary has been taken ill, one has been asked to have a look at him, run-of-the-mill stuff.

'Do we understand each other correctly?' Preuss asks.

The professor gets up. Below the bookcase are doors; he opens one and looks for his brown leather doctor's bag.

'It's in the cupboard,' says Elisa Kirschbaum.

He takes the bag out of the cupboard, opens it, checks the contents, then holds it out to Preuss, who doesn't bother to look inside.

'Medical equipment.'

'Good enough.'

Elisa Kirschbaum opens the cupboard again: a scarf, she holds it out to her brother.

'I won't need it. It's warm outside,' he says.

'You will need it,' says Elisa Kirschbaum. 'You don't know how chilly it gets after eight.'

He stuffs the scarf in his pocket, Meyer opens the door, the parting is at hand.

'Goodbye, Elisa.'

'Goodbye.'

That's what a parting looks like.

Then, outside the building, they get into the car, no doubt according to a preplanned seating arrangement: Preuss and the professor in the back, Meyer in front beside the uniform. Elisa is standing at the window, the whole street is standing at windows, but only the one is open. The car makes a U-turn, driving over the low kerb; a pale blue cloud hangs in the air for a few seconds. At the end of the street the car turns left, heading for Hardtloff.

Preuss snaps open a silver cigarette case and asks: 'Care for one?'

'No, thanks,' says Kirschbaum.

Meyer shakes his head without turning round and casts a sidelong glance at the uniform to see what it thinks of this farce; the uniform merely grins while looking straight ahead. Preuss observes the two in the rear-view mirror, but Kirschbaum doesn't; he sits there as if reluctant to waste a single movement.

'Why don't you put your bag on the floor?' Preuss asks. 'We've still quite a long way to go.'

148

'About how long?'

'Oh, about half an hour.'

Kirschbaum keeps his bag on his knees.

They reach the ghetto gate, they stop. Meyer winds down the window. A sentry sticks his helmet in and asks: 'Who's that old codger you've got in there?'

'Don't tell me you don't know him!' cries Meyer. 'Why, that's the famous Professor Kirschbaum!'

Preuss shows the sentry a permit and says, very formally: 'Open the gate. We're in a hurry.'

'Right away – no harm meant,' says the sentry, giving a hand signal to another sentry, who releases the barrier and pushes open the gate.

They drive on, now in the free part of the town; the street scene changes. Pedestrians not wearing yellow stars will catch Kirschbaum's eye, shops displaying goods, not exactly overcrowded but with customers going in and out, and, above all, trees lining the streets, I imagine. The Imperial in the market square is showing a German film. From time to time a car in the opposite direction, a tram, soldiers in walking-out uniform with a girl on each arm. Kirschbaum looks on with moderate interest; the sights cannot tell him much, cannot evoke memories, as they would with Jakob, for instance, for this is not his town.

'Come to think of it, you must actually be quite glad to get your hands on a new patient again, at long last,' says Preuss.

'May I know how you came to choose me?'

'That wasn't difficult. Hardtloff's personal physician had done all he could and asked for a specialist to be brought in. But try and find a specialist these days! We looked through the lists of inhabitants and came across your name. Hardtloff's doctor knows you.'

'He knows me?'

'Not personally, of course. Only by name.'

They reach the better-class residential areas; the buildings are lower, stand apart with more green and more trees. Kirschbaum opens his leather bag, takes out a little glass tube, unscrews the cap, and shakes two tablets into his palm. A questioning look from Preuss.

'For heartburn,' Kirschbaum explains. 'Care for some too?'

'No.'

Kirschbaum swallows the tablets, screws the cap back on, into the bag again, resumes his former posture.

'Feeling better now?' asks Preuss after a short interval.

'The tablets don't work that fast.'

They drive out of town, another barrier, and continue more or less through open country: Hardtloff has picked himself a secluded spot. Birch woods on either side. 'Naturally you will be driven back again, after everything has been taken care of,' Preuss says.

Now Kirschbaum does put the bag down on the floor. All through the drive it has been on his knees; but so close to their destination, down on the floor. With a deep breath he leans back.

'If you would let me have a cigarette now?'

Preuss gives him one, and lights it. We might point again to Meyer's exaggerated display of bafflement. Kirschbaum suffers a mild coughing fit, soon recovers, and throws a half-smoked cigarette out of the window.

'On the other hand, I can in a way understand your misgivings,' says Preuss, taking up what seems to have been a long-lost thread of conversation.

'I no longer have any misgivings,' Kirschbaum says.

'Oh, but you do, I can tell from looking at you! Your situation isn't exactly enviable, I can see that. If you succeed in saving the life of the Stormtroop Leader, you won't be very popular with your own people, I imagine. And if you don't succeed. . . .'

Preuss breaks off his pithy analysis, the rest would be tactless, as well as superfluous; he has said enough for Kirschbaum to grasp the value ascribed to Hardtloff's survival. For the first time during the drive, Meyer turns round. His expression makes it plain that he, too, knows how Preuss would have continued; above all it conveys his opinion of that continuation. With this in mind, so to speak, he turns round for a moment. Kirschbaum ignores him; he seems sufficiently preoccupied with himself. Preuss attempts one or two more trivial remarks, but Kirschbaum no longer responds.

They arrive at the Hardtloff villa. A driveway through an overgrown park, then round a circular flower-bed containing a dried-up ornamental-fish pond: all somewhat neglected, but magnificently laid out, quite magnificently.

'We're here,' says Preuss to the still absent-minded Kirschbaum, and gets out.

Hurrying down the flight of steps comes Hardtloff's personal physician, a bald-headed little man in shiny boots and unbuttoned tunic, looking as unkempt as the garden. His haste indicates worry or fear, presumably fear; he bears the responsibility here – for Hardtloff's health and, as we have heard, for today's bold experiment. While still on the higher steps he calls out: 'He's worse again! What took you so long?'

'We had to wait, he wasn't at home,' said Preuss.

'Hurry, hurry!'

There being no movement inside the car, Preuss opens the door on Kirschbaum's side and says again: 'We're here. Will you get out, please.'

But Kirschbaum just sits there, as if still a long way from sorting out his thoughts; he doesn't even turn his head towards Preuss. Delayed rebelliousness or a professor's proverbial absent-mindedness: the worst possible moment to have chosen, whichever it is. Impatience sets in. Meyer would have no problem deciding what should be done.

Preuss grips the professor by the arm and says in a low voice: 'Don't be difficult now,' punctilious to the last, and pulls him out with gentle force.

Kirschbaum's exit from the car proceeds in a surprising manner: sliding unhurriedly towards Preuss, who is too surprised to hold him up, Kirschbaum falls out of the car onto the neglected ground.

'What's going on?'

Hardtloff's doctor pushes his way between the two, bends down over the Jewish patient, and with no effort arrives at the unequivocal result of his examination.

'The man is dead!'

He is telling Preuss nothing new, not by this time. Preuss takes the leather bag out of the car. The usual brown leather doctor's bag. 'Do you need to take anything with you?' 'Medical equipment.' 'Good enough.' Perhaps it was he who had given Kirschbaum the idea.

Preuss opens the bag, finds the little tube among the contents. He hands it to the doctor.

'For heartburn,' says Preuss.

'Idiot,' says the doctor.

Now for the promised explanation.

Superfluous, really, but I imagine that some people will ask suspiciously how I can account for having been in that car. Hardly via Kirschbaum, so where was my informant sitting, and from the questioner's point of view the question is perfectly legitimate.

I could, of course, reply that it's not up to me to explain, I am telling a story I don't understand myself. I might say that I know from witnesses that Kirschbaum got into the car, that I managed to find out that by the end of the trip he was dead; the part in between can only have happened in such-and-such a way, anything else being inconceivable. But I would be lying, for the part in between could very well have happened differently, I would even say that it is far more likely to have happened differently. And herein, I suppose, lies the real reason for my explanation.

So: some time after the war I made a trip to our ghetto, on my first holiday. My few friends had advised against it, the trip would merely ruin the whole of my next year, memories were one thing, living something else. I told them they were right, and went. Jakob's room, the military office, Kurländischer Damm, Mischa's room, the cellar: I took my time looking at them all, measuring, examining, or just looking. I also went to Jakob's shop, where a shoemaker had moved in temporarily: 'Until I find something better,' he told me.

It seemed to me that mixed with the smell of leather there was also a scorched smell, but the shoemaker didn't think so. On the last-but-one day of my holiday, I wondered as I was packing whether I had forgotten anything; I would probably never return to this town, and this was the last chance for anything I had overlooked. All I could think of was Kirschbaum's journey by car, but I didn't see how I could check on that; besides, I didn't consider it essential to the story for whose sake I had come. Even so, I went that afternoon to the Russian *Kommandatura*, probably out of boredom, or perhaps because I couldn't find a restaurant open.

The duty officer was a woman of about forty, with the rank of a lieutenant. I told her that I had lived in the ghetto, that before the war my father and Kirschbaum had been close friends and so I was interested in Kirschbaum's fate. I made a proper Red Cross action out of it. Then I explained the connection between Kirschbaum and Hardtloff: all I knew was that Kirschbaum had entered the car, beyond that nothing, which was the truth. The two men who came for him were, I thought, called Preuss and Meyer or something like that. And I went on to say that, even if she couldn't tell me what had happened to the professor, maybe she could at least tell me something about those two men: that might provide a starting point. She made a note of the names and asked me to come back in two hours.

Two hours later I learned that, a few days before the Red Army marched in, Meyer was killed, by partisans, during a night raid.

'And the other man?' I asked.

'I have his German address here,' she replied.

Just as I was about to reach for the slip of paper, she gave me a worried look and said: 'You wouldn't be planning anything foolish, would you?'

'No, of course not – what an idea!' I said.

She handed me the paper; I looked at the address and said: 'That's a bit of luck. I'm also living in Berlin now.'

'You didn't leave Germany?' she asked in surprise. 'Why was that?'

'I don't really know,' I answered truthfully. 'It just happened that way.'

Preuss was living in Schöneberg, which is part of West Berlin. Nice wife and two children, the wife has only one arm. I went out there on Sunday afternoon. When I rang the bell the door was opened by a tall, brown-haired, good-looking man, a bit on the soft side, scarcely older than myself.

'Yes?' he asked.

'Are you Mr Preuss?'

'Yes?'

'I'm sorry to bother you,' I said. 'Might I talk to you for a few minutes?'

'Come in,' he replied, then led me into the living room and sent the children out after a few complications. On the wall hung a reproduction of Dürer's *Hands* and a photograph of a little girl in mourning crape. He asked me to sit down.

I began by telling him my name, which obviously caught his attention, although he couldn't make too much of it. But he could with my question, which was whether I had been correctly informed that he had worked for Hardtloff. I could observe him turning pale before he asked in a low voice: 'Why have you come?'

'I'm here on account of a story,' I said. 'To be more precise, on account of a gap in that story which you may be able to fill.'

He got up, started rummaging in a cupboard, soon found what he was looking for, and placed a piece of paper on the table in front of me. It was his certificate of denazification, duly stamped and signed.

'You needn't show me that,' I said.

However, he left the paper lying in front of me until I had finished reading it; then he picked it up, folded it, and locked it away again.

'Can I offer you something?' he asked.

'No, thank you.'

'A cup of tea, perhaps?'

'No, thank you.'

He called out: 'Ingrid!' His wife came in, and it was obvious that she still wasn't used to having only one arm.

'This is my wife,' he said.

I stood up, and we shook hands.

'Would you mind running down to Sebald's and fetching the siphon of beer? He promised me two litres for the weekend,' he told her.

After she had left the room I said: 'Do you remember a Professor Kirschbaum?'

'Oh yes,' he replied at once. 'Very well indeed.'

'You went to pick him up, didn't you, because he was to examine Hardtloff? You and someone called Meyer?'

'That's correct. Meyer caught it some time later.'

'I know. But what happened to Kirschbaum? Was he shot, after Hardtloff died?'

'What makes you think that? The two never met.'

I looked at Preuss in surprise and asked: 'Did he refuse to examine him?'

'I suppose you could call it that,' he answered. 'He took poison in the car. As we were driving, right before our eyes.'

'Poison?' I asked, and he noticed that I didn't believe him.

'I can prove it to you,' he said. 'You need only ask Letzerich, he'll confirm every word.'

'Who is Letzerich?'

'He was the driver. He was there the whole time. I'm sorry I haven't got his address, all I know is that he was from Cologne. But it should be possible somehow or other to get hold of his address.'

I asked him to describe this drive to me in more detail; the result is known. It took quite a while; at some point his wife brought us the beer, I drank a glass, it tasted horrible. I hardly interrupted him because he was giving me the details without prompting. He attached special importance to the fact that Kirschbaum had offered the tablets to him too. 'And I really do sometimes suffer from heartburn, quite often in fact. Just imagine if I had taken one of them!'

'It was a blatant attempt at murder,' I said.

He continued his story, driving out of town, the last part of the trip, the last cigarette, Meyer's meaningful looks, until they reached the villa, until Hardtloff's doctor came, until Kirschbaum lay dead on the ground in front of him. How he suddenly grasped what had really happened, how he took the little bag out of the car, the glass tube, handing it to the doctor, how the doctor had said: 'Idiot.'

For quite some time we were silent; he must have assumed that I

154

was profoundly shaken, but actually I was wondering what else I could ask him. He had told the story well, graphically and omitting nothing, and I felt there were enough convincing reasons for him to have remembered that drive so well.

Finally he felt an irresistible urge to confide to me his present thoughts about those ill-fated times, to talk to a sensible person and get the whole rotten business off his chest. But I really hadn't come to listen to that. I said I had stayed much too long anyway, I still had a few things to do, as no doubt he did too, so I got up and thanked him for his co-operation.

'And remember the name, in case you want to double-check,' he said. 'Egon Letzerich. Cologne.'

In the passage we met his wife, who was just taking the children to the bathroom. They were already in their pyjama trousers, their top halves naked.

'Come on now, what do you say?' Preuss asked them.

Both put out their hands simultaneously, curtseyed and bowed, and said: 'Goodnight, Uncle.'

'Goodnight,' I said.

All three disappeared into the bathroom. Preuss insisted on accompanying me out of the building. In case the front door was already locked.

The front door was still open. Preuss walked ahead of me into the street, took a deep breath, flung out his arms, and said: 'May is almost here again!'

I had the impression that he was slightly drunk; after all, he had consumed two litres of tepid beer, minus one glass.

'Ah yes,' I said, 'can you tell me anything more about his sister?'

'Kirschbaum's sister? We never had anything to do with her. I only saw her that one time. Is there any more to tell?'

As I was finally leaving he said: 'Would you answer a question for me too?'

'Of course,' I replied.

He hesitated a moment before asking: 'How did you find out my address?'

'From the British Secret Service,' I said. Then I really did leave.

Hardtloff is dead, died of a weak heart. The news has come all the way to us here at the freight yard. It must have happened last night. When we left the station yesterday after work, the flag was hanging limply at its normal spot on the red brick building, but this morning when we turned up for work it was fluttering gaily at half-mast, so it happened some time in between. Of course the flag in itself is only a vague clue, betraying merely that someone high up has passed on, without giving any name. The name was supplied by a sentry while he was talking to another sentry: at some point during the morning Roman Schtamm overheard the revealing conversation. He approached a stack of crates, with nothing reprehensible in mind, and the two sentries were standing behind it discussing Hardtloff's death. It was a fluke. Roman took a little longer than usual over the lifting of the crate, only managing to complete the job when the two sentries changed the subject.

By this time every one of us knows for whom the flag is flying at half-mast, Roman having seen no reason to keep it to himself. It can be said that we bear the news with composure; it will scarcely mean any change for us. If there is ever to be any, it won't be as a result of Hardtloff's death; nevertheless, worse things can be imagined. Only Jakob regrets that it was Roman Schtamm and not he who overheard the sentries' conversation: the Stormtrooper's misfortune would have yielded an excellent radio report. Not only because of the content: it would have been the first report that didn't have to be accepted in good faith. Everyone would have had a chance to verify its truth, with his own eyes and without effort – the confirmation has been flying from the flag-pole since early this morning. To tell them now that one had heard about Hardtloff's death on the early morning news would be pretty senseless, what's past is past, a radio has its pride, it doesn't come limping in the wake of events.

When the Whistle blows punctually for soup-time, Jakob finally abandons this pleasant train of thought. The little cart with the tin bowls is pulled over, and we form the customary impeccable queue.

Someone behind Jakob asks softly: 'Were you listening again last night?'

'Yes,' says Jakob.

'Did they say anything about Hardtloff?'

'Don't be daft! Do you imagine they're concerned with such trivial stuff?'

Someone in front of Jakob asks: 'What stations do you listen to?'

'Whatever's available,' says Jakob. 'Moscow, London, Switzerland, depends on the weather too.'

'Never any German stations?'

'What for?'

'Do you sometimes listen to music too?'

'Not very often,' says Jakob. 'Only when I'm waiting for the news. I'm not keeping the radio for entertainment, you know.'

'I'd give anything to hear some music again. Any music,' says someone in front of the man in front of Jakob.

The cauldrons of soup are a long time coming, yet the line is as straight as an arrow, word of honour. The men automatically continue to correct any irregularities, even the almost imperceptible ones, but that doesn't bring on the cauldrons this time. Instead the window in the gable of the brick building opens, a hand commands silence, a voice calls out from above sounding like the irate Almighty in person: 'Ten-minute break! No lunch today!'

The cart with its bowls is pushed away again, the hungry line loses its neatness and spreads out over the yard. Unused spoons are returned to pockets, a few oaths, curses, and angry looks, the Russians will show you bastards.

Kowalski comes up to me and asks: 'No food for us because Hardtloff is dead?'

'Obviously,' I say.

'If you ask me,' says Kowalski, 'it's worth it.'

He wasn't exactly rewarded with gales of laughter; no midday meal, that really hurts, like a blow to the stomach. But Kowalski in his kind way attempts another modest joke, 'Just imagine if every time one of us kicks the bucket the Germans get nothing to eat – what a fine starvation that would be!'

No response.

As Jakob walks to the spot he has chosen for those ten minutes he is followed by a faithful little bevy of Jews. Kowalski drops back to join them before Jakob actually misses him. Jakob knows they are behind him; the meal has been cancelled so a word from him will

157

have to do instead. He goes to an empty rail car where they can all find a place to sit down, a thoughtfulness that has long become a habit. Jakob doesn't feel quite comfortable: he had intended to rest a bit on yesterday's laurels, on the liberation of the little town of Tobolin. With our enthusiastic approval, Major Karthäuser had set his name with a flourish to the document of surrender, the fortress had fallen, but that was yesterday. No one could have foreseen the desperate need of the following day. Jakob sits unprepared in the midst of his flock.

Suddenly, so I am told, as they are sitting there looking at him, for he is expected to start his report right away, he is struck by a wicked thought that drives out Tobolin and all victories. Suddenly he realizes that two pieces of news have reached the railway station today, although only one of them was immediately grasped: Hardtloff. The other, the bad one, has been ignored, although it has been in the air, clear and unmistakable: the only thing needed was the effort. 'The news isn't that good at all, I'm sorry to say,' Jakob announces gravely.

'What news do you mean?'

'That Hardtloff is dead.'

'Did you care about him?' comes a mocking voice.

'Not about him,' says Jakob, 'but about Kirschbaum.'

Reluctantly one must agree, it's not easy, a convincing correlation that most of them understand without any further explanation. The way things are, a Jewish doctor is not likely to survive his Aryan patient for long, in this particular case not at all. 'Who's Kirschbaum?' someone asks; one can't know everyone. It is explained to him, a leading light, at one time a famous heart specialist, here Jakob's neighbour, was picked up and taken away to cure Hardtloff. Now belatedly a quiet grieving for the professor; the ten minutes pass without questions or reports of successes. Jakob could have wished for a different distraction. He feels an urge to dispense some sort of consolation, one can't let them sit there hungry like that. The old story about the secret German plans that fell into Russian hands in the fortress of Tobolin flashes across his mind. But the Whistle preserves him from this folly by putting an end in the usual way to the midday meal that today was so singularly lacking in flavour.

Thus in spite of Hardtloff's death the day passes dismally, and continues to do so. In the midst of work a tank wagon appears, drawn by two scrawny horses, the sight is familiar as is the rattling that can be heard a long way off. On an average it turns up once every three months, less often in summer, somewhat more often in winter, when the ground is frozen, but always on a Monday. Its visit has to do with the little German hut with the heart in the door: for three months the hut can manage without it, but no longer than that, or it will overflow.

The wagon is driven by a farmer from somewhere in the surrounding countryside; no one knows how he came by this honour. We can't stand him. On his first visit the Germans forbade him to talk to any of us, and he strictly obeys this rule. At first, long before Jakob's radio, we tried to coax a word out of him, we didn't know ourselves what kind of a word, any tiny detail from the outside. There would have been no danger, but he would sit there with compressed lips, not saying a word and squinting over at the distant sentries. He probably feared for his head or his manure. Or he is anti-Semitic, or quite simply an idiot.

He stops his wagon behind the privy. A German comes out of the brick building and mingles with the men, who all pretend to be terribly busy as soon as the hateful rattling is heard. The job for which four men are now to be picked is no easier than lugging crates; afterwards you stink to high heaven and can't wash till you get home.

'You, you, you and you,' says the German.

Schmidt, Jakob and two strangers grit their teeth as they walk behind the privy and begin the filthy job. They take the two shovels and the two buckets hanging from the side of the wagon, and Jakob and the lawyer lift the cover off the pit. They they proceed to shovel the muck into the buckets, which the other two empty into the tank. Schmidt's disgusted expression doesn't help matters. It'll take about three hours, and at half-time they change over, shovels for buckets.

'Have you ever done this before?' asks Schmidt.

'Twice.'

'I never have.'

The farmer is seated on the wagon with his back to them. He takes a little parcel out of his pocket, grease-proof paper, unwraps it, bread and bacon. The sun low, the world well forgotten, he enjoys his noon or evening meal, Jakob's eyes fill with tears.

The older of the two bucket-carriers begs the farmer for a mouthful, with a muttered explanation as to what happened to his lunch, just a little piece of bread, we won't even mention bacon. The farmer seems undecided; as Jakob shovels he observes the farmer's oafish eyes raking the yard for watchers, of whom none is interested in the proceedings behind the privy.

'Don't be scared,' says our man. 'You don't have to speak to us. Just drop a piece of bread, you know, by mistake. No one can blame you for that. I'll pick it up so no one'll notice. . . . D'you hear? No one, not even you, will notice it!'

'Could you eat in this stench?' Schmidt asks.

'Yes,' says Jakob.

The farmer puts his hand in his pocket again, brings out the grease-proof paper, carefully wraps up what's left of the bread and bacon, and stows it away. Either he has had enough, or he really has lost his appetite. Just an ample gulp from his canteen, and he wipes his mouth with his dirty sleeve.

'Arsehole,' is what he has to hear, but not even this filthy epithet makes him come alive.

Shortly before the change-over, Schmidt slows down noticeably in his shovelling. Finally he stops entirely, claiming that he can't go on, that everything is turning before his eyes, black spots. Sweating, he leans against the back wall of the privy.

'It's because you haven't had any food,' says Jakob.

That's no help to Schmidt; big drops of sweat run down his face, he tries to throw up, but nothing comes. Jakob fills a bucket in his place, the carriers are forced to wait, not a long-term solution.

'You have to keep going,' Jakob says.

'That's easy for you to say,' gasps Schmidt, leaning back and very pale.

'Either you keep going now, or you might as well just lie down and die,' says Jakob.

This appeals even less to Lawyer Schmidt. He picks up his shovel again and on unsteady legs starts filling the waiting bucket. He groans, it looks like a desperate effort doomed, one fears, to failure. The shovel pokes around on the surface, not going as deep as it should, so that it is pulled out of the muck only half full, more work for Jakob.

'By the way, I've heard something from your Mr Churchill,' says Jakob, in an undertone so that the farmer can't understand anything no matter hard he tries.

'From Winston Churchill?' says Schmidt, weakly yet with audible interest.

'He has a cold.'

'Is it serious?'

'No, no, just an ordinary cold. He sneezed through half the interview.'

'A whole interview?'

'A short one.'

'And what did he say?'

Jakob indicates that this is not a suitable place for a chat: those sentries over there, at the moment they are concerned with other things, but in three hours one of them is sure to come over and check, and by that time the pit must be empty. So a report only if it can be camouflaged with work. Schmidt sees the point, his grip on the shovel grows firmer by necessity, the drops on his forehead remain the same, what did Churchill say?

Jakob tells him; the cellar conversation between the reporter and the British prime minister is still in his memory, although no longer quite so fresh. The situation on the eastern front, without naming any towns, in any case desperate for the Germans, those were his own words, a great colourful bouquet of good prospects. And Mr Churchill can well afford an opinion, wouldn't you say, from his vantage point? Of course, there are still some problems here and there – I ask you, in what kind of a war does everything go without a hitch?

And there are also differences between Schmidt and Lina, considerable ones, that must be taken into account. One isn't sitting with a little girl in a dusky cellar, for fun, as it were, or for love; one is standing in the sunshine with the highly educated Schmidt, every word must be weighed, in three hours the pit must be empty of muck.

On the morning of this day, which has been earmarked for the advance on the district town of Pry – the Russians won't quite reach it but will come a good deal closer to it, Jakob has decided – on the morning of this promising day Mischa while on his way to work notices an agitated little group standing in the street. They point first in one direction and then another, two of them are talking excitedly, the others are listening in dismay. Mischa is not going to walk past without finding out what's going on. Then he hears the name of a street, Franziskaner; Mischa grabs the man nearest him by the arm, pulls him out of the hubbub, and insists he tell him for heaven's sake what's happening in Franziskaner-Strasse. He is quickly told, a disaster has overtaken it, the people living in that street are being lined up in rows of three. A house-to-house search is under way, they have just got as far as Number 10, in a few hours there won't be a soul left living there, off to camp or God knows where.

'And the Russians are said to have already taken Tobolin,' the man says.

Mischa dashes off. The fate of Franziskaner-Strasse affects him more than in a general way, for that street is a very special one: Rosa lives in it. The man said they had just reached Number 10, which means only a few minutes ago, normally by this hour Rosa is already at the factory. Mischa blames himself for not having simply made her stay with him every night, especially last night. He will go to her factory, the sentry at the gate won't let him in, but he can hang about close by. Until they come off work, Mischa himself will be a sentry, because Rosa must be prevented from going home. He hopes to God he won't have to spend the entire day watching an empty factory; if Rosa left home on time, she must be in there, that's his only hope. Mischa runs, why so fast, he doesn't know himself, Rosa won't be coming off work for a long time, he runs.

Outside the building, a grey brick garment factory, the world looks quite normal. Mischa stands on the opposite side of the street, no one else is about. He prepares himself for a long day, but it proves to be much shorter than expected. A Jewish girl emerges from the factory, and Mischa wonders why she is coming out during working hours; she strolls aimlessly across the roadway, past him. Mischa stands there hesitating until she has almost reached the next corner, then follows her. She soon notices it, coquettishly turns her head, once, then again; a blue-eyed, broad-shouldered young man is, after all, a rarity in the ghetto, and in broad daylight at that. She slows down at once, she has no objection to being overtaken, and that finally happens too; just past the corner he is standing beside her.

'Excuse me,' says Mischa. 'Do you work in that factory?'

'Yes,' she says with a smile.

'Do you happen to know whether Rosa Frankfurter is still in there?'

She considers this for a few seconds before saying: 'You're Mischa, aren't you?'

'Yes,' he replies. 'Is she inside?'

'She left a few minutes ago. She was told she could go home today.'

'How many is that, a few minutes?' his voice already shrill. 'How many, exactly?'

'Ten, maybe,' she answers, surprised at his sudden agitation.

Again he rushes off, feverishly calculating that he can make it if ten minutes is correct. From here to Franziskaner-Strasse would take Rosa barely half an hour, more if she's not hurrying, and she's not likely to be. They told her she could go home, without giving any reason, the bastards, so there's no need to hurry. All at once Mischa turns on his heel, dashes back the same way, an oversight must be corrected, an unforgivable one. The girl is slowly coming towards him and smiles again.

'Did they send you home too?' he calls out while still some distance away.

'Yes.'

'Don't go home! Hide somewhere!'

He hears her calling after him: 'But why?'

'Because Franziskaner-Strasse is being deported!'

'But I don't live there, I live in Sagorsker-Strasse!'

This awkward exchange costs him far too much time. So Sagorsker-Strasse too. He has told her all he knows, she can draw her own conclusions and save her life or not. If she's smart she'll stand outside the factory and tell each of the women being sent home: 'Don't go home, hide somewhere, never mind where you live!' All this is going through his head long after he has started running again, to catch up with Rosa, and that Franziskaner- and Sagorsker-Strasse don't even meet: between them is Blumenbinder-Gasse, which doesn't have many houses, mostly open storage places that are not being used these days, except for a few. And beyond each new corner he looks for Rosa, maybe she isn't even taking the shortest route, maybe she's going for a stroll in this nice weather and wants to make the most of the unexpected free day. If she is really taking her time, he can't fail to reach Franziskaner-Strasse ahead of her, and he could occupy one end and intercept her. But only one end, Franziskaner-Strasse has two ends, which of those ends do you propose to occupy, and at this hour you won't find anyone to help you at any price. A new glimmer of hope flares up for a few moments: Mischa is banking on Rosa's instinct for self-preservation. Regardless of which end she appears at, she will see what's happening to her street. Perhaps she'll turn round then, run to his building, stay hidden in the courtyard and wait until he arrives in the evening with the key. But Mischa doesn't rely too heavily on that, he knows her too well, his crazy Rosa won't be able to banish her love for her father and mother from her head, all that useless girlish stuff. The best she'll be able to manage at that sight will be a hesitation, then she'll burst into tears and run straight into her doom, to where her parents are, who can well do without her, and all this won't help a soul.

All calculations come to an end when at last he sees her in a long, dead-straight street. In Argentinische-Allee, whose linden trees have been carefully chopped down, close to the ground, resulting in a wide, clear vista. The street is virtually empty; he recognizes her rust-coloured dress when it is still only a dot, then her blue head-scarf, her walk – slow, as he had foreseen. What luck, Mischa thinks.

Within a short distance of her he stops running and follows her quietly for a few steps. Rosa is looking at the fine old gables in this once-prosperous merchants' area, Rosa is out for a stroll. His last thoughts before making himself known are that his behaviour must seem perfectly natural, he happens to be on his way to her home because he has heard that the factory has given her the day off. Nothing about great anxiety, not a word about the fate of Franziskaner-Strasse, that would only remind her of her love for her parents.

He intends to put his hands over her eyes from behind and in a disguised voice ask her to guess who it is; that would be a harmless enough way to begin. He notices that his hands are sticky with sweat, his face too; he wipes it dry with his sleeve and says with forced casualness: 'Fancy meeting you here!'

She quickly turns round, startled at first, then smiles, the prettiest girls smile at Mischa. 'What are you doing here?' she asks.

'And what are you doing here?'

'I'm on my way home,' she says. 'Just imagine, I'd been at the factory less than an hour and I was allowed to leave!'

'Why?'

'No idea. They simply told me I could go home. A few others too, but not everyone.'

'The same thing happened to me,' Mischa says.

'Have you got the day off too? The whole day?'

'Yes.'

'Wonderful!'

She links her arm through his; a solitary passer-by looks in wonderment at young love.

'We'll go to my room,' says Mischa.

'But how do you happen to be here of all places?'

'Because I wanted to fetch you from the factory. When they gave me the day off, I thought maybe they'd let you off today too.'

'You're a clever one.'

'But you had just left. A girl told me so, a cute-looking girl with red hair.'

'That was Larissa,' she says.

They go to his place, in no hurry, for the direction doesn't worry him, Franziskaner-Strasse being off to the left. Rosa tells him about

Larissa, that she had sometimes spoken to her about Mischa, she hopes he doesn't mind, they sew at the same table, and the day is long. Larissa is still water that runs deep, one mustn't be deceived by her dreamy eyes. For instance, she also has a boyfriend, his name is Najdorf, Josef, she calls him Jossele, he works in a tool factory, Mischa wouldn't know him. They live in the same building, Larissa has a mother and two grown-up brothers, and a funny thing happened with the two brothers. They once gave Josef Najdorf a beating when they caught him with their sister in the attic, doing what, do you suppose? Necking and kissing, of course, but Larissa let them have it all right. Meanwhile they've calmed down, they realize she is no longer a child; Jossele is sometimes even allowed to visit her at home, just for a chat of course. And abruptly, in the midst of her flow of talk, Rosa stops and asks: 'Why on earth would they suddenly give us a whole day off?'

'How should I know?'

'But there must be a reason.'

He shrugs, he had hoped she wouldn't bring up the subject. He can't give her an answer, but she's right, it is strange.

'I wonder if it has anything to do with the Russians,' she says.

'With the Russians?'

'I mean, if they feel that the game is up and they want to try and make themselves popular while there's still time?' says Rosa. 'Don't you see? Thinking ahead.'

'Maybe,' says Mischa, having no better explanation to offer.

So on they stroll towards his place, Rosa chattering away as never before, out of sheer light-heartedness. Mischa lets her chatter on without interruption; she is far from having shot her bolt with Larissa: Klara and Annette and above all Nina are having affairs, and what affairs! Furthermore, her father is at last beginning to have some tentative thoughts about the future. Two evenings ago he placed a curious piece of paper on the table, says Rosa. On it, divided into three groups, were theatrical roles corresponding to his ideas of what he hopes one day to perform, God willing; the theatre management has denied them to him long enough. Rosa doesn't know the details, she doesn't understand enough about the theatre for that, but there were at least twenty.

At the front door an unpleasant thought strikes Mischa: no work means no midday meal today. He asks Rosa whether she happens to have her ration card with her. Sorry, she's left it at home, wouldn't you know it, he thinks. Should she quickly go and get it, no she shouldn't. He gives her the key, he'll follow in a few minutes, and goes off with his own ration card.

In the shop Mischa is the only customer; normally after work there's never less than a half-hour wait.

'So early?' asks Rosenek the well nourished. His scales are suspected of inaccuracy, always in the same direction, only they could have provided him with that pot-belly. Although he tries to hide the little monster with an outsize overall, overall and Rosenek cannot deceive: no overall, no matter how big, can hide those pudgy cheeks.

'They've given us the day off,' says Mischa.

'Day off? What does that mean?'

'A day off.'

Mischa puts his food coupons down on the counter in front of Rosenek, all of them.

'It's only Tuesday,' says Rosenek in surprise, as a reminder.

'Never mind.'

'Well, it's up to you.'

From a floury drawer behind him Rosenek takes out a round loaf that doesn't smell of bread like in the old days, puts it on the counter, groans as he cuts it in two with a serrated knife, then places one half on the famous scales, the deceitful brass weights ranged like organ pipes.

'Please weigh properly,' Mischa says.

'What's that supposed to mean? I always weigh properly!'

Mischa is not about to engage in hair-splitting, which will lead nowhere, so he says: 'Be sure to weigh properly. I have a guest.'

'A guest? What does that mean?'

'A guest.'

Rosenek discovers his heart and gives Mischa the other half of the loaf, the alleged half, without placing it on the scales. Two pocketfuls of potatoes come next, Mischa having nothing else to carry them in, then a small bag of ground dried peas, some sausage, more so in appearance than in essence, and a little package of malt coffee.

'The coupons also say something about fat,' Mischa says.

'So they do! Do they also say where I'm supposed to get it from?'

'Mr Rosenek,' says Mischa.

Rosenek looks at him as if faced with the most difficult decision of his life, you'll be the death of me yet, my boy. 'Do you need the coffee?' Rosenek asks.

'Not that badly.'

Rosenek persists for a while longer in his long-suffering pose, finally

picks up the little package of coffee from the counter, and goes off
into an adjoining room. He returns bearing a piece of grease-proof
paper. At first sight it appears to be nothing but a folded piece of
paper, but then it is clear that there is something wrapped in it. Fat.
To judge by his expression, Rosenek has cut it out of his own belly.

'Because it's you,' says Rosenek. 'But for heaven's sake don't tell
anyone!'

'What do you take me for?'

Mischa arrives upstairs with his spoils. Rosa marvels at what he has
brought; she has opened the window wide.

'Otherwise the sun will think no one's home and will go away again,
Mother says,' she says.

Mischa puts Rosenek's largesse away in the cupboard and empties
his pockets of the earth from the potatoes. Rosa calls him to the
window: he doesn't like the sound of her voice. Leaning out beside
her, he sees a grey procession approaching, still too distant to make
out details. So far the only sound is of the dogs barking, intermittently
and unnecessarily since no one is getting out of line.

'Which street is it today?' Rosa asks.

'I don't know.'

He pulls her away from the window and shuts it, but he can't
prevent her remaining behind the window-pane and waiting for the
procession to pass by. 'Let me look,' Rosa says. 'Maybe there'll be
people we know.'

'Are you hungry?' he asks. 'Shall we make ourselves something?'

'Not now.'

He saves himself the trouble of further offers, knowing that her
answer to any suggestion from him would be: 'Not now'. Only force
could separate her from the window – quite silly, really, because she
has no idea whom she will see in the procession, but she fancies that in
such situations she mustn't hide her head in the sand. A kind of rule
of the game for Rosa: that's how she is. The simplest would be to grab
her, throw her on the bed, and start kissing her as if obeying an
uncontrollable impulse. Mischa takes his first step in this direction,
but at the second his courage deserts him, Rosa knows him too well
and would immediately see through his ruse. He has no choice but
to leave her standing there until the terrible sight: there is no way she
can be spared that.

He sits down on the bed and tries to look composed, a total waste
of time since Rosa continues to look fixedly out of the window. Her
forehead leans against the glass so she can obtain the earliest possible

view of the transport. A little patch of mist forms on the pane; she is breathing through her mouth, as excited people do.

'Come on over here!' he says.

Did those idiots have to pick on his street of all streets? There are enough others. Mischa feels an urge to get up and go out into the corridor, or at least into Fajngold's half of the room which, needless to say, had resumed its former appearance the day after Rosa's intervention. What in the world will she do? The yapping of the dogs becomes louder; when it subsides for a moment one can hear footsteps, even a single voice calling out: 'Step lively now, step lively!'

'Mischa,' Rosa says softly.

'Mischa!' she screams seconds later. 'Mischa, Mischa, Mischa, it's our street!'

He is standing behind her now; the thought that her parents must be in that transport doesn't seem to have occurred to her yet. In a whisper she counts off the names of neighbours whom she recognizes; each of them is carrying something, a bag, a suitcase, a bundle of whatever was worth taking along. Mischa has time to look for her parents; he discovers them before she does, Felix Frankfurter with his inevitable scarf wound about his neck. His walk somehow expresses confidence; his wife, a head shorter, is walking beside him. She looks up at their window; Mischa had never been a secret.

Rosa is still counting off names; her mother's upward glances gives Mischa the push he needs. He grips Rosa tightly in his arms and carries her away from the window, intending to put her down on the bed and keep her there by force. But nothing comes of that; on the way they fall to the floor because Rosa is struggling. He lets her hit him and scratch him and pull his hair while he just keeps his arms gripped tightly round her waist; they lie on the floor for an eternity. She screams for him to let her go, maybe twenty times she screams nothing but the words: 'Let me go!' Until they can hear no more barking, no more footsteps; her blows become weaker and finally cease. Cautiously he lets go of her, ready to grab her again the next instant. But she lies there without moving, with her eyes closed, breathing heavily, as if after some great exertion. There is a knock at the door, and a woman from the building asks whether she can help, she thought she'd heard someone screaming.

'No, no, it's quite all right,' says Mischa through the closed door. 'Thank you.'

He gets up and opens the window, otherwise the sun will think no one's home and will go away again, so we've been told. The street is

168

silent and empty. He looks out for a long time, and when he turns round Rosa is still lying on the floor, her position unchanged.

'Come on, get up.'

She gets up – not, it seems to him, because he has told her to. So far not a tear has been shed. She sits down on the bed; he dare not speak to her.

'Your neck is bleeding,' she says.

He goes over to her, squats down in front of her, and tries to look into her eyes, but she looks past him.

'That's why you came to fetch me,' she says. 'You knew.'

He is shocked at the reproach in her words. He wishes he could explain that there was no time to warn her parents, but at the moment she won't accept any reasons.

'Did you actually see them?' he asks.

'You wouldn't let me,' she says, and at last begins to cry.

He says he didn't see them either, not even right at the end of the transport, maybe they sensed the danger in time and found a safe place to go. He knows how ridiculous this is; after three words he realizes the futility of lying, but he finishes his sentences like an automaton.

'I'm sure you'll see them again,' he adds. 'Jakob said. . . .'

'You're lying!' she screams. 'You're all lying! You talk and talk and nothing ever changes!'

She jumps up and tries to run out of the room, but Mischa manages to catch her just as she flings open the door. In the corridor the woman straightens up, from keyhole level. 'Are you sure I can't help?' she asks.

'For God's sake, no!' Mischa screams; now he is screaming too.

Offended, the woman withdraws; one must assume that her desire to help has been quenched for ever, at least as far as this screaming maniac is concerned. However, the appearance of a third person has brought Rosa to her senses again, it seems; she goes back into the room without Mischa having to force her. He closes the door. Dreading her silence, he sets to work immediately to take renewed possession of Fajngold's fallow half of the room: the cupboard against the wall, precisely covering the big square of still-clean wallpaper, the curtain down from the ceiling and in front of the window again. For Rosa is going to be living here now: that much at least is clear.

'Have you been hearing anything recently about the deportations?' Mischa asks.

'No, I haven't,' Jakob replies.

'They've not only evacuated Franziskaner-Strasse. They're in Sagorsker-Strasse too and. . . .'

'I know,' says Jakob.

They walk on for a bit without speaking, on their way home from the station, having shaken Kowalski at the last corner. He had held back with his questions in Mischa's presence.

Since that day, five men have failed to show up at the station, maybe even more; one only misses the five one knows personally. Jakob had thought there were six, having included Mischa among them because he didn't show up for work that day. Luckily that was a mistake.

'How are things goings with Rosa?' Jakob asks.

'How should they go?'

'Are you managing with food?'

'Splendidly!'

'But she can't go and get any more ration cards, can she?'

'Don't I know it!'

'Couldn't someone in the building help out? I have the same problem with Lina. Kirschbaum always used to let me have something for her.'

'I can no longer believe this will end well,' says Mischa. 'They're combing street after street now.'

Jakob seems to hear a veiled reproach in his voice.

'Maybe,' says Jakob. 'But think for yourself. The Germans are in a state of panic. The transports are the best proof that the Russians must already be really close! Seen in that light, they're actually a good sign.'

'Some good sign! Try explaining that to Rosa.'

On one of her deadly boring and tear-filled afternoons, Rosa leaves the room, although Mischa has strictly forbidden her to do so. Actually he would have liked to lock her in, regardless of her protests; the only reason he hasn't is that the toilet is in the courtyard.

She has no fixed destination; all she wants to do is stretch her legs after a whole week of prison. The dangers Mischa is always talking about seem to her exaggerated; in his room she is no safer than anywhere else, it can be this building's turn any day. And who is there to recognize her? There is hardly anyone left whom she knows, and the street patrols don't show up until the evening, round about curfew time. Besides, none of that really matters to her, and besides, Mischa needn't find out about the walk she's taking, she won't stay away long.

Later when, as it happens, he arrives home long before her, it doesn't necessarily have to be the truth when she tells him that she happened to have the key to her old home with her, and that, without really intending to, she found herself in Franziskaner-Strasse, her feet having taken that route by force of habit, she says.

The street seems eerily empty to her; people also avoid walking through it, as if it had been smitten by the plague. Rosa looks into deserted ground-floor rooms, into rooms of people she had spoken to only the other day. Through one window she notices a boy, about fourteen years old. He is kneeling in front of an open cupboard and hurriedly stuffing whatever he can lay hands on into a rucksack – dishes, bed-linen, trousers, a wooden box without checking its contents for usefulness. Rosa stands stock-still as she watches him, the sole living creature apart from herself. The cupboard appears to be completely empty, but the rucksack is not yet full; the boy straightens up and carefully surveys the room. Then he sees the wide eyes outside the window; at first he gets a shock, then he also sees the yellow star on Rosa's chest, and a conspiratorial grin spreads over his face. He probably takes her for a harmless competitor.

Rosa hurries on, wondering whether someone like that has meanwhile been in her home too: she can't think of any other word, a looter. While she feels no rage, mere tolerance is not enough. What bothers her is the thought that behind the walls there exists a second, secret life, at first sight not discernible, slowly wiping out all traces.

She quietly opens her front door and listens with a beating heart. She wishes she had Mischa with her, perhaps he could have been persuaded to come, but now she happens to be here without him. One can never be sure, but after a lengthy silence she assumes that there is no one else in the building. She walks quickly up the two flights and looks through the keyhole before unlocking the door. Then she is standing in the room, which looks very tidy. The dust hasn't had much time to settle; the four chairs are standing neatly round the table, which is covered with a yellow cloth, a tassel at each corner. The tap is dripping. So far no one with a rucksack has been here, Rosa can see that right away, also that her parents must have left without haste.

The first thing she looks for is some kind of a message: this only occurs to her when she remembers that her mother never went out for a second without leaving a message. But this time she had broken with her old habit, evidently; this time there is no scribbled note, which anyway could say no more than: 'I don't know where to, I don't know for how long.'

Then Rosa looks again, this time no longer for a message, simply looks around. Mischa tells me she is a sentimental little thing and wanted to get some idea of what her parents had taken with them. Probably she wept buckets as she did so. The brown-and-white checked shopping bag is missing, as is the black cardboard suitcase, nothing else in the way of containers. Since Rosa knows exactly what had been in the room, she would have been able at the end of her search to draw up a list of what her parents had taken along. Including the album of photos and reviews, the book about Felix Frankfurter's true life.

Her own things lie untouched, among them the ration card, part of which has already expired. Rosa puts it in her pocket; otherwise there are no objects to which she feels especially attached. She forces herself to think in practical terms. A briefcase has been left behind; into it she stuffs her other dress, underwear and stockings, finally her winter coat, wondering as she does so how she can manage to think as far ahead as next winter. With the coat in it, the briefcase won't close. Rosa considers wearing it, but then she would have to unpick the yellow stars from her dress and sew them on the coat. So she crams it as best she can into the briefcase, which she then ties up with the belt from her coat. If she should run into that boy in the street, he will be envious of her rich booty.

Rosa firmly turns off the tap; she is finished here. As she goes she leaves the key in the door, for the boy or anyone else, as if putting paid to her past.

'I'll give you ten guesses,' Mischa says to me, 'but you'll never guess where she went next.'

Rosa goes to see Jakob, whom she doesn't know, except from Mischa's accounts, though from them quite well. Since Bezanika they have never spent an evening together without talking about him, about his radio, his courage, about the Russian successes at the front. At the time, when the first rejoicing over the news reports had subsided, Rosa had asked why this Jakob person had waited until now before beginning to pass on reports; after all, they had been living in the ghetto for three years, and if he was keeping a radio hidden he must have had it from the very beginning.

'Most likely the Germans were advancing all the time until just recently. Was he supposed to tell us that things were getting worse and worse every day?' Mischa answered, and that sounded convincing.

So here she is standing outside his door, not, so she tries to persuade herself, out of any desire for revenge or personal resentment. No doubt he is nice and kind and well meaning, but those reports, day by day more encouraging, and then the empty room in Franziskaner-Strasse, the whole district in fact – she's going to ask him how one can be reconciled with the other. She's going to put it to him, is it permissible to raise such hopes in their situation, don't start telling me about the radio, that can report what it likes, but he had only to look around.

Rosa knocks several times, with no result. Why hadn't it occurred to her earlier that Jakob must come home at about the same time as Mischa? The waiting saps her confidence; by the time she confronts him her head will feel hollow. There is still time for her to leave and get back to their room before Mischa and avoid the argument that is bound to arise if she doesn't. The longer she waits, the more clearly she has to admit to herself that she has come with the vaguest of intentions. Jakob will persist in citing his radio, regardless of what she blames him for. She had hoped to survive these times intact; now things have turned out differently, and that, when one gets right down to it, is her whole reason. 'She plays faster than she thinks,' her father once said after a game of draughts; her father. The thought crosses Rosa's mind that Jakob may be spreading news other than what he hears on his radio.

Suddenly Lina is standing at the end of the corridor, just back from the street and Rafael. She sees a young woman with a bulging briefcase outside a certain door, and she approaches, full of curiosity. They eye each other for a few moments, neither of them suspicious. Lina asks: 'Are you looking for Uncle Jakob?'

'Yes.'

'He should be here soon. Wouldn't you rather wait inside?'

'Do you live here, then?' Rosa asks.

For an answer, Lina takes the key from behind the door frame, unlocks the door, and gestures invitingly and a little proudly. Rosa enters with some hesitation, a chair is promptly pulled out for her, she has fallen into the hands of an attentive hostess. Lina sits down too, and they continue to look at each other, approvingly.

'You're Lina, aren't you?' said Rosa.

'How do you know my name?'

'From Mischa,' says Rosa. 'You're good friends, I hear.'

'Of course. And now I know who you are.'

'Do tell me!'

'You're Rosa. Right?'

They exchange whatever information they have about each other. Lina, incidentally, is still cross with Mischa because the whole time she was ill in bed he didn't come to see her once, just sent his love via Jakob. Rosa looks round surreptitiously – not that she expects the radio to be standing there in full view to regale every chance guest.

'What do you want to see Uncle Jakob about?' Lina asks, any other topic having soon been exhausted.

'Let's wait till he's here.'

'Have you brought a message from Mischa?'

'No.'

'It's all right to tell me. He has no secrets from me.'

But Rosa refuses to budge; she smiles and says nothing. Now Lina tries a roundabout approach.

'Have you ever been here before?' she asks.

'No, never.'

'I mean, lots of people have been coming here lately, and you know what they want?' Lina pauses, to give Rosa a chance to appreciate this special proof of trust, before divulging: 'They want to hear the news. Is that why you're here too?'

Rosa's smile vanishes: she certainly hasn't come for that reason; on the contrary, rather. She already regrets having come at all, has regretted it increasingly from the first moment. She feels she is in the wrong place with her despair; here everything is being done honestly and in good faith. She wonders what she would do if Jakob were to come in now and tell her that the transport with her parents on its way to so-and-so had met up with the liberators. And she dare not give an answer, nor to the second question either: whether she has been deceiving herself all along as to the real reason for her coming. She doesn't exclude the possibility.

'Well?' said Lina. 'Is that why you're here too?'

'No,' says Rosa.

'But you've heard about it?'

'About what?'

'That everything's going to change soon?'

'Yes.'

'So why aren't you glad?'

Rosa sits up straight; the threshold has been reached where one either turns round or speaks the truth, but what is the truth, apart from her misgivings? 'Because I don't believe it,' she says.

'You don't believe what Uncle Jakob has been saying?' Lina asks, in a tone implying that she must have misheard.

'No, I don't.'

'Do you think he's fibbing?'

Rosa likes the word and wouldn't have thought of it in this context. She would quite like to discuss nice things with this nice child. On no account continue in the direction already taken; how could she have done that, with a child? Without any conclusive reasons to offer, she is suddenly convinced that she has made a mistake which, she hopes, will have no bad effects. She can't just calmly get up and leave. So she sits there forlornly, waiting – now no longer for Jakob – but for some convenient opportunity to bring to an end a visit which she now perceives to be wrong. But that opportunity is moving further and further away. After her first shock, Lina becomes almost alarmingly worked up, for her uncle is most certainly not a liar. But Rosa hadn't said that, yes, that's exactly what she has said, how can anyone say such a thing? Since she'd heard for herself on his radio that the Russians will soon be here, with her own ears, what do you say to that? A man with a very deep voice had told that to another man, she can't remember his name but she remembers his voice exactly, word for word he had said that the whole mess would soon be over, in another few weeks at most. Did Rosa think he had been fibbing too, what had got into Rosa anyway, to accuse her uncle of telling lies? Just wait till he came home, *he'd* give her the right answer!

Before she has got it all off her chest in a torrent of verbal indignation, Lina suddenly breaks off and stares past Rosa, with a startled look. Rosa turns her head towards the door: Jakob is standing there, stony faced; no one had noticed the door opening.

Rosa gets up. Regardless of how much or how little he may have heard, she feels he has seen through her, such is the dismay in his eyes. With lowered head she goes to the door, no chance now for a breezy departure; she has put her foot in it. Jakob takes half a step aside for her, but back she must go to the chair for the briefcase lying forgotten on the floor. The whole length of the corridor Rosa doesn't dare look back. But on reaching the stairs she does: Jakob is still standing there motionless, watching her go. Soon the little girl will tell him what he no doubt already knows.

Let us stay with Rosa. She comes out into the street, in the early dusk, where the next unpleasantness is waiting. What meets her eyes is wild excitement, Jews fleeing into hallways, yet again. At first Rosa can't make out why. Then she sees a car approaching, a small, dark-green van with a man in uniform standing on the running board. Without thinking, Rosa dashes the few metres back into Jakob's building, caught up in the panic. She leans against the wall and keeps her eyes closed, then opens them when she hears hurrying footsteps. An old man, gasping for breath, stops beside her, also coming in from the street.

'What do they want?' he asks.

Rosa shrugs her shoulders. The van will drive on and soon be forgotten; the scene with Mischa awaits her. The man assumes that it is a matter for the highest authorities, otherwise they would come on foot, as apparently happens every few days. To their horror there is a screeching of brakes; the frightened old man clutches Rosa's arm so tight that it hurts.

Two men in uniform come into the very hallway they are standing in, leather straps under their chins. The old man clings desperately to Rosa's arm. Outside, the engine has been left running. At first the Germans think they are alone in the semi-darkness, but when they have almost reached the stairs one of them says: 'Look!'

They turn towards the two figures against the wall. Rosa seems to interest them more than the man does, but maybe she is just imagining that. They come a few steps closer, then one of them shakes his head and says: 'No, no.'

The other man tells them: 'Get out of here!'

Then the Germans walk up the stairs, the clatter of their boots alarming the whole building. A door is slammed. Agitated voices sound confusedly from everywhere, though it would have been better to stay calm. A child is crying.

'Come on!' whispers the old man.

Rosa follows him. In the doorway he hesitates, afraid of the van, but they must pass it if they are to obey the German's order.

'Go on, get going!' says Rosa.

They hurry straight across the road, towards the building opposite where the door is already being opened for them from the inside. The old man sits down exhausted on the bottom stair, groaning as if he had run round the entire block and massaging his chest over his heart. Rosa sees three other men and a woman in the hallway, which is even darker than the first one; she doesn't know any of them. She looks towards the door, which is of metal; a fourth man, fairly young, is peering out through the keyhole and reports for the benefit of all.

'Nothing yet,' he says.

'Who are they looking for over there?' the woman asks the old man.

'How would I know?' he says, continuing to massage his left chest.

'Does someone special live there?' asks a bald-headed man.

At first he receives no reply; they are all on their way home from work and strangers in this street, until Rosa says softly: 'They've come for Jakob Heym.'

Who is Jakob Heym, which Jakob Heym? The scout at the keyhole straightens up and asks: 'Jakob Heym? Is he the one with the radio?'

'Yes.'

'Nice mess,' he says, without much sympathy it seems to Rosa, 'it was bound to come out sooner or later.'

At that the old man on the stairs flies into a rage, to Rosa's surprise; he had appeared to be fully occupied with his fear and his heart. Now his veins are swelling. 'Why did he have to be found out, you young pip-squeak? Eh? Why? I can tell you why he was found out. Because somebody ratted on him! That's why! Or do you imagine it happened all by itself?'

The embarrassed pip-squeak submits to this dressing-down without protest. He bends over again to the keyhole and says after a short pause: 'Still nothing.'

The old man summons Rosa to him with a movement of his head and, when she is standing in front of him, moves slightly to one side, so she sits down beside him.

'Do you know him?' he asks.

'Who?'

'That Jakob Heym?'

'No.'

'Then how do you know he lives there?'

'From friends.'

'They're still inside,' the pip-squeak reports. The old man ponders for a few moments in silence, then says in the direction of the door: 'When they bring him out, let me know. I'd like to see what he looks like,' a remark that, right at this moment, Rosa finds in poor taste; then she doesn't.

'He has taken a great risk,' says the old man admiringly, now back again to Rosa, who nods. And wonders what she will tell Mischa now. Let him scold her all he likes about her visit to her old home, she couldn't keep that a secret even if she wanted to; the tell-tale briefcase and ration card would be enough without any confession on her part. But she would rather not mention Jakob; she doesn't dare face Mischa with that, especially after what's happening now. And, bitter as it is, she runs no risk if she doesn't mention her encounter with Jakob: Jakob will be in no position to give her the lie with Mischa.

'Perhaps he isn't even at home,' says the old man.

'He is at home,' Rosa says without thinking.

The old man looks at her in surprise, a question already in his eyes, but before he can voice it the pip-squeak calls from the door: 'You were wrong – they're bringing out a woman!'

Let us permit ourselves a closer look and go out into the street. The woman being led away is Elisa Kirschbaum. She is being made to pay for her brother's incompetence, for the fact that, contrary to expectations, he was unable to cure the Stormtroop leader: it has taken them long enough to think of that.

For some time now, people living in the building have been afraid that events might take such a turn; anyone can put two and two together. Someone had mentioned the hitherto unknown expression 'clan liability' in conversation. The very evening of the day when the station flag was flying at half-mast, Jakob had gone to see Elisa Kirschbaum. He had put it to her that it might be better for her to go into hiding with friends she undoubtedly had, at least for the time being, until it became clear whether the threatened reprisals would actually be carried out. For, however painful it might be, one must assume the worst for her brother, and if by some miracle he should, in spite of everything, return unharmed, Jakob promised to let her know at once. But she wanted none of all that and told Jakob: 'It's very kind of you, my dear Mr Heym. But let that be my worry.' As if she still held a trump card that nobody suspected.

Now she is walking ahead of the two Germans, briskly so there can be no excuse for pushing or touching her. And briskly also, as Jakob behind the window suspects, so as not to offer any spectacle to the street which, although apparently deserted, is full of hidden eyes. The display of concentrated power being exuded by the two men behind her appears excessive for so frail a prisoner. Elisa Kirschbaum stops behind the van without looking round at her escorts. One of them lets down the tailgate, on the inside of which is a narrow step. Just as she is about to put her foot on it the van moves forward, and Elisa Kirschbaum steps into a void and falls onto the street. The van is merely making a U-turn so it can wait on the other side of the street; the driver has already stuck his head out of the window in preparation.

Jakob's vantage point is not near enough for him to make out the expressions of the participants. People living closer by report later that the Germans had grinned as if at an oft-repeated practical joke. Elisa Kirschbaum gets up immediately, with surprising agility; she is on her feet again, waiting, before the van has completed its turn, for which it has to make two attempts. Then she climbs in; it is rather high for her, and in spite of all her efforts she is given a shove. The two Germans also climb into the back, the tailgate is pulled up, Elisa Kirschbaum has finally disappeared behind the dark-green tarpaulin. The van drives off, and after a safe interval many of the front doors open. The narrow pavements gradually fill up again with people, some silent, some debating, most of them on their way home from work, as we already know, and strangers to this street.

M eanwhile, according to the radio the Red Army has advanced to the outskirts of the district town of Pry. Pry is not to be compared with Bezanika; anyone can visualize Pry, no one has to ask where in the world Pry is. Pry is exactly one hundred and forty-six kilometres away from us; most of the local inhabitants know the little town from occasional visits. A few have even lived there and were moved here after the outbreak of the war, for due to its fortunate population structure Pry has no ghetto of its own.

The position of the Russians becomes the subject of an argument. Kowalski has a quarrel with his three room-mates, whose names I don't know. Now, as both the easy-going Jakob and I have good reason to know, it is the simplest thing in the world to disagree with Kowalski, but in this particular case one is inclined to agree with him. The issue is no trivial one: what is involved is that this one man, for simplicity's sake let us call him Abraham, this Abraham claims that the Russians have already passed through Pry on their way to Mieloworno. Someone at his factory, let us assume the brickworks, has said so. Kowalski, on the other hand, swears up and down that they haven't even reached Pry. But Abraham sees no reason whatever to believe Kowalski more than his fellow worker.

'Who's working at the railway station?' Kowalski asks angrily. 'You or me? Who hears everything first hand? You or me?'

For Abraham this is no valid proof, presumably because his version sounds so much better than Kowalski's. Anyone can make a mistake, he says. Nor will he accept the logical objection that whatever this mysterious fellow worker at the brickworks claims to know must, in some way or other, originate with Jakob.

'Or are you suggesting there is another radio?'

'How should I know?' says Abraham.

It might not matter to Kowalski – let Abraham think what he likes, let him be taken in like a naïve child by crude rumours – except that somehow he feels partially responsible for the truth. For the radio is, in a way, also his radio, given his long-standing friendship with Jakob, as strong today as it ever was, the radio had actually come within an ace of landing in his room, at the time of the power failure. So he patiently explains the long route that every news item has to take from Jakob's mouth to the factory, via so many people, the dangers it is exposed to along the way, dangers of mutilation and enhancement. How everyone adds something to it, turns something good into something better, which means the news finally arrives, as it turns out, in such shape that even its own creator won't recognize it.

'Anyway, the Russians are on their way to Mieloworno,' Abraham says stubbornly. 'Maybe you got it wrong, or he got it wrong. You'd better ask him again tomorrow.'

Kowalski doesn't ask Jakob tomorrow; excuses for a leisurely chat with Jakob are scarce enough, so Kowalski goes to Jakob then and there.

He finds him in the worst possible shape: weary, apathetic, taciturn. Half an hour ago they took Elisa Kirschbaum away.

'Am I intruding?' Kowalski asks, conjuring a smile that, as soon as he has peered into Jakob's face, he feels is all wrong.

'It's you,' says Jakob. After closing the door behind Kowalski, he lies down fully dressed on the bed, where he obviously had already been lying before the knock at the door. He clasps his hands behind his head and stares at the ceiling. Kowalski wonders what has suddenly got into him. Only a little while ago, on their way back from the station, he had still seemed quite cheerful, if one may even use the word 'cheerful' in these times.

'Has something happened?' asks Kowalski.

Happened or not happened: Jakob feels a strange new weakness, alarmingly sudden. Before, on his way down from the attic, where he had gone up with Lina, he had had to hold on to the banister. He has tried to account for this new condition with that perpetual hunger, but that could explain only the trembling of his knees, scarcely the origin of that other weakness, equally tormenting, his sense of discouragement. This is what he is now attempting to analyse while staring at the ceiling, trying to dissuade himself from minimizing it; it is too massive and weighty for that. The incident with Elisa Kirschbaum was probably only a small component; it had unquestionably shaken Jakob, but it would be too much to describe it as *the* experience which robbed Jakob of his courage from one minute to the next. Certainly of greater impact was Rosa's visit, having to hear Lina defending him with lies, with his own weapons, although even that visit should not be held wholly responsible, either, for Jakob's dwindling powers. It is a number of things coming together from all sides – mainly, perhaps, just contemplating the situation all round. More and more often someone takes you aside and says, Jakob, Jakob, I can no longer believe this will end well, and by the time you have offered one person some modest consolation by way of the very latest news, there are already six other people waiting to tell you the same thing. According to the radio, the Russians are exerting pressure on Pry; God alone knows who they are really exerting pressure on, or who is exerting pressure on them. According to the radio, one should soon be able to see the first artillery flashes in the distance, but day after day all you ever see is the same scene, that repulsive desolation. You will gradually have to consider some withdrawal tactics, for in your enthusiasm you have allowed the advance to proceed at a speed that unfortunately won't stand up to grim reality.

And Kowalski stands around idly, waiting in vain for an inviting look.

'Do you want me to go away again?' he asks after an appropriate interval, and sits down.

Jakob remembers that he has a visitor; he abandons the ceiling and says: 'Sorry, I'm not feeling too good.'

'Has something happened?'

'Yes and r⌐,' says Jakob. 'They've just taken Kirschbaum's sister away. But aட ⌐rt from that, I'm beginning to feel my age.'

'Kirschbaum's sister? After all this time?'

'Yes, just imagine.'

Jakob gets up; his ears buzz with suspicious signals, and these are combined with giddiness and nausea. All he needs now is to become seriously ill. From quite far away he hears Kowalski saying: 'Are you all right?'

He quickly sits down at the table; fortunately he begins to feel better. He thinks of Lina and what is to become of her and that it's preferable to stay well. And when he finally looks at Kowalski he is reminded of a little cardboard sign, a little white sign with green lettering: 'Closed temporarily due to illness'. He got it from Lajb Pachman when he bought the shop from him, together with a lot of other stuff in the inventory. Only once did he ever use it, during all those twenty years spent over potato pancakes, ice-cream and comparatively minor worries, only once did the little sign hang on the shop door. And it wasn't even a proper illness, Jakob having the constitution of an ox: while trying to repair a stuck blind he had fallen off the ladder and broken a leg. The best health in the world is of no help there. That had been long before Josefa Litwin's time; she could have been very useful as a nurse, but in the event he was looked after by a wizened old witch from the building across the courtyard. For money, of course, since he had no one else. But as for looking after him, all she did was push the table with his meals close enough for him to feed himself, occasionally empty the ashtray and air the room, and in the mornings straighten the bed. Beyond that, all she did was say: 'And if there's anything else you need, Reb Heym, just call me, I'll leave my window open.' Jakob took her up on this once or twice, but either she had closed her window or she was as hard of hearing as an old mule. And every second or third evening Kowalski would drop in with a small bottle and express his sympathy for Jakob having to lie there with his leg in a splint, unable to move. Would sit there until the bottle was empty, neither of them being great conversationalists. Jakob thanked God that the fracture healed without complications. A few days longer, and the boredom would have killed him. And shortly after that he threw the blameless little sign into the stove, watching with grim enjoyment as it was consumed by the flames. The threat had such a lasting effect that to this day he has never again had to be confined to bed.

'Are you sure you don't want me to leave?' asks Kowalski, at the end of his patience and interrupting Jakob's thoughts.

'Don't go,' says Jakob.

Kowalski looks at him with raised eyebrows. He has a feeling that Jakob intends to tell him something, most likely nothing good to judge by the past few minutes and the sluggish introduction. Yet all he had had in mind was a completely innocent visit, for on his way here he had decided not to bother about a confirmation regarding Pry, an error being out of the question – that fellow Abraham must have been hoodwinked by a busybody. He had merely wanted to drop by

182

and say hello and talk a bit about the old days and the days to come, with whom else if not with his only old friend, if he doesn't come to you, you come to him.

'What do you think, Kowalski, how much can a person endure?'

So he wants to philosophize, Kowalski must be thinking. He waits for a clarification of the question, for it to be narrowed down in one direction or another, but Jakob appears to have asked it in quite a general sense. 'Well?' he says. 'What do you think?'

'If you put it like that,' Kowalski replies, 'a lot. An awful lot.'

'But there is a limit.'

'Of course. . . .'

'I'm sorry,' says Jakob, 'but I have now reached that limit. Perhaps someone else could have gone on longer, but I simply can't.'

'What can't you?'

'I can't go on,' says Jakob.

Kowalski lets him take his time. He doesn't know that Jakob is preparing an unconditional surrender, the worst of all admissions. He sees only Jakob's gaunt face, propped on his hands, maybe a bit paler than usual, possibly a bit more weary, but it's still the face of that same Jakob he knows better than anyone else. He is worried, because such attacks of melancholy are completely foreign to Jakob; he can be grouchy and quarrelsome at times, but that's different. He's never been known to moan, moaning is what all the others do, whereas Jakob has been something of a spiritual comforter. Quite often, whether consciously or not, one went to him for one's own weaknesses to be exorcised. Even before the days of the radio, actually even before the days of the ghetto. At the end of a particularly foul day, after standing from early morning to late evening behind the shop window, watching in vain for customers, or when some enormous bill arrived and one hadn't the slightest idea out of which pocket it was to be paid: where did one go that evening? To Jakob's shop, but not because his schnapps tasted any better. It was the same schnapps as anywhere else, besides being illegal because it was served without a licence. One went there because afterwards the world looked just a bit rosier, because Jakob could say something like 'Chin up', or 'Things are going to be all right', with just a bit more conviction than other people. But also because he alone among one's scanty acquaintances made the effort to say such things. Kowalski lets him take his time.

Now Jakob starts to speak: judging by appearances, to Kowalski, there being no one else in the room; judging by the words, to a larger audience, that's to say just thinking out loud, into the room, with a wistfulness in his low voice and that new tone of resignation, the last of an extravagant diversity of messages to everyone. That, if their vanishing strength permits it, they shouldn't be angry with him: the fact is, he doesn't have a radio, he has never possessed one. Furthermore, he doesn't know where the Russians are, maybe they will come tomorrow, maybe they will never come, they are in Pry or in Tobolin or in Kiev or in Poltawa or still farther away, maybe by this time they have suffered a crushing defeat, he doesn't even know that much. The only thing he can say with certainty is that so-and-so many days ago they were fighting at Bezanika. How can he be so sure? That's a whole separate story, no longer of interest to anyone, but at least that is the truth. And he can well imagine how devastating this confession must sound to their ears, so once again his plea for forbearance, he had only acted for the best, but his plans went awry.

Then there is a long silence in the room as if a king had abdicated. Jakob tries in vain to discover some emotion in Kowalski's face, but Kowalski looks straight through him and sits there like a pillar of salt. Needless to say, Jakob feels pangs of conscience the moment he comes to the end of his speech. Not because of the message itself, which was overdue and could no longer be delayed, but mightn't he have conveyed it more gently, perhaps tucked in with a Russian retreat, instead of shifting the whole load all at once onto other shoulders, shoulders no broader than his own? Was he sure Kowalski had been the right man in whose presence the curtain had to be rung down, Kowalski of all people? If he had heard it from a stranger, or from someone not that close to Jakob, he would undoubtedly have taken it for an error or spiteful slander. After a night filled with doubts he would have said to you: 'Do you know what those idiots are telling each other? That you haven't got a radio!' 'That's true,' the answer would then have been, which would also have hurt him but perhaps less so because during the previous night he would have at least considered the possibility. And it could somehow have been arranged like that, exactly like that; it was Kowalski's bad luck that he had to turn up this very evening.

'You're not saying anything?' says Jakob.

'What can I say.'

From unfathomable depths Kowalski brings his smile to the surface; without this smile he would not be Kowalski. He looks at Jakob again. Although his eyes smile less than his mouth, they still do not proclaim the end of all hope. They have more of a sly look, as if this time too, as always, they could see beyond appearances.

'What can I say, Jakob? I do understand you, I understand you very well. You know, I'm what you might call the opposite of a hero, you've known me long enough. If I'd had a radio here, I don't suppose a single soul would ever have heard a word. Or more likely still, fear would have simply made me throw it in the fire, I have no illusions about that. To keep an entire ghetto supplied with news! I would never have gone that far – how does one know who else is listening? If I have ever in my life understood anybody, I can understand you now.'

Jakob could not have expected such a flight of fancy; cunning old Kowalski has surpassed himself, has even made his calculations where there was nothing to calculate. How are you going to convince him that at least now you are telling the truth? All you can do is suggest that he ransack every nook and cranny in this room and the cellar. But to protest with upturned palms, 'When did I ever lie to you?' – that you can no longer do. And if you actually do urge him to search the place and tell him that whatever radios you find here, Kowalski, you can keep, he will give you a knowing wink and respond with something like, 'Let's not play games, Jakob, haven't we known each other for forty years?' He will intimate that any attempt at hide-and-seek is a waste of time. The impossible can never be proved. Jakob, alarmed, says: 'You don't believe me?'

'Believe, disbelieve, what is the difference?' says Kowalski in a low voice and more absently than expected, in a tone similar to Jakob's just now in his little speech to all. That's all he says for the time being, as his fingers drum a measured theme on the table, his head tilted back, sunk in private thoughts.

Jakob considers further ways of justifying himself. It means a lot to him that he be judged with leniency, and for that the reasons for his actions must be known, as well as the reasons for the sudden cessation. But these are still not entirely clear to himself; and because of this, and because he realizes that not only his standing but Kowalski's, too, is at stake in all this, he says nothing and saves his request for extenuating circumstances for some later date.

This is followed by the sobering thought that his own standing is not at stake at all; no one in the ghetto is less important than he, without a radio. The only people who matter are his recipients, Kowalski among a great many others. And they couldn't care less about excuses, however plausible; they have other worries, and not minor ones either – they want to know, for instance, what is going to happen now after Pry.

Kowalski stops his drumming and brooding, gets up, and places a friendly hand on Jakob's shoulder. 'Don't worry, old man,' he says. 'You're safe with me. I won't ask you any more.'

He goes to the door, reviving his smile. Before opening the door he turns round once more and actually winks with both eyes.

'And I'm not angry with you.'

And leaves.

Next morning, after the most sleepless night for a long time, Jakob is on his way to work. Before stepping out into the street he had furtively pressed down the handle of Kirschbaum's door, for whatever reason, but the door was locked. Horowitz, his neighbour caught him at the unrevealing keyhole and asked: 'Are you looking for something in particular?'

Of course Jakob hadn't been looking for anything in particular, just looking, human curiosity, and with a vague explanation to Horowitz he left. Then there had been that iridescent patch in front of the building, on the road, where the small German van had stood yesterday. A few drops of oil had seeped from it and were now gleaming in thin streaks on the dwindling remains of a reservoir deposited there by Siegfried and Rafael, first by way of their rolled-up shorts, then, when their sources had dried up, with the aid of a bucket of water. They had set to work immediately after Elisa Kirschbaum's departure, for with so little motor traffic such opportunities were few and far between. Jakob had still been at the window observing them with Lina, who was disgusted at the boys' indecency.

But back to Jakob on his way to work: from a distance he can already see a fair-sized crowd at a street corner, right in front of the building where Kowalski lives. Jakob's first thought is that Kowalski must be at the centre of the crowd; his best friend will have come out into the street and, true to his nature, been unable to keep his mouth shut. Either, in thinking it over last night, he has come to the conclusion after all that he has been told the truth, or, as is more likely with Kowalski, he still doesn't believe it but outwardly pretends to do so, for true friendship means sticking together. Has come out of the building and has lost no time in scaring the Jews to death with his dire news, since he must at all costs be the first; whether on the road to hell or to paradise, Kowalski always in the lead. Has thereby cut off all one's paths of retreat – not that, after giving it much thought, one meant to take any such path, but what business was that of Kowalski's?

Jakob feels inclined to turn back, he tells me, and to make a short detour; it's going to be hard enough anyway, they'll give him a gruelling time at the station. Let Kowalski cope with this on his own, that's his problem, this is a good opportunity to stay out of it. Now Jakob notices, while still some way off, that those people are hardly speaking, yet surely they should be agitated after the presumed revelation. As he approaches he sees that most of them are standing in shocked silence. Some are looking up at an open window which, at first sight, does not seem to have anything unusual about it, being merely empty and open. Jakob is not quite sure whether it is Kowalski's window or the one next to it. But on looking closer he does see what is unusual: a short piece of rope, fastened to the crossbar of the window and no longer than a finger, hence unnoticed until now.

Jakob, forcing his way through the crowd, dashes into the building. He tries to take two stairs at a time but manages only the first two; luckily Kowalski lives only one floor up. The door is open, like the window, so there is a draught. Kowalski's three neighbours, one of whom we arbitrarily called Abraham, are not at home. Only Kowalski is at home, and two complete strangers are in the room, the first passers-by to have seen him hanging. They have cut him down and laid him on the bed; now they are standing about helplessly, not knowing what to do next. One of them asks Jakob: 'Did you know him?'

'What?' Jakob asks, standing by the bed.

'I said, Did you know him?'

'Yes,' says Jakob.

When after a while he turns round, he is alone; they have closed the door. Jakob walks to the window and looks out into the street: nothing left of the crowd, only people walking past. He tries to shut the window, but it jams: first he has to remove the rope with its double knot from the crossbar. Then he draws the curtain shut; in the subdued light, Kowalski's face seems easier to bear. He pulls up a chair, not wanting to sit on the bed, and sits down for an indefinite period. I say indefinite because later he is unable to tell me anything about how long he stayed there.

The sight of a dead person is far from unfamiliar to Jakob; it is not uncommon to have to step over somebody, a victim of starvation, lying on the pavement and not yet removed by the clean-up squad. But Kowalski is not just somebody, dear God, no he isn't. Kowalski is Kowalski. A confession has resulted in his death, a confession, moreover, that he pretended not to believe. You crazy fool, why didn't you stay on last night? We would have had a calm discussion about everything and scraped up that little bit of courage needed to go on living. Haven't we scraped up enough together, rightfully or wrongfully? If it works, no one asks how it was done. Why did you have to behave like a poker player on your last evening? We could have helped one another, but only you knew what was going on inside both of us, you hid from your friend Jakob Heym, you showed me a false face, yet we could have gone on living, Kowalski, we could have managed.

By profession a barber, had some money stashed away, as we know, intending to change his life one day but would probably have gone on being a barber; was equipped with various questionable attributes, was suspicious, quirky, awkward, garrulous, too clever by half, but, all in all, with hindsight, suddenly endearing. Once rescued Jakob from a horrendous situation, from a German privy, subscribed to the *Völkischer Kurier* for the advertisements, could sometimes put away seven large potato pancakes at a sitting but couldn't tolerate ice-cream, would rather borrow than pay back, wanted to seem calculating but wasn't like that at all, except once.

As is to be expected, self-reproaches are whirling round in Jakob's head: that he had Kowalski on his conscience, that he with his petty fatigue was to blame for Kowalski's resorting to the rope, once one starts something one has to see it through, one has to estimate one's strength in advance. Here I interrupted Jakob and told him: 'You're talking nonsense. You didn't overestimate your strength because you had no way of knowing that it would go on so long.' And I told him: 'The point is not that you're to blame for Kowalski's death but that he has to thank you for having stayed alive up to that day.' 'Yes, I know,' was Jakob's response, 'but none of that helps.'

Finally Jakob gets up. He pulls the curtain aside again and, when he goes, leaves the door wide open so that one of the neighbours returning from work will see what has happened and do the necessary. It is far too late to go to the station; one can hardly tell the sentry at the gate that one was delayed on the way, and there'll definitely be no midday meal for him today. Jakob goes home, his only hope being that Kowalski kept his reasons to himself, that for once he held his tongue. For Jakob has rediscovered his radio.

N o matter how often Jakob rediscovers, reports, invents battles and circulates them, there is one thing he cannot prevent: inexorably the story approaches its infamous ending. Or rather, it has two endings; actually, of course, only one, the one experienced by Jakob and the rest of us, but for me it also has another ending. Without wishing to boast, I know an ending that could make a person turn pale with envy; not exactly a happy one, somewhat at Jakob's expense, yet incomparably more satisfactory than the real ending. I devised it over the years. I said to myself, What a terrible pity for such a beautiful story to peter out so miserably. Find a halfway satisfactory ending for it, one that will hold water; a decent ending allows many a weakness to be forgotten. Besides, they all deserved a better ending, not only Jakob, and that will be your justification, in case you need one. That's what I told myself, and so I spared no effort – successfully, if you ask me. But then I was beset by misgivings as to its veracity; by comparison it simply sounded too good, and I asked myself whether attaching a peacock's magnificent tail to some miserable animal, merely out of love, has any hope of success, whether that wouldn't be just creating a monster. Then it seemed to me a weak comparison, but I never could make up my mind. And now here I am with the two endings, not knowing which one to tell, mine or the ugly one. Until it occurs to me to get both off my chest, not because I lack decisiveness but merely because I think that this way we will both have our say. On the one hand the story that is independent of me and, on the other, myself with all the effort I would like not to have made in vain.

So, first the ending that never happened.

Kowalski is allowed to celebrate his resurrection; he completely ignores crossbar and rope, Jakob having foregone his confession. The evening in question they chat about irrelevant things, although

Jakob has something else on his mind. However, Kowalski needn't be aware of that. Only later, when he is alone again, does Jakob realize that it is beyond his dwindling strength to carry on with the radio lies, especially with no end in sight. Nevertheless, the true state of affairs must not come to light. Jakob imagines the consequences that would have: he might have to fear, for example, that the series of suicides, which for some time has mercifully been at a standstill, would flare up again and increase by leaps and bounds.

The following nights – which, of course, are now free because he need not reproach himself with Kowalski's death – Jakob spends trying to come up with a final credible lie. Its purpose is to explain why the radio has stopped playing; he has to get rid of this worst of all torments, but the lie simply won't come to him. It is proving harder to find than all the others.

I imagine for a moment that Jakob might have hit upon the obvious idea of announcing that the radio had been stolen from him. A lot of things are stolen in the ghetto, why not a radio too? Objects of less value and usefulness have gone missing. I imagine an entire ghetto hunting for the unscrupulous thief. People eye each other suspiciously; visits are now made only to camouflage inspections. In the evening each person listens at the door of his neighbour – perhaps he has just tuned in to the BBC, perhaps he is this contemptible person: hasn't there always been a strange look in his eyes that your inner voice warned you about? Only one thing is a mystery: what advantage does the thief derive from his crime? None at all; even now he won't find out any more than he would have heard anyway from Jakob or one of the intermediaries. Just that the rest of us are left groping in the dark: what sense is there in that? How else can one explain his motives than by a thoroughly evil disposition? I go on to imagine that the search for the thief assumes alarming proportions, that a sort of illegal committee is formed which combs through the ghetto building by building after work. And let us assume that, among the several thousand inhabitants, there is one other person like Felix Frankfurter, just one, who also keeps a radio hidden and, unlike Frankfurter, has not destroyed it.

I am well aware that this one person would present a problem for the whole story; for either, like Frankfurter, he was always too scared to listen, or he did listen and must therefore know that Jakob's daily reports were a tissue of lies, except for the battle of Bezanika. And all this time said nothing. However unlikely either of these two possibilities may be, let us accept one or other of them for the next three sentences, since that person is a mere figment of my imagination, an ephemeral fancy. During the search the radio is discovered at his place; he is killed by the enraged searchers, a fine fancy one might say, or he isn't killed, it's of no consequence. The radio is taken to Jakob, the rightful owner: just the thought of his face is worth the whole idea. Now things resume their normal course, Jakob listens and reports, and for days the talk continues to be of the outrageous incident, how any person can behave so despicably, for no good reason.

But enough of that. Jakob doesn't come up with the idea of the theft, neither in the actual ending, which surprises me, nor in mine. In mine, no matter how hard he tries he can't rid himself of the radio, so he decides to rid himself of the Jews. He stops receiving visitors, simply doesn't open the door; at the station he goes off by himself to eat his midday soup near the Germans' brick building, where he can't be asked anything. And as soon as work is over he vanishes like a ghost, even taking the long way round so as to dodge those lying in wait for him. Now and again he does get waylaid, in spite of all precautions, and he is asked what has suddenly got into him, why he's stopped telling them anything.

'There's no news,' he says then. 'Don't worry, if there is any I'll tell you.'

Or, even more effective, he'll say: 'It's become too dangerous for me, I don't want to run any risk so close to the end. Do me a favour and stop asking me.'

This doesn't make him exactly popular; there are only a few who feel for him in his situation, and yesterday's great man rapidly declines in prestige. He's called a coward and a bastard, also because he stubbornly refuses to hand over the radio to someone else, someone with more guts. Soon glances come his way that could scare a person; words are whispered behind his back that are better not heard, but Jakob sticks to his guns. Let them look upon him as the wicked one, he would feel exactly the same in their place, never mind if they take every opportunity of letting him know the taste of contempt: anything is better than telling them the truth.

Not that he has been entirely deserted by well-wishers. I would think that Kowalski and Mischa remain faithful. Mischa goes on carrying crates with him, and Kowalski says sometimes, although less often than before: 'Well, what's new, old man? Surely you can give *me* a little hint? No one need notice.'

Jakob always refuses, even if it means losing his oldest friend. He doesn't lose him; Kowalski proves to be a tenacious friend.

One day Mischa says: 'Jakob, I hate to tell you this, but they're talking about taking away your radio.'

'Taking it away?'

'Yes,' says Mischa gravely. 'By force.'

Jakob looks across to the others. So there are one or two among them who are prepared to resort to intimidation; Jakob doesn't want to know who it is.

'Can't you stop them?' he asks.

'How?' asks Mischa. 'I'd be glad to. But can you tell me how?'

'Tell them I've hidden it so well that they'll never find it,' says Jakob.

'I'll tell them,' says Mischa.

At home Jakob strictly forbids Lina to be in his room when he is not there. As a precaution he no longer leaves the key in the hole in the wall behind the door frame, not for Lina and not for anybody. As far as possible she is to remain in her attic and stay put. To offset her boredom he lets her take the book about Africa upstairs; she can use it to learn to read, which will do her more good than hanging around doing nothing.

The next few days prove to be a strenuous test of Jakob's sorely tried nerves. Twiddling his thumbs he has to sit still and wait, for liberators and intruders, in both cases uncertain whether they will come or not. Mischa tells him he has no idea whether the opposition has changed its mind; ever since his loyalty to Jakob has been noticed, in spite of all that has happened, ever since he has offered his services as a go-between, he has been excluded from the deliberations. Moreover, something of the general contempt has rubbed off on him too. The same goes for Kowalski.

I have not given any thought to my own attitude in this matter, on whose side I am, whether I am Jakob's friend or enemy. But knowing myself, and considering how much the steady flow of information has meant to me, I would say I am his enemy, one of the worst, in fact. Let us assume that I strongly plead that no one be confused by all this talk, that the sooner his radio is taken away the better. Many people share my view, but there are also some Jews who think differently and want to be heard – those, for example, who right from the start have regarded the radio as a danger. Basically they are delighted with Jakob's change of heart. 'What's all the fuss about?' they say. 'If the Russians come at all, they'll come, radio or no radio.' And others again say: 'Let's hold our horses, maybe Heym will come to his senses. We must give him a little more time.'

In any event, the break-in does not take place, not in my ending.

These bad days are a test of Jakob's nerves in another respect, too. At some point he has to acknowledge that he has clung to what is by now almost an old habit, that once again he has overestimated his own strength. He was convinced that the wave of hostility, which he obviously had to count on, would not affect him very much, that he could survive it intact. He found encouragement in the thought that he was experienced in such matters, that all his years in the shop had, after all, been little more than a struggle of one against all. That was a facile and mistaken conclusion. What Jakob overlooked was the period after Bezanika during which he had been showered with good will, affection and respect, with every indication that he was indispensable, to all of which one becomes accustomed with absurd rapidity. And now the exact opposite: after ten days at most, that wave of hostility threatens to engulf him; the cold shoulders become unbearable.

Lina notices changes in Jakob that she cannot account for. Because she obediently heeds his instructions and keeps to her attic, she hears nothing. She merely notices that, whenever Jakob is with her, he sinks into a gloomy abstraction, hardly speaks, doesn't even show the proper surprise when she reads out a whole sentence from the Africa book, unaided. Whenever she sits on his lap she might as well be sitting on a chair, and only a short while ago he would gladly take her on his knees. Now he seems not to notice her at all. When she asks him for a story he says he can't think of any and puts her off till such time as he remembers one.

'Are you angry about something?' Lina asks.

'Angry? Why angry?'

'Because you're so queer.'

'Me, queer?' says Jakob, lacking the strength to avoid an unmerited sharpness in his voice. 'Look after your own business and don't bother me.'

Lina continues to be mostly alone and has very little to look after – except Jakob, to whom something incomprehensible must have happened.

One important evening in my ending, shortly after the first of the month because that is when the ration cards are always distributed, Jakob knocks on Mischa's door. He has to wait a while before it is cautiously opened. Mischa says in surprise: 'Jakob?'

Jakob enters the room. The first thing he says is: 'If you really want to hide her you shouldn't leave two cups on the table, you donkey.'

'You're right,' says Mischa.

He goes to the wardrobe and lets Rosa out. Rosa and Jakob stand facing each other wordlessly, until at length Mischa finds the situation embarrassing.

'Do you two know each other?' he asks.

'We once saw each other very briefly,' says Jakob.

'Won't you sit down?' Rosa says quickly, with a smile, before Mischa can ask about that once. Jakob sits down and looks for a way to begin, for he hasn't just dropped in: what he has in mind is quite a tall order.

'The reason I'm here,' he says, 'I want to ask you a favour, and if you say No I'll fully understand. I just couldn't think of anyone else to turn to.'

'I'm listening,' says Mischa.

'The thing is, these last few days I've been feeling rotten. Physically, I mean. I'm not as young as I was, my heart's starting to act up, so's my back, and my head aches all the time – it's rather sudden and a bit much all at once.'

Mischa still can't think what kind of a favour it could be and says: 'That's bad.'

'Well, not that bad really, it'll pass. But until it does, Mischa, I was wondering whether you could take Lina in for a while.'

The general awkwardness results in a pause, during which Jakob doesn't look up; probably he's expecting a bit too much of the young man. Two illegal womenfolk in his room; but after all Jakob did say he wouldn't blame him if he refused.

'Well, you know,' Mischa says slowly, his intention being quite clear.

'Of course you can bring Lina here,' says Rosa, with a reproachful look at Mischa.

'I would never have come to you if you'd been alone,' Jakob tells the unhappy Mischa. 'But since Miss Frankfurter is here all day, and Lina is always alone too. . . .'

'I'm looking forward to having her,' says Rosa.

'How about you?'

'He's looking forward to it too,' says Rosa.

Mischa gives himself time to rearrange his expression – they all know he isn't exactly happy. 'All right,' he says, 'bring her here.'

Relieved, Jakob puts the ration card down on the table; it is intact except for one coupon, so Mischa need no longer fear that Jakob is also demanding full board, free of charge.

'When can I bring her?'

'When did you have in mind?'

'Tomorrow evening?' asks Jakob.

Although Jakob assures him that it is entirely unnecessary, Mischa accompanies him for a few steps out into the street. When Jakob holds out his hand to say goodnight and Mischa keeps it in his a shade longer than necessary, Jakob detects a vital question in Mischa's blue eyes. Mischa is absolutely right, Jakob concludes, one good turn deserves another, especially when it is sought so modestly.

'You'd like to know what the situation is?' he asks.

'If you don't mind,' says Mischa.

Jakob divulges that Pry has meanwhile been taken but that half-way to Mieloworno the Germans have established a fortified line which will be fought over for quite some time, it appears, but which has already been breached at several points, this in turn leaving room for hope. And he asks Mischa to keep this news to himself, otherwise there'll only be endless questions at the freight yard, why is one person told and all the others are not. Mischa promises, no doubt hoping for further periodic news items. That is how I account for his tactics.

The following evening Lina moves. Jakob has given her the same reason as he gave Mischa, a separation for only a few days, and Lina accepts it calmly enough. After all, she is fond of Mischa, it's almost a secret love, and he is presumably fond of her too, only that Rosa woman sticks in her gullet because of that visit and those reproaches – she might have some trouble with her. But Jakob again assures her on the way to Mischa's that Rosa is very easy to get along with, helpful and kind, that only last evening she had told him she was looking forward to having Lina. It would be best not to say a word about that stupid visit the other day.

'You're a big girl now, so don't disgrace me.'

After delivering Lina, Jakob goes straight home, ostensibly to lie down. For a long time he sits in the dark room, brooding over whether his decision, for the sake of which Lina had to leave, is justified. He doesn't want to have to reproach himself later, if there is a later; he has made enough wrong decisions recently. To have the Russians come almost within sight was a mistake, to discontinue the radio broadcasts was a mistake, the radio itself was the first and biggest mistake, it seems to him: too many mistakes for one man. There is still a chance of undoing some of that, to get back to the old routine. In three or four days he could feel better, illnesses of this kind can be cured at will, then he could bring Lina back, play the part of the converted at the station, and go on supplying reports, both good and bad, to the news-hungry, but where would that all lead, Jakob wonders?

After a couple of hours, I imagine, Jakob has made up his mind. He hangs the cloth in front of the window, turns on the light, then picks up a knife, takes off his jacket and removes the yellow stars from front and back. He does this very carefully, even unpicking the little white threads so they won't betray the infamous places. That done, Jakob puts on the jacket, which now seems strangely denuded. His eyes roam the room for objects that might be useful for his undertaking: the pliers, of course, which he puts in his pocket. Nothing else catches his eye, so he turns out the light and gives a last look out of the window, into the black, deserted street. It is long past eight o'clock and curfew time, probably already midnight. In the distance he might, if you like, recognize his searchlight as it ranges duty-obsessed and aimlessly over the roofs.

Since there are no limits to my arbitrary inventions, I say that it is a cold and starry night. Not only does that sound pleasing, it also comes in handy for my ending, as we shall see. Accordingly, Jakob, without his yellow stars and long after eight o'clock, walks along the street, or rather, he slinks along close to the buildings, trying to resemble a shadow; after all, he has no intention of forfeiting his life. One street, and another, and yet another: what they all have in common is that they represent the shortest route to the boundary of the ghetto.

Then the boundary. I have chosen the most favourable spot of all, the old vegetable market, a small cobbled square with barbed wire drawn across it. Previous escape attempts have succeeded or failed almost invariably at this place. To the right, at the very end of the square, is the watch-tower, this one without a searchlight. The sentry on top doesn't move while Jakob observes him from a doorway on the far left side. The distance may amount to a hundred and fifty metres. Along the whole length of the barbed wire, which surrounds the entire ghetto without a gap, there is no other spot that far from a watch-tower. Only here have they left that much space, either for the sake of economy or because of the unimpeded view.

On the tower all is as quiet as on a monument, so that Jakob is already beginning to hope that the sentry has fallen asleep. Jakob looks up at the sky, waiting prudently until one of the few clouds drifts across the inconvenient moon. When the cloud finally does him the favour, Jakob takes the pliers out of his pocket and starts running.

Let us pause briefly at this highly dramatic moment in my ending, to give me a chance to admit that I cannot provide the reason for Jakob's sudden flight. In other words: I don't take the easy way out and declare: 'In my ending he just wants to escape, that's all.' Obviously I am in a position to offer several reasons, all of which I consider plausible; I just don't know which one to choose. For instance: Jakob has given up all hope of the ghetto being liberated while there are any Jews still left in it and therefore decides to save his own skin. Or: he is fleeing from his own people, from their persecution and hostility, and from their thirst for news too, an attempt to find a refuge from the radio and its consequences. Or a third reason, for Jakob the most creditable one: he has the daring plan of returning to the ghetto some time during the following night; he only wants to get out now so as to obtain some useful information to feed through his radio.

Those would be the chief reasons. None of them to be ruled out, one must admit, but I can't bring myself to commit Jakob to any one of them. So I offer them as a selection; let each reader choose the one which, according to his own experience, he finds the most valid. Maybe some readers will come up with even more plausible ones. I merely wish to remind them that almost anything of importance that has ever happened has had more than one reason.

Under cover of the cloud Jakob reaches the barbed wire unobserved. He lies down flat on the ground; his simple plan is to crawl out under the barrier, which, of course, is easier planned than done, the lowest of the many strands being only ten centimetres above the ground; but that is no more than was expected, hence the precautionary pliers. These are now put to work, rapidly snipping away at the thin wire that can't resist them indefinitely and splits more quickly than expected. But then there is that noise, for the wire is taut, an appalling whine which Jakob imagines capable of rousing a whole town from its sleep. He holds his breath and listens in fear, but everything remains as calm as before. Gradually, however, the light increases, for no cloud lasts for ever. The next strand is ten centimetres higher, thus twenty above the ground. Jakob calculates that to crawl under it would entail some risk to body and clothing; after all, though he has become terribly thin, he still is a fully grown man. On the other hand, he would rather not risk breaking the silence by twanging the second wire, which will be not a jot quieter than the first one, and he can't for the life of him think of any third option.

Jakob is still lying there undecided, plucking cautiously at that second strand to see if it can be loosened and the noise thus reduced as the pliers cut through it, when the decision is taken out of his hands by a higher authority. I said at the beginning that this ending of mine is rather at Jakob's expense. A raucous burst from a machine-pistol shatters the night silence: our sentry hasn't been that fast asleep. And there is nothing more to calculate, and Jakob is dead, all his endeavours at an end.

But there's more to come; what kind of an ending would this be anyway? I imagine further that tranquillity is far from returning to the ghetto. I visualize a revenge for Jakob, this, I have decided, being the cold and starry night when the Russians arrive. Thus the Red Army succeeds in surrounding the city in no time at all; the sky is lit up by flashes from the heavy artillery. Immediately following the salvo aimed at Jakob, an ear-splitting, thunderous roar starts up, as if inadvertently triggered by the unfortunate marksman on the watch-tower. The first ghostly tanks, shells hitting the military office, the watch-towers in flames, tenacious Germans defending themselves to the last bullet, or fleeing Germans unable to find any hole to crawl into – dear God, what a night that would have been. And, behind the windows, weeping Jews for whom everything has happened so suddenly that they can only stand there in disbelief, holding each other by the hand, Jews who would give anything to rejoice yet find themselves unable to; there'll be a time for that later. I imagine that by dawn the last battles are over, the ghetto is no longer a ghetto but merely the most run-down part of town. Anyone can go wherever he likes.

How Mischa thinks that Jakob is sure to be feeling better now; how he tries to take Lina back to him but doesn't find him in his room; the taste of the bread given us in ample quantities; what happens to the poor Germans who fall into our hands: all that and more is, to my mind, not important enough to be accorded a place in my ending. Only one thing is important to me.

Some of the Jews leave the ghetto by way of the old vegetable market. There they see a man, not wearing stars, lying on the ground with the pliers still clenched in his right hand, under the barbed wire of which one strand is cut – obviously caught while trying to escape. They turn him over on his back, who is this poor fellow, they ask, and someone is there who knows Jakob. Preferably Kowalski, but it could also be a neighbour or myself or anyone else from the freight yard, just someone who knows him, except Lina. This person stares in horror at Jakob's face; perhaps he had heard the first good news from Jakob the very day he himself was preparing to forego the rest of his life, and he now murmurs words of incomprehension. Someone asks him: 'What do you mean, you don't understand? The poor fellow was trying to escape because he didn't know the end was so near. What's so hard to understand about that?'

And, with a lump in his throat, that one person makes the hopeless attempt to explain what will for ever remain inexplicable to him.

'But that's Jakob Heym,' he says. 'Don't you understand? It's Jakob Heym! Why was he trying to escape? He must have gone out of his mind. He knew perfectly well that they were coming. He had a radio. . . .'

That, roughly speaking, is what he says; then, shaking his head, he walks with the others out into freedom, and that, roughly speaking, would be my ending.

B ut, finally, after the invented ending, here is the pallid and depressing, the true and unimaginative, ending that makes one inclined to ask the foolish question: What was the point of it all?

Kowalski is irrevocably dead, and for the time being Jakob goes on living, with no thought of foisting Lina upon strangers, does not strip his jacket of the prescribed stars, leaves the pliers in the drawer (assuming he even owns any), consequently does not tempt any sentry at the old vegetable market, on a cold and starry night, to fire shots capable of setting off such a mighty echo. That day, and we know why, he missed going to work; the friend who had hanged himself haunts his mind but must by next morning give way to some hard thinking. Jakob could see with his own eyes what the elimination of the radio can lead to; perhaps not in such extreme form in every case but quite possibly in one or two, and for that reason there will be no change regarding the radio. The grieving for Kowalski, whom suddenly he misses more than he ever wanted him around while he was still alive, must be put aside for now. Instead, the little news factory that feeds its man so laboriously starts working, for tomorrow there will be questions again, as there are every day. Like it or not, life drags on.

So next morning Jakob, tight lipped, walks past Kowalski's building, his eyes fixed firmly on a safe point at the end of the street. Yet, as we know, any attempt to force oneself not to think of something specific is doomed. Jakob sees him lying there exactly as if he were still standing beside him in the room; once again he unties the remains of the rope from the window, pulls up the chair because he doesn't want to sit on the bed and, as if that were not enough, can hear the end or the beginning of a conversation.

'In that building there.'

'Number fourteen?'

'No, sixteen. The corner building.'

'And do they know who?'

'Not really. A name like Kaminski or something.'

While still some distance from the station, Jakob realizes that something unusual must have happened: the Jews who have arrived for work are crowding round the entrance because the gate is locked. Why they are not being allowed in is at first a mystery to him; a mystery also why the first man to notice him points in his direction, says something, and the others turn to look at him. Fifty or sixty men have been waiting for Jakob, myself among them: we are watching the only person who can still, we hope, stand between us and disaster as, looking puzzled, he hesitantly approaches us. We make room for him, forming a narrow lane to allow him to walk right up to the gate and read the notice on it, then tell us that things aren't that bad. Beside me, Lawyer Schmidt shifts his weight from one foot to the other, and I hear him muttering: 'Get a move on, can't you?' because Jakob is walking with such maddening slowness and looking at people's faces rather than straight ahead.

Punctual for work, Jakob reaches the locked station gate and reads the notice attached to it. That today, at 13.00 hours sharp, we are to assemble in the square in front of the military office, five kilograms of luggage per head, all rooms to be left unlocked and in clean condition, anyone still found in his building after the appointed time . . . , the same applies to the bedridden and the infirm. Further details at 13.00 hours at the location indicated.

And now try and give them some more comfort, where to find it is your look-out, make them believe it's all a bad joke, that actually it's going to be a mystery trip with lots of nice surprises; after all, that's the kind of thing they're waiting for behind your back. Not to worry, brothers, is what they want to hear, just forget about that scrap of paper. Anyone who is curious can, if he likes, go to the military office at one o'clock if he has nothing better to do. Either way, nothing can happen because – of course you don't know this yet, stupidly I forgot to tell you – the Russians are waiting round the corner and will take care that not a hair of the head of a single one of you will be harmed.

Jakob stands so long in front of the sign without moving that one would think he is learning the few lines by heart. Why is he standing there so long, we silently wonder and begin to fear the worst? What will his face look like when he shows it to us again, and what will he say? He'll have to say something. I also notice the first few starting to drift quietly away. With dreadful certainty I know they are right, there is nothing more to hope for here, yet I go on hoping and stay rooted to the spot like most of the others.

A waste of time. After an eternity Jakob turns round, presenting us with two vacant eyes, and at that same moment even the stupidest must recognize that the last hope of salvation is gone. Jakob has no time, he tells me, for any private horror at the course of events, this being pushed aside by the horror of the others who are looking at him like bilked creditors, as if he were someone for whom it was now time to redeem the pledges he had so carelessly distributed. Again he stands for a long time without daring to raise his eyes, and they don't make things any easier for him either, by leaving, say. For the five kilos of luggage to be selected there is still plenty of time, the rest of their lives so to speak. The narrow lane that had opened for Jakob on his way to the gate has closed up behind him; now he is standing in a tight semicircle – to use Jakob's own words, like an entertainer who has forgotten his lines at the crucial moment.

'Haven't you lot anything better to do than stand there gaping?' asks a sentry on the other side of the fence.

Only now do we notice him standing a few metres from the gate; he alone knows how long he's been there. In any case he won't have heard much, though everything that matters has already been said. We finally move off, why annoy him unnecessarily, and silently go our separate ways. The sentry shakes his head in amusement at these strange creatures. Jakob is almost grateful to him for the unintentional help.

On reaching home Jakob immediately goes up into the attic, expecting to find Lina still in bed, but she is not even in the room, although the weather is by no means ideal, with only a few patches of blue visible in the sky, but Jakob can imagine that his instructions are not taken too seriously. Her bed has been neatly made, the piece of bread has disappeared from the plate on the chest of drawers. Right after he had said goodbye to her this morning she must have got up and hurried off to some project or other that one is never told about. Jakob decides to look for her later and first to pack her things, then his own. When that's done, he can still go and find Lina. He wastes no time wondering whether the notice on the gate applies only to those employed at the station or to all inhabitants of the ghetto. For he has no choice but to take Lina with him; leaving her behind would not mean hoping for an uncertain fate for her, that's pretty obvious.

The maximum luggage allowance proves to be fairly generous, the total of her usable belongings amounting to scarcely more than a handful. Jakob stuffs underwear, stockings and scarf into his pockets. While he is folding her winter dress, Lina shows up, holding what remains of the bread in her fingers. She is very surprised to see Jakob but is immediately aware of his disapproving look, which she has no trouble interpreting: he won't like her having left the attic against his wishes.

'I just went to the pump. I was thirsty,' she explains.

'Never mind,' says Jakob.

He finishes folding the dress and gives it to her to hold, then looks round and once again opens the cupboard doors to see whether he has forgotten anything.

'Am I going to stay with you again downstairs?' asks Lina.

'Come along,' he says.

They go down to his room. On the stairs they meet Horowitz, the neighbour, who has apparently come up from the cellar and is lugging a heavy leather suitcase whose locks fail to keep the lid shut.

'What is your opinion about it?' Horowitz asks.

'Have a guess,' Jakob replies.

For the first time he knows with certainty that the proclamation on the station gate applies to the whole ghetto; Horowitz's inane question and the suitcase he is carrying mean that the same notice will have been posted overnight at every factory entrance.

'Did you happen to hear where they are taking us?'

'No,' says Jakob.

He hurries into his room with Lina before he can become involved in any lengthy discussions; the only thing he might have liked to know was what Horowitz, a single man, hoped to gain by that enormous suitcase – his notice can hardly have mentioned four hundredweight per person.

When the door is closed behind them, Lina confesses that she can't stand Horowitz. She always gives him a wide berth because he invariably has some admonishment ready for her, such as not to hang about, to say good-morning nicely, not to look so cheeky, to stop making that noise: there's always something he can think up. Once he even shook her by the arm because she had slid down the banister and landed at his feet. Jakob says: 'Well, fancy that.'

After taking Lina's things out of his pockets and putting them on the table, he starts packing. But first he has to choose between suitcase and rucksack; there's plenty of room in either one. Because of its handiness the rucksack wins, for on a journey of uncertain length, when one hand must constantly be available for Lina, a suitcase can become a nuisance.

For quite a while Lina patiently hopes that Jakob will volunteer an explanation for his strange actions, but all he says from time to time is Hand me that, Hold this, and not a word to satisfy her curiosity. So she must ask: 'Why are you packing all those things?'

'Well, why does anyone pack?'

'I don't know,' she says, emphasizing her words with an exaggerated shrug, the kind already known to us, pulling her shoulders up to her ears.

'Then think about it.'

'To go on a trip?'

'Exactly, you clever dick.'

'We're going on a trip?' Lina cries, and it sounds a bit like: And you're only telling me now?

'That's right, we're going away,' Jakob says.

'Where are we going?'

'I don't know exactly.'

'Far away or not so far?'

'Quite far away, I think.'

'As far as America?'

'No.'

'As far as China?'

'No.'

'As far as Africa?'

Knowing from experience that she is capable of keeping up this game for hours, Jakob says: 'Yes, about as far as Africa.'

She starts skipping round the room, hardly able to grasp her good fortune, and Jakob doesn't try to stop her – after all, the child has never been on a real trip. The hardest part comes when she suddenly gives him a kiss and asks why he isn't glad too.

'Because I don't like travelling,' he answers.

'You'll see what fun it will be!'

As he is finishing up with the rucksack, putting two spoons on top, and is about to fasten it, Lina lays her hand on his arm and says: 'You've left out the book.'

'What book?'

'The one about Africa.'

'Oh yes. Where is it?'

'Under my pillow. I'll run and get it for you!'

Lina hurries out of the room, and Jakob can hear her cheery voice in the corridor and up the stairs: 'We're going on a trip! We're going on a trip. . . .' From sheer joy, or to annoy grumpy old Horowitz a bit while under Jakob's protection.

Then we are on our way.

It is very cramped and stuffy in the boxcar. The Jews are squatting or sitting on the floor beside their five kilos, at least thirty of them, I would think. Sleeping at night, if the journey should take that long, will be a problem, for we can't all lie down at the same time; we'll have to do it in shifts. It is dark, too; the few narrow openings right under the roof let in only a meagre light, besides being almost permanently occupied. There is hardly any conversation to be heard; most people look as if they had terribly important and serious matters to reflect upon, yet with the noise of the rumbling wheels it would be possible to talk, if one wanted to, without being overheard, despite the close quarters.

I am sitting on a checked pillowcase that contains all my stuff, and I am bored; beside me a very old woman is weeping, quietly, out of consideration for others. Her tears have long since been used up, yet from time to time she sniffs so violently that it would seem whole torrents were being held back. And her husband, with whom she is sitting on their suitcase, looks round apologetically each time, because no doubt he is embarrassed, because he wants to convey that there's nothing he can do about it.

To my left, where I now switch my attention, Jakob has managed to get hold of a spot by one of the narrow openings, but I can truthfully state that this proximity is pure coincidence. I didn't push my way next to him; I don't go as far as some idiots who make out he is partly to blame for this journey, but I can't deny a feeling of unwarranted resentment towards him because everything I built up on the foundations he supplied has collapsed. I didn't push my way next to him; I don't care who I'm next to: it simply happened that way. Looking between Jakob's legs I can see Lina, who so far I have known only from hearsay; she is sitting on the rucksack. Because of Lina I find myself liking him a little more again. Who else, I think, would have taken on the burden of a child, and that, I think, almost outweighs my disappointment.

I would so much like to be friends with her, by winking or making funny faces, the kind of thing one does, but she takes no notice of me whatever. She is looking dreamily at the floor, her mind doubtless occupied by thoughts that are remote from everyone else's, for she occasionally smiles to herself. Or her lips form soundless words, or she grimaces as if she were not sure of her ground. I enjoy watching her. On the floor I find a little pebble and flick it against her arm. She comes out of her reverie and gazes round to see who it could have been, in every direction except mine. Then she looks up at Jakob, who is beyond all suspicion as he stands motionless at the little opening, his whole attention absorbed by the passing countryside. She taps his leg.

He looks down and asks: 'What is it?'

'Do you remember the fairy tale?' asks Lina.

'Which one?'

'About the sick princess?'

'Yes.'

'Is it true?'

It is clear from his expression that he finds it strange for her to be thinking of that just now.

'Of course it's true,' he says.

'But Siegfried and Rafi wouldn't believe me.'

'Maybe you didn't tell it properly?'

'I told it exactly as you did. But they say there's no such thing in the whole world.'

'No such thing as what?'

'That a person can get well again by being given a piece of cotton wool.'

Jakob bends down and lifts her up to the little window. I stand up too: the wheels make quite a racket, and I'd like to hear how it goes on.

'But it's true, isn't it?' says Lina. 'The princess wanted a piece of cotton wool as big as a pillow? And when she had it she got well again?'

I see Jakob's mouth widen, and he says: 'Not exactly. She wished for a cloud. The point is that she thought clouds are made of cotton wool, and that's why she was satisfied with the cotton wool.'

Lina looks out for a while, surprised, it seems to me, before asking him: 'But aren't clouds made of cotton wool?'

Between their heads I can make out a bit of sky with a few clouds, and I must admit that there really is an amazing resemblance: they do look like tufts of cotton wool.

'Then what *are* clouds made of?' Lina asks.

But Jakob promises to give her an answer later, probably partly because she is getting too heavy for him. He sets her down on the rucksack again, then resumes watching the landscape slip past.

This, I think, is my moment. I sit down too, move closer to her, and ask whether she would like me to explain what clouds are made of. Of course she would, and I tell her about rivers and lakes, and about the ocean, about the never-ending cycle of water, about that almost incredible process of evaporation, how water flows invisibly into the sky, in tiny droplets, and forms clouds there which at some point become as heavy and wet as soaking sponges until they lose the drops again as rain. I tell her about steam too, from locomotives for instance, and from chimneys and all the various kinds of fires. She listens attentively but sceptically; I know that the whole lengthy story cannot be covered in one lesson. And I see Jakob casting a friendly eye on me; perhaps that lesson is responsible for his singling me out, a few days later, to tell me an even crazier story. For there is nothing from my appearance to show that I would be one of the few to survive.

When my knowledge about the formation and composition of clouds is exhausted, I tell Lina not to be shy about asking if there is anything she hasn't understood. But she makes no use of this offer; with her face cupped in her hands, she takes her time thinking through the whole matter again. After all, she has to come to terms with a very significant mistake: clouds are not made of cotton wool.

'You don't know what you're letting yourself in for,' Jakob whispers in my ear.

'Why?'

'Because you have no idea the kind of questions this child can ask.'

I look at her and say: 'I'll manage all right.'

His eyes tell me, Just wait and see. Then he asks me whether I would like to look out of the opening for a bit.

'Thanks, I would,' I say.

I stand up expectantly and look out until darkness falls. I see villages and fields, once even a little town in the distance; at a half-overgrown pond I see a group of soldiers resting among lorries, cannon and cows. And I see a few sleepy stations with platforms and barriers and railwaymen's cottages with green window-boxes overflowing with flowers, and I wonder whether these are regulation window-boxes because they are attached to each cottage and each one is green. And I see people whose faces I can't make out watching our train pass, but above all I see trees, which I had almost forgotten although I'm still a young fellow, vast numbers of trees. Beeches and alders and birches and willows and pines – my God, look at all those trees, there's no end to them. A tree was responsible for my not becoming a violinist, and under a tree I became a real man: the wild boar came too late to prevent it. And at an unknown tree my wife Chana was lost to me, and an ordinance tried to deprive me of trees for all time. Some say that trees have confused my mind, I go on standing there, and to this day I sometimes get into a train passing through a thickly wooded area, best of all a mixed forest. Till I hear Jakob's voice: 'Aren't you ever going to get some sleep?'

'Let me stand here a little longer,' I say.

'But there's nothing more for you to see,' I hear him say.

'Yes, there is.'

For I can still see the shadows of trees, and I can't sleep. We are heading for wherever we are heading.